Dragons Fire

Christine Morgan Douglas

Published in 2013 by FeedARead.com Publishing – Arts Council funded

Copyright © The author as named on the book cover.

First Edition

The author has asserted their moral right under the Copyright, Designs and Patents Act, 1988, to be identified as the author of this work.

All Rights reserved. No part of this publication may be reproduced, copied, stored in a retrieval system, or transmitted, in any form or by any means, without the prior written consent of the copyright holder, nor be otherwise circulated in any form of binding or cover other than that in which it is published and without a similar condition being imposed on the subsequent purchaser.

A CIP catalogue record for this title is available from the British Library.

Dedication

I would like to dedicate this book to my husband for the endless help and encouragement he has given me and to the rest of my family for the inspiration they gave me to write it.

Chapter One

The hedgerows of the Somerset countryside were rich with the autumn fruits. The little wren was busy pecking at a ripe blackberry when the sound of footfall startled her and she soared into the sky chirruping angrily.

A group of men were making their way along the road towards Camelot. They had been part of the king's army when they had repelled the invasion of the Vikings to the north and Saxons to the south east of his borders. They did not follow the road all the way to Camelot but left and made their way back to their own farms and cottages in the surrounding villages.

In the garden of a small cottage, twin brothers, David and Thomas paused in their labour to watch the distant road.

Although they were only in their teens the boys were well built. Both had fair, unruly, hair that had a tendency to curl when damp. They were identical except that Thomas's hair had a definite red sheen to it. Their steely blue eyes missed little as they watched the men making their way home.

'I suppose the king and his knights will be following in a few weeks,' David observed. 'That means we will have more work in the stables.'

'I wish we could go to court and serve as Knights of the Round Table,' Thomas said, wistfully, as the last man disappeared from view.

'Fat chance,' David replied. 'We aren't nobles and anyway we couldn't afford to buy all the horses and armour that we'd need.'

'At least we could serve in the army next time they have to go anywhere.'

David stared at his brother. 'What about Freya?'

'What about her?'

'We couldn't just go off and leave her on her own. Who would do all the hard work?'

'She's not an old woman,' Thomas retorted. 'I'm sure she could look after the garden on her own whilst we're away?'

'That's not the point; we promised that we would always be there for each other.'

'David, you always worry too much. Anyway let's not argue, after all we won't be going anywhere at the moment.'

'Who's not going anywhere?' a soft voice asked. Freya, their sister, was beautiful with dark hair and green eyes. She had softly come up behind them. 'I thought you two would be going to find out what all the fuss is about.'

'What fuss? We've just been discussing the return of the King and his army.'

David and Thomas started to clear up and put the tools away in the back of the stable area as Freya collected some beans for their evening meal.

'From what I've just heard in the village,' she continued, 'there has been something going on at 'The Moon Inn' while the men have been away and now as they are returning they are getting quite excited. I thought you could go and find out what is going on.'

'We don't mind,' Thomas immediately replied, 'but can we have something to eat first as I'm starving.'

Freya laughed. 'Oh course you can, the meal won't be long. By the time you've both washed and changed, it should be on the table.

The three of them made their way up the path, through the rest of the vegetable garden, to the back door of the pretty cottage. The sun was setting and the little dormer windows glowed in the golden light of the last days of September.

The meal, once ready, was eaten in silence until Freya lay down her knife and fork and smiled at her brothers.

'I know you are bored with living here and I don't want you to think you have to stay with me. You need your own lives. I just don't think the army is the answer.'

'What is the answer then?' Thomas snapped back.

'I don't know at this moment, I just have the feeling that something is going to happen.' Freya paused then her face lit up. 'Talking of things happening, about the fuss I mentioned to you before dinner. Well, when I was making my way home from the market, earlier today, I overheard two men talking. They were on about a new opportunity to earn big money. I heard one say that George Miller was recruiting men in "The Moon" this evening and as they moved away I thought I heard dragon mentioned.'

'I thought George worked for Mordred,' David pondered.

'Yes he does, so that's a very good reason for you to go and find out what they are planning,'

'Come on David lets go and see what's happening,' Thomas said jumping up with a smile once more upon his face.

Chapter Two

The week previously.

In the castle at Camelot, Morgana, King Arthur's half-sister, hurried up the back stairs to her special room on the top floor of the turret. It was dark up there, except for the flickering light of the fire.

Once in, she started pacing up and down as she brooded on the meeting she had just attended with Aelle, the Saxon king.

Having been told, by her spies, of her brother's disbanding his armies until the next spring, she had wasted no time in taking this knowledge to Arthur's biggest adversary.

They had plotted together and agreed on a plan to attack a village near to Camelot.

The person to raise the alarm, one of Morgana's men, would assure the king that the attacking army was only small; therefore he would ride out with just his local force. On arrival he would find a large army in waiting. The ensuing battle should kill King Arthur and allow Morgana to become Queen.

She knew that Aelle, mistakenly, thought she would marry him and he would become king by default, but she was confident she would be able to deal with him when the time came.

Moving to the centre of the room she became more visible by the silver white glow of a crystal ball that she uncovered. She crouched over it and stretched out her arms wide making herself look like an evil bird of prey hovering over its victim. She started chanting one of her spells as her black eyes gazed into the depth of the ball. The light became more intense and the shadows deep within began to take shape. She saw a flickering picture of herself at her coronation; she was wearing a purple robe and on her head, a golden crown. The priest handed her a golden orb and then held out the sceptre. Once she had that in her hand she would become the true queen.

As her image's hand started to close on this last item, Morgana smiled in triumph, then her alabaster face took on a truly terrible look as she watched the images change into a large, fire breathing dragon. The light died and the room returned to darkness. She let out a hideous scream.

'No, it will not be! I shall destroy every dragon in the land: I shall be queen. I pledge by all that is darkness, as sure as my name is Morgana. I will rule this land.'

She strode from the room, the darkness surrounding her, and as the door slammed, the fire seemed to become brighter and the shadows no longer as menacing. The lady of darkness glided down the stairs to one of the main rooms of the castle.

'Mordred, where are you?' she called. 'You are never around when I need you.'

A young man, with her dark good looks, lazily arose from a chair by the fire where he had been lounging.

'What do you want, mother?' he asked as he stretched himself and went across to embrace her.

'I need your help to kill the dragons. My powers will not work directly against them as they are incorruptible and will not do my bidding. But they must go!' she snarled, abruptly pulling away from him.

'What will be my reward for helping you?' Mordred's eyes gleamed as he slyly smiled at his mother.

'I will instruct you fully in the arts of magic, also I will give you two hundred pieces of silver for every dragon killed.' she paused, 'we will need a great many people to help in the slaying of the dragons but first we need someone to spearhead this operation. Who is your most trusted servant?'

Mordred thought for a moment, and then he smiled.

'I think I have the very man you need for the job. He has recently come into my employ. He is from the village and therefore the locals would trust him. Shall I go and fetch him now?'

'The sooner the better,' she replied, an evil smile spreading across her face.

Once he left she returned to her room, closed the door and fetched a large book from one of the many shelves. She placed it on the table and lit a candle before opening the old leather-bound cover, she began to search through the pages until; giving an evil chuckle she found her place. She read quietly for a few moments, and then started to bustle about the room, gathering various objects from her bottles and jars lining all the other shelves in the alcoves on each side of the fireplace. Quickly measuring the amounts of their contents needed from each, she deposited these into a cauldron that she then hung over the fire. Adding some water, Morgana started to stir the contents as they heated up. After a few moments steam started to rise up and she began to chant: -

'Herbs and spices, saps and bark,
Dim the sunshine bring the dark,
Hide their reason in the mist,
Change the people with a twist,
Bring the shadows, night and day,
Let the darkness have its way,'

The steam darkened and grew thicker and slowly started to move around the room turning into the forms of shadowy men. Soon there were dozens of the creatures flickering around the room, faster and faster.

Morgana made a number of strange passes over the cauldron; the door flew open with a crash and the shadows slid out of the room, down the stairs and under the main door, into the night, where they were lost from sight.

No sooner had they gone than Morgana drained the remaining liquid from the cauldron into a small glass flask and placed it on a silver tray with some goblets and a decanter of wine. She finished just in time, as downstairs, the door banged and two sets of footsteps were heard mounting the stairs to her room.

'Welcome back, my son, and who do we have here?'

'Mother, I'd like to I introduce my newest recruit, George Miller. George this is my mother, the Lady Morgana. I think we are all going to get along famously.'

Crossing the room she held out her hand to Mordred's companion and smiled her most beguiling smile.

'It is so good of you to come out at this time of night. We must give you some refreshment.'

She returned to the tray and with her back to her guest poured out three drinks; to one she added some of the magic potion. The lady turned back, smiling, and handed out the drinks, making sure the one with the added potion was handed to George.

George took a deep drink, and a gleam of satisfaction came over Morgana's face.

'Now to business. Please do seat yourself and have some more of the wine.'

She quickly refilled George's goblet before he had a chance to object, and then seating herself by the fire, indicated the two chairs on the other side of the hearth.

'We need someone to lead a band of men to rid the land of all the Dragons. They are becoming a great nuisance and a danger to farmers.'

George started to say that he had never heard of any stories of trouble with the beasts, and how they were gentle with humans, when he found his thoughts clouding and darkening. Yes, he thought, they were a danger. They must be destroyed.

'I'm your man.' he found himself saying as he gazed at Morgana with adoration in his eyes.

On the table a piece of paper appeared and on it was written:

Why work for a pittance?
You could sign up with
GEORGE THE DRAGON SLAYER
Earn a fortune and become famous.
50 pieces of silver for every dragon killed.
Sign below and become rich!!

'Why, that's my name.' George declared

'Yes, and Mordred will give you one hundred pieces of silver per dragons head.

Both men looked very happy with the arrangement.

'How will I persuade the locals to join me? Will the money be enough?' George was beginning to worry. Morgana lifted up her hand, pointed to the corner and beckoned. A shadow man who had not left with the others detached itself from the dark corner and flitted across behind George. It attached itself to his real shadow, so now he had two. It seemed to bend and whisper in his ear. George shuddered, and then smiled as a vacant look came upon his face.

Seeing that her work was done here Morgana rose and taking her guest by his hand led him to the doorway.

'I think we can rely on gentle persuasion to make the others see sense. Now I have much to do and so have you. I will bid you both a goodnight.' She turned to her son. 'Please show our friend out, Mordred, and leave me to my work.'

The men wished Morgana a goodnight, left her to return to her spells and potion as she concocted more of her evil helpers.

Mordred, having seen George out, watched as he hurried to the local inn where he could start to recruit his men. Smiling he closed the door before going to his room to think of all the riches he would soon have.

Chapter Three

As the darker evenings of autumn set in the villagers usually sat around their home fires or gathered together at the local inn called 'The Moon'. This alehouse was situated a short distance from the castle walls. There was one big main room, with benches and tables spaced around. The room was made welcoming and cosy with one wall being taken up by a large fireplace complete with cheerful flames blazing in its hearth.

The walls had lanterns hung at intervals, giving a warm, yellow light, altogether a pleasant place for the villagers to spend an evening.

There were quite a few men drinking and being served by the innkeeper and his serving maids.

George entered calling out greetings to one or two of the men already gathered there. He ordered a drink from the nearest serving maid, and went to sit by the fire. Putting down the piece of paper Morgana had given him, he looked up just as the first shadow man slid through the doorway and fluttered to the nearest drinker. The man shivered. He had been thinking of going home but now paused as if listening to someone.

'It's cold outside I had better have another drink of cider, to warm up, before going,' he thought.

Without realising what he was doing the man held up his tankard and the girl filled it for him, from the large jug she was carrying around.

Taking his drink he walked across and joined George. One more would not hurt, he reasoned, especially as the girl hadn't asked for any payment. There seemed to be a darker shadow behind her, strange, but that didn't matter. His mind was foggy, perhaps he had drunk more than he had realised. As he looked around, he noticed the piece of paper on the table. Picking it up he read it and immediately felt he had to add his name to it. No sooner had he finished doing this than the other men in the bar came across to join them, all pushing to have their names added to the growing list.

As George added each name he couldn't help smiling as he thought of all the profit he was going to make he worked out that if each man only brought back one dragonhead, he would make more money than he had ever seen in his life, and he was doing something for mankind. Perhaps they would make a saint of him, St George and the Dragon, now that sounded impressive.

'Come on my lads, sign up and make your fortune. There's plenty for everyone. I need you to go and fetch your friends and neighbours to bring them here to sign on with me. There will be free drinks for you all.'

George had no sooner uttered his words before the men, who had already signed, left the hostel to do George's bidding.

Hurrying towards their homes they knocked on their friends' doors to encourage them to go and sign up for the untold wealth. It was not long before there was a crowd of men hurrying down the road to the hostel.

At the same time the two brothers were happily making their way to the village Inn. Fifteen minutes later they arrived at their destination and Thomas glanced in through the window. What he saw made him stop in his tracks; it was so sudden that David, who was following him around the corner, nearly fell over him.

'Why did you stop?' he asked, laughing at his brother.

Thomas did not answer immediately as he was staring into the window.

'That's strange. Look David, the people have two shadows.'

'There is nothing strange in that, two sources of light can cause two shadows.'

'No, take a look again. One shadow is light and it goes across the floor, but the other is dark and is almost leaning on the peoples' shoulders.'

David slid past his brother and leaned towards the window to get a better look.

'I see what you mean,' he mumbled, beginning to feel a little worried.

They stood watching as the men all gathered around a table and took it in turns to sign a piece of paper that was placed on the table.

'Isn't that George, the man we were talking about?'

'I think you are right. Freya is always saying there is something evil going on at the castle. One of us had better try to find out what is going on.'

They had a good view of the entire room and even as they watched, the men who had signed left and more arrived from the surrounding area. As each entered the hostelry the dark shadow in the corner nearest the door seemed to writhe and separate. This part attached itself to the newcomer as an extra shadow.

'Did you see that? What on earth is happening?' David asked really alarmed now. 'I am going to have to go and find out what is happening and we need to see what the men are signing.'

Thomas looked at his brother, and then nodded.

'You take care. We don't want one of the shadows to attach to you, as we don't know what they do,' Thomas replied frowning.

'Don't worry; I think I know how to get in. If I wait for the next person and go through the door at exactly the same time as him, I then move quickly around the room on this side. The shadow will be busy with my companion. They seem to attach one at a time,' David said moving nearer the doorway.

'I shall watch you from the window, ready to help you,' Thomas said, remaining where he was.

Even as they were speaking a young man approached the door; not waiting to think anymore, David rushed forwards and went through the doorway at exactly the same time. He quickly separated from the other man and hurried around the walls to look over George's shoulder and read the piece of paper.

Having taken in the words he looked up anxiously, just in time, he saw a black shape moving towards him. He glanced about him and realised his only chance of escape was through the window, he just had to hope it would open easily. Without a second thought, he raced across the room and opened the catch on the window. He pulled with all his might. The window flew open and he dived through in one fluid movement, or rather he went half way through before he stuck, caught by his shirt snagging on the window catch.

Thomas grabbed his brother's arms and heaved, for a moment it looked as if David was going to be caught by the shadow as it drew closer. Desperation added strength to Thomas who heaved with all his might. There was a ripping sound and David's garment gave way and he tumbled out on top of his brother.

Wasting no time to check if either off them was hurt, they scrambled to their feet and set of, at a run, towards their home, without looking back.

If they had, they would have seen a dark shape slide over the windowsill and vanish into the night's shadows.

Chapter Four

The front door slammed behind the brothers as they rushed into their home.

'Light all the lights. We need to see if any shadows come in.' Thomas shouted.

'I'm already doing it.' replied David as he ran around the room turning up the lanterns that were on and lighting others.

'What's all the commotion?' Freya asked, as she came in to the room looking puzzled at her two brothers.

'We will explain everything as soon as the room is as bright as it can be.' David replied, closing the curtains and shutting the doors leading to the kitchen and stairs.

David stirred the flames of the fire into a warm blaze before glancing around the room to see if there was anything unusual. There was nothing so he relaxed a little and turning to his brother and sister he quickly explained what he had read.

'There were shadows attaching themselves to the men as soon as they entered, I think they were the cause that made the men sign up to kill the dragons.'

'Why are they going to kill the dragons?' Thomas asked puzzled. 'They don't hurt anyone.'

Freya looked thoughtful for a moment then replied, 'I don't know, but it must have something to do with Morgana, because only she could have made the shadows do her bidding. She will know about you by now so the best thing I can think of is for you to go to Cornwall, to Grandmother, and enlist her help as we need to warn the dragons and think of some way to stop

Morgana. I will try to find out what her plans are. Then I will follow you as soon as I can.'

The twins looked doubtfully at each other.

'Will you be safe here on your own?' Thomas asked.

'I think so; Morgana would not think I could do anything against her. She does not realise I have any powers of my own. Not yet anyway.' Freya replied. 'The shadows shouldn't be able to enter our house,' she continued, 'as I've put some protecting herbs and potions around the windows and doors. Always a good idea when you don't want anyone to know what you are doing. Now off to bed as you had better make an early start in the morning and I've some preparation to do.'

Realising it was no use arguing with their sister, the boys went off to their room and Freya went through into the kitchen where she took some bottles and jars out of her cupboard. Taking a deep blue flask, she went over to the fire, removed the stopper and poured a little of the powder onto the flames. As she did this she concentrated hard on what she wanted to see.

The fire burned with a beautiful blue flame and a vision appeared: It was Morgana with Aelle plotting the king's death. The vision clouded then cleared again. This time the flame showed the evil woman as she conjured up the shadow men.

Freya stood transfixed, for a moment, as she tried to think what to do next. The obvious thing was to send the boys to Cornwall to enlist the help of their Grandmother immediately, also the further away they were from Morgana the safer they would be. First she had to make some protection for them. Leaving the flames she set to work and before very long had prepared two separate pouches. These she hung onto lengths of leather. Once she had finished she decided it would not be safe to wait until the morning so went and woke her brothers. She told them what she had seen.

The boys, realising the gravity of the situation, did not argue with her but set about collecting all the supplies they would need for the three-day journey to Tregardock, a small village near Camelford on the north coast of Cornwall.

As they gathered everything together they were all quiet with their own thoughts of the coming adventure.

On finishing his packing, David turned to his sister.

'Freya, I am still worried about leaving you here on your own.'

'Don't be, I have my magic to protect me. Talking of protection I have these for you,' she replied and picking up the pouches she handed them to each of the boys in turn.

'Wear these around your necks and they should keep most evil things away from you on your journey, and I promise I will follow in a few days' time as soon as I can arrange it.'

David went outside and saddled up three ponies, the extra one to carry all the supplies and equipment they would need for the journey. Once ready he led them around to the front of the cottage. He and Thomas hugged their sister before mounting the animals and set off on their journey.

As Freya watched them go she realised it was darker than it should have been as there was a full moon, but it appeared to give no light. There was evil around already she realised.

Back in the kitchen, Freya had forgotten to calm her flames, so she had left a portal open for observation.

In her room at the castle, Morgana was watching through her crystal ball.

As the brothers left their home she smiled to herself. 'So they think they can warn the dragons and stop me do they? Once they are away from Freya's protection, we will see how far they get.'

She walked across the room to her book of spells and immediately went to the one she needed and began to cast a spell to capture the brothers.

'Come, my helpers, with this mark. (Using her wand she drew a line on the table.)

Wake the demons of the dark

Bring the goblins from the hill

Come to life and do my will!'

As she finished her chanting, Morgana used her wand again to make a pass in the air. In reply there was a trumpet sound from some far off hill. Smiling she returned to her crystal ball and watched as the stones on the hills around Camelot, rolled back to reveal the black slime underneath each one, this begin to bubble and writhe about and slowly began to take the shape of Hobgoblins.

They were stocky, thickset beings, with closely shaved heads and strange marks and pictures tattooed on their forearms. Some had rings in their ears and noses. All had scruffy, dark attire and heavy footwear. They looked exactly like what they were, trouble.

Once they were all formed they grouped together and ambled off in a westerly direction, following in the brothers' footsteps.

Chapter Five

David and Thomas rode away from Freya, both of them worrying a little at the thought of leaving her alone but they had no way of knowing about the dangers that were following them. Even so they had a good start on their enemy but the advantage would not last forever. Hobgoblins only stop for two reasons; one was drinking and the second for a good fight.

Making good time on their fresh horses the brothers travelled a long way on the first day and as early evening started to darken the sky David pulled his mount to a halt at the top of a rise and looked across at a large town a short distance away.

'I think we should find somewhere to stay for the night and have a meal.'

'That's a good idea.' Thomas agreed, 'I am parched and hungry, do you realise we have been riding steadily all day and not stopped for any refreshments?'

'I know. I have been concentrating on getting to Grandmother so that we can do something about whatever is spreading across the land.' David replied as he urged his tired mount onward again.

Ten minutes later they entered the town and followed a short street into the market square, where a large Inn stood on the corner.

'None of the shadows seem to have reached this far, thank goodness,' David said, as they both dismounted stiffly and led the horses in to the stabling area.

'Perhaps it's only our village that has been affected,' replied Thomas, 'in that case it will not be too hard to put right,' he added hopefully.

David smiled in agreement as he handed the animals over to an ostler to be fed and watered. The brothers went in to find the landlord and arranged for a room for the night before they ordered a meal.

They moved into the taproom and sat down where they were served by the friendly staff.

'I hadn't realised how hungry I was,' David said, as he leaned back when they had finished the meal. 'I think we deserve another drink before we turn in for the night.'

'I agree,' Thomas said, and beckoned the waiter over. 'Two more of the same, please.'

As soon as they finished this they started to rise when a movement caught David's eye.

'Oh no!' he exclaimed, 'look over there, by the door!'

Thomas turned in time to see the shadow, as it became darker, turn into a shadow man and attached itself to an unsuspecting customer as he walked in through the entrance. The man shuddered and paused as if listening. He smiled and went over to a group of men standing reading a poster on the wall; pushing through them he took up the charcoal and put his mark on the paper. Meanwhile the doorway had become alive with flittering shapes as the shadow men detached themselves and went over to the other patrons of the inn.

'We had better leave whilst we can,' David said. 'If we can.' he added, as two of the shadows came over and slid behind the brothers before they could make a move.

Then a strange thing happened. It was as if the sun had come out as a glow surrounded each of them and dissolved the shadows into nothing.

'The talisman works!' exclaimed Thomas.

'Let's go whilst the going's good,' David replied, as he started grabbing their things. They left some money on the hall table to pay the landlord as they went and quickly collected their poor tired animals to make their way out of town.

The sunshine glow stayed around them until they were well clear of the market place. When, at last, the glow faded David sighed in relief.

'At least the shadows aren't actually following us, if you take notice of the glow from these pouches.'

'I suppose we're going to have to avoid towns in future to be sure we are safe.'

'If the shadow men have come this far, it makes me wonder what other troubles there are in store for us?' David mused. 'Perhaps Morgana sent other threats. Freya could be in trouble.'

'Don't worry about her, she's not silly and I wouldn't be surprised if she's actually on her way to follow us now,' Thomas reassured him.

'We should've insisted she came with us.'

'It's too late to worry now; we'll just have to press on as fast as we can. Grandmother is sure to know what to do.'

Urging their horses into a canter they headed out into the countryside. By this time he ponies were getting very tired, so after a while they dismounted and started to lead them.

It was not long before the natural darkness of the evening began to overtake them and as they entered a wooded area it became even harder to see clearly.

'Look, there's a fairly sheltered spot by that oak tree and a small copse of trees beyond for firewood.' said David pointing to a small clearing.

'Perfect,' replied Thomas and made his way over to it where he unsaddled the animals. He fixed hobbles to their front legs, to allow them to graze the lush grass, whilst the brothers both set up camp. Thomas collected a large bundle of firewood and taking some of the smaller twigs and some ferns he made a small pile then using his flint he lit the tinder. As it caught alight he added bigger pieces of wood until he had a good fire going lighting up the clearing.

They were busy laying out their blankets by the fire when there was a noise in the distance.

David straightened up and stared intently back the way they had so recently travelled.

'I think we have company coming.'

Thomas stopped what he was doing and walked over to join his brother.

'What have you seen?' he asked, peering into the darkness.

'Look over at that hill we came down, before we came into the woods. I am sure I saw movements over the top.'

'The moonlight's not very bright, I don't see anything... hang on... yes, there is something... there's a man, and.... no, look there're lots of them.' Thomas spun round and rushed over to their things where he retrieved his longbow and arrows. 'We'll have to stay and fight, if it's necessary, as the horses are too tired to go very much further and at least we know what is coming.'

'Perhaps Freya's spells will be a help. I'd hate not to be able to get to warn the dragons of their danger,' David replied, also collecting up his sword and standing facing the oncoming mob.

The hobgoblins were now quite clearly seen in the dull light of the moon. They had upped their speed to a shambling run once they saw their pray in front of them.

'We're going to be a little outnumbered. There seem to be about ten to fifteen of them,' David muttered, after counting them.

'If we stand shoulder to shoulder with the fire behind us, we'll have the light on our side, so a slight advantage,' Thomas replied.

They took up their positions and waited. Within five minutes the first of the hobgoblins arrived and stopped at the edge of the firelight.

'Why don't they start?' Thomas asked as he drew back his bow and fitted in an arrow.

'Hold on, Tom, I think they can't reach us,' David laughed. 'No. Look. They can't step into the light.'

Even as he spoke three of the gathering enemy attempted to rush them only to be knocked back, literally, as if they had hit a wall. Unnoticed by the brothers the area around their camp had taken on a bright glow, the talismans that they each wore around the neck were working again.

'We don't want these things following us, even if they can't hurt us. We mustn't lead them to Grandmother,'

'We can't just sit here and wait for the power of the magic to weaken though.'

'I know, we'll have to think of something but in the mean time you get some rest, David. I will keep watch for a couple of hours and then you take over. In the mean time I shall try to think of a plan to outsmart them.'

David seeing the wisdom of Thomas's idea rolled himself in the sleeping blanket he had laid out by the fire. He didn't think he would sleep at all, not with the worry of all the danger such a short way away, but within moments he was fast asleep leaving his brother to keep his lonely watch.

Thomas sat with his back to the flames and watched the hobgoblins as they roamed around the perimeter of the light. Every few moments one of them would try to step across only to jump back quickly.

After some time he noticed one of them was crouching down and trying to reach something. It was one of the packs they had offloaded from the ponies earlier.

Even as he watched the goblin picked up a stick and using it, he hooked the strap and started to pull it back towards himself.

Thomas jumped up and rushed across. He was too late. The hobgoblin had the bag. He went back a few feet and sat down to open it and take out the bottles of drink Freya had sent with the boys, as a present for their grandmother.

The drink was a special sloe gin that Freya had had a lot of success with. It was very, very strong.

The thief hooked the top off and took a drink; the Hobgoblin smiled, and took another drink.

A moment later another of his kind had come over and taken out another of the bottles. He too began drinking. He was followed by more of his companions, opening new bottles or snatching one from their companions. This behaviour continued for some time until most of the bottles were empty, and then they started fighting between themselves, each, trying to take the last of the drink.

One of them was taking no notice and lolling against a tree. Thomas watched for a moment, and then a smile spread across his face. The hobgoblin was asleep. The drink was beginning to take effect. In the short time he was watching he saw one after another fall over and within moments they all appeared to be asleep.

Seeing the opportunity, Thomas immediately woke David, he had to put his hand over his mouth, to keep him as quiet as possible, while he whispered to him what had happened. They quietly repacked their things and loaded the ponies. They sneaked away into the night not noticed by the few hobgoblins, which were still more or less, on their feet.

To make as little noise as possible they led the animals along the grass verge beside the road. As soon as they were out of sight they mounted and galloped off to resume their journey west.

Determined to keep the lead they had established, they took a slight risk at the first town they came to and exchanged the ponies for fresh ones. This enabled them to make good time through the beautiful countryside as they made their way across Devon and then finally across the Tamar river into the county of Cornwall.

The rest of the journey passed without incident as they pushed further west going as quickly as they could. Even so it had taken them a full three days before they arrived near Tintagel, King Arthur's birthplace, on the North Coast of Cornwall.

That last night, David and Thomas finished off most of their supplies for their final meal.

'What do you remember about Grandmother?' Thomas asked David as he licked his fingers.

'Not a great deal. Mainly feeling safe when she was holding me after our parents disappeared. It's a long time ago; after all we were only four at the time.'

'I can remember she used to make a beautiful strawberry pie for us after we had gathered the berries from the garden.'

'Oh yes and once you had so many helpings you were sick,' David added, laughing.

'Why did we have to leave her? '

'Freya said it was to keep us all safe. That is why we didn't have a proper home for a long time. We travelled around the country for years before we came to Camelot and Freya found us the cottage so that she could start to grow plants and things.'

'I don't really understand what we were being kept safe from.'

'No, neither do I. At least we will get the chance to talk to Grandmother and find out. We don't even know what happened to our parents.'

'I don't know if Freya knew any more than we do, as she always said we would all be told when we were ready.'

'Well I don't know about you but I think I am ready now.'

'Hopefully lots of questions will be answered tomorrow. Now I think we had better get some rest.'

'Right I shall take the first watch, whilst you sleep. I shall wake you in three hours. After all we don't want to be caught now, so near our goal.' David added, but they did not think to look to the sky where a great dark shape was making its way towards them.

Chapter Six

The final morning dawned dry with a misty sun gracing the area with its gentle light. David was putting their bedding rolls on the back of the saddles when the ponies all started showed signs of panic, A very large dark shadow covered them, they pulled and pranced as they tried to pull the tethers out of his hand.

'Whoa, whoa,' he said, in a calming voice, not wanting to convey the panic he felt himself. He looked up and saw a large dragon; it was at least three metres in length. It looked very fierce with a mouth full of large teeth and sharp claws glinting in the sunlight as it circled around in the sky.

'Don't be scared, I shan't hurt you,' the dragon called down to them, as he made a final circle around before landing on the other side of some rocks. He poked his huge head around the rocks, hoping that hiding his great body would calm the ponies.

'My name is Greor. I live with your grandmother, she sent me to guide you on the last part of your journey.'

The ponies did quieten down after the dragon had landed. This in turn helped David and Thomas feel more relaxed. They had never met a dragon before and had not realised how big they were.

'We're pleased to meet you,' David said, politely. 'I'm David and this is my brother, Thomas. Is Grandmother well, and how did she know we were coming?'

'Your grandmother is very well. She's been watching you for the last two days, ever since Merlin sent her a message saying that something evil was in the air, unfortunately he did not know where it was coming from or for whom,' he replied. 'Now if you are both ready, we had better set off.'

David had many more questions he wanted to ask but decided that they would wait until they reached their journeys end. He turned to the ponies and saw that they had calmed enough to go back to cropping the grass.

Thomas brought the rest of their belongings across to the pack animal where David helped him load the saddlebags. Once this was done, they climbed back into the saddles and waited for Greor to direct them onwards.

The dragon unfurled the great wings from where they had been lying, neatly, along his back. With two beats he went high above the brothers' heads.

'Follow me,' he called down. And set off towards the distant coast.

David and Thomas urged their mounts into a fast canter over the heathland as they followed the great beast's lead.

Greor led them along the coast, skirting around the villages, then off towards the cliff tops at Tregardock. They crossed the fields and went between the hills, ever downwards, until they reached the very cliff edge.

Reigning in the ponies, they looked for a way down, but there was none. The tide was all the way in with the waves crashing on the rocks below.

David turned in is saddle and watched Greor as he landed behind them.

'Where does Grandmother live? You've brought us to the sea but there aren't any houses here. I don't understand'

'This way,' Greor called moving forward towards a passageway that had just appeared in the side of the hill.

'Wow! I wasn't expecting that,' Thomas said, laughing. He urged his pony forward into a large caved area. David followed behind both of them looking around in wonder.

Their way was lit by lanterns, each one set onto brackets set into the walls on each side. No sooner were they inside than the entrance closed behind them.

'Where are we, It's so big and light?' Thomas asked, in amazement.

'You're in my home,' a soft voice replied. 'Last time you were here we gave you a special drink to make you forget where you had been. That is why you can't remember much about me either. Now you're old enough to know everything.'

In front of them stood their grandmother, a woman of indeterminable age, grey hair piled on top of her head, her blue eyes sparkled as she regarded them in amusement.

'Grandmother?' the boys asked, and slid off their steeds.

'Yes I'm your grandmother but you must call me Rowena, as everyone else does. It's been far too long since I last saw you,' she sighed, 'why does it take trouble for us to meet again?'

David laughed at her.

'Yes, Rowena, we'll have plenty of time to catch up once we've told you why we've come for your help.'

Her face became grave.

'This must be something to do with Merlin's message. Come with me we can sit down and then you can tell me everything,' she said, leading them through an opening on one side of the cave. Here, they were surprised to find a comfortable seating area. It was warm and cosy with a wood burning stove on one side, blazing away merrily and a sheepskin rug in front of it with the chairs arranged around this.

David could not wait until he had seated himself and started telling of the plot to kill all the dragons. About the shadow men and the hobgoblins who had followed them on their journey to Cornwall.

Once Rowena had taken all this in, she looked from David to Thomas and asked anxiously, 'Where's Freya? I thought she would be with you.'

David glanced at Thomas and they both looked a little bit edgy.

'She told us to go ahead as she'd be fine. She was going to find out as much as she could before following us here.'

'She's so headstrong, I'll be happier when she's with us. Now I must go and arrange to send messengers immediately to all the different bands of dragons, to warn them of the danger.'

She hurried off, calling for Greor. A few minutes later she returned.

'I've arranged for messages to be sent to the nearest Dragon camp and then they, in turn, will spread the word of the coming danger.' She stood in the entrance for a few moments and sighed, 'I would've liked time to just sit and just talk with you, but that will have to wait as there's so much to do. First things first, put your ponies in over there,' she said, indicating a stable across on the other side of the middle cavern.

'Once they are settled, both of you come down to the kitchen for some food.'

Their grandmother disappeared down another passageway leaving the brothers to take care of the ponies. Once in the stable the animals were rubbed down, fed and made comfortable. When this was finished the twins set off to find their grandmother.

Following the path way, they went deeper into the cavern. The way went downwards until they must have been level with the beach. The boys looked about them in wonder at a wall which looked like water. To the left of them were two openings. The left one emitted a warm glow and a mouth-watering smell of food being prepared.

They started towards this when a movement in the right hand opening halted them.

Emerging was a small green Dragon, hardly bigger than a pony.

'Hello,' she said, 'I'm Shimmer. You have already met my father, Greor. You must be Thomas and David. Rowena told me all about you.'

She sat there in the soft light of the cave and her scales seemed to shimmer with a silver green light.

'Hi, it's nice to meet you, even if the circumstances aren't so good,' David said, and then asked, 'perhaps you could tell me how it's so light down here?'

'You had better ask Rowena'.' Shimmer replied, as the lady came out of the other entrance and joined them.

'Ask me what?' she enquired, 'I'm glad to see you have introduced yourselves.'

'We were wondering about the tide and the light.' David said.

"The light comes from the pool and it also stops the water coming in. It's rather a good spell, don't you think?' she replied, pointing across the way.

The boys' looked where Rowena had indicated and they realised the wall really was water.

'Wow! That's a brilliant spell.' Thomas said, as to his astonishment he realized that he could see through it and watch the fish swimming around quite oblivious of their audience.

'From the other side it just looks like the back of the cave, it also feels like the back of the cave so no one going in at low tide would be able to see or hear us. We can go in and out by using a special key to open the entrance.' She handed both of them a little gold key on a chain and pointed to a key hole set in the rock beside the water feature. 'Now come on, let's go and have something to eat before it all gets cold,' she said, leading them into the kitchen.

The boys said goodbye to Shimmer and followed Rowena through into a large room, with a table, in the centre, fully loaded with food.

On seeing this, the boys realised how hungry they were. Rowena sat in a chair and indicated to the boys to sit down. They did that and not much was said as they tucked in. When they had eaten their fill, they were shown to their quarters and told to rest whilst they waited for news of the dragons.

Both David and Thomas were both too worried to sit still and were soon pacing about the room as they tried to make sense of all the events that had taken place in the last few days.

'I just hope we were in time to warn the dragons.' David fretted.

'We couldn't have come here any quicker.' Thomas said, trying to soothe him.

'If we'd known where the dragons lived around our home, surely we could've warned them earlier?'

'But we didn't know where they lived, so it's not much use worrying about 'what if's' now.'

David moved to sit on the bed, and then rose again to resume his pacing up and down the room anxiously waiting for any news. At last he could stand no more.

'Come on I'm not going to wait here anymore. Let's go and see if Rowena's heard anything yet.' He pulled open the door and went out. Thomas eagerly followed his brother back to the area where they had met Shimmer.

They had only just arrived when Greor returned.

'The news is not good,' Greor stated, without preamble, 'as winter approaches, many of my kind make ready for hibernation. Most dragons don't like the cold so they make themselves a cosy nest and sleep from the first frost until springtime. The men knew this, so it was easy for them to sneak up and kill them, as they lay half-asleep. Dragons don't like to hurt humans, so they did not fight back until it was too late.'

'I was afraid of that. What have you arranged to happen now?' Rowena had arrived as Greor had started speaking, she sounded very worried.

'I have told them to go and warn all the other dragons. They are going to tell them to go away into the mountains, well away from the humans. I also told them that, if they preferred, they could come to join us here,' Greor replied.

'That's a good idea. I hope they come soon and then perhaps we will be able to find out why the people are doing this, because I've no idea. Humans and dragons have always lived quite happily together before now.' Rowena turned to her grandsons. 'When did Freya say she was coming to join us?'

'We're not sure. She said she was going to find out what Morgana was doing, and then she would join us. Hopefully she's on her way now, so I would think another day at the most,' David replied, frowning. 'I'll be glad once she's here as I'm a bit worried. Someone knew we were coming here; otherwise why send the hobgoblins after us?'

'I'll attempt to oversee her in my magic pool,' Rowena said, 'just to make sure she is all right.'

She left the little gathering and made her way back into her quarters.

'I do hope Freya has got away okay and isn't in danger,' David said, looking worried.

It was not long before their worst fears would be realised.

Chapter Seven

Freya watched as her brothers disappeared from view. She turned to go back inside her cottage as the first rays of dawn peeped over the top of the hills in the distance. She paused; certain that she had noticed something. Puzzled she tried to make out whatever it had been to catch her attention. Then she saw it. There definitely was movement in the shadows; some people were coming down the hillside. Whoever they were, they were moving in a westerly direction. That was the same direction as Thomas and David. As the light improved she recognised them and a feeling of horror washed over her. They were hobgoblins. She had to do something, but what?

Hurrying into the cottage, she immediately went into the kitchen to the fire where the flames were still burning with a blue light.

She bent to peer into the heart of the flames and asked

'Who sent the hobgoblins?'

A vision of Morgana calling them appeared, then the vision changed and she saw Morgana looking into her crystal ball. Even as she watched, Morgana lifted her dark head and stared straight at Freya. The look she gave her was so evil that Freya recoiled in fright. With a quick pass of her hand she returned the flames to normal but was it in time?

Freya, realising her danger, decided the best thing she could do was to follow the boys immediately. She went out to the sable and saddled a pony then rushed back to pack all the things she would need for the journey, she had no time to spare.

Back in the castle, Morgana observed Freya as she started her preparation.

'So they think that they can meddle in my affairs. They will rue the day they tried to cross me. I think I have underestimated you, Freya, but I shall no longer. I need to know more about you and what you are planning. I think you need to come and visit me then I can stop you and your ideas once and for all,' Morgana muttered to herself.

She immediately went back to her spells and called up a few more goblins. These she quickly sent to Freya's cottage to capture her.

Freya had collected the few things she needed for the next few days. Once finished, she returned to the kitchen where she poured water over the fire to put it out but to be on the safe side she put a fire guard around the hearth. Glancing around the room for the last time, she could not think of anything else so she left, locking the door behind her. Carrying her bag, she pulled her cloak tight around her shoulders; she turned to walk down the path only to find that her way was blocked by one of three hobgoblins. Without thinking, she swung the bag at him. He had not expected any resistance so was caught off his guard and the blow sent him spinning to land in a heap in the flowerbed.

Freya jumped over him and made a run across the grass towards the stables where her horse was waiting for her.

One of the other goblins ran after her. The other, realised where she was going ran up the street towards the stable door. Even so, Freya arrived first and pulled the bridle from the hook, threw herself into the saddle, pleased that she had had the forethought to make sure the animal was ready first. The horse set off at a run with Freya low over the animal's neck and exploded out of the doorway as the two hobgoblins arrived. The first grabbed at Freya's leg as she went past. She kicked out and sent him reeling backwards. The other one caught the bridle and held on tightly. The extra weight was enough to bring the animal to a prancing stop.

Freya could not reach her capture, as the horse plunged about, which gave the first hobgoblin time to regain his feet; he was joined by the one they had left at the cottage door. Between the three of them, she had no chance, they dragged her out of the saddle as she kicked and scratched, trying to break free until, exhausted, she was overcome. Her hands were tied behind her back before she was unceremoniously thrown; face down, across the saddle she had so recently left.

In this uncomfortable position they led her through the, still deserted, lanes until they arrived at the large wooden doors that led to Morgana's quarters. The doors were flung open by the lady herself.

'You,' she indicated the hobgoblin leading the horse, 'take the animal to the stable and put it amongst mine so no one will know it belonged to anyone else. You other two bring the girl.' She finished and swung around on her heels.

'I have some lovely quarters for you my dear, with a lovely view,' Morgana said, over her shoulder, as she led them in to the hall and up a very long flight of stairs that eventually led to a turret in the castle.

There was a heavy wooden door with a small opening in the top to allow a view of the inside of the cell.

There, Freya's bindings were untied, and she was pushed violently through the open doorway, sending her sprawling. She struggled to her feet and turned only to hear the door clanging shut and the key turn in the lock.

'I shall leave you to cool down, my dear, but I will be back later to see to you.' Morgana said, as she and the hobgoblins left her.

Freya looked around her cell; there was only a large heavy bed, a chair by a table and a window that had no bars. Hope filled her breast and she went over to look out. The view was magnificent, looking over the lovely countryside, with the hills in the distance, but Freya was not in the mood to admire it. She looked down at the walls but they were completely smooth. Feelings of despair washed over her. She was trapped. She went over to the bed and threw herself down as tears of frustration gathered in her eyes. Pulling herself together she rolled over on to her back and lay there as she tried to think of a plan to escape. It was no use relying on her brothers, they would not worry until she did not turn up in Cornwall and they did not expect her for days.

She also knew she must not let Morgana know where the boys had gone or why.

Freya was convinced that Morgana had been behind the death of her parents and would have no compulsion about killing her and her brothers if she found out their real name. They had taken the name of Lightfoot when they had left Cornwall, all those years ago, in the keeping of a traveller's family. They had stayed with them until Freya was old enough to take care of her brothers and she had set up home for the three of them, near to Morgana, hoping one day to find some proof to bring the witch to justice. Now she was in the clutches of the very person she wanted to punish. If Morgana found out their Grandmother was Rowena, all would be lost.

Chapter Eight

The first morning in Cornwall dawned bright and crisp. After an early breakfast the brothers decided to go for a walk along the shoreline. For some time, they seemed content to watch the rolling waves sending up columns of spray as they crashed against the many rocks in the bay. A beautiful blue sky reflected its colour in the sea as it sparkled in the autumn sunshine.

Thomas and David walked slowly along the sand avoiding the odd wave that sent its water further up the beach. The wind whipped at their hair and their clothes although it was not cold.

From the inside of the cave Rowena watched her grandsons. How she had missed seeing them over the years, missed them growing up from toddlers into the strong young men they were today. Their mother would have been so proud of them. One day she would have to tell them what really happened to cause the death of their parents. But right now there were more pressing things on her mind. She walked out on to the sand and over to where the boys stood.

If only they could just enjoy the relaxing Cornish air, David thought as he watched the old lady make her way over to them. Then he sighed and pushed his hair out of his eyes.

'I can't wait any longer,' David said to Rowena, 'what did you manage to find out?'

'I don't have very much to report as I couldn't see anything; it was just dark shadows whirling around over the whole of your village,' she replied tiredly. 'I tried and tried all night but could raise nothing. The only person, I can think of, who could block out that much is Morgana.'

'But why are they killing the dragons? Morgana must have something to gain; otherwise she wouldn't be doing it.' David mused.

'We'll know more when Freya arrives; I'd expect her sometime today. I must admit that I'm a little concerned about her travelling on her own. When we left, we'd no idea that someone was chasing us; otherwise we would've insisted that she travelled with us... I suppose she's all right,' Thomas answered his twin.

'I think I should go and try again also I'll ask Greor to fly out and look for any sign of her,' Rowena said, turning around and walking quickly back to the cave.

The boys followed her part of the way.

'I know, let's go and find Shimmer; Talking to her will take our mind of Freya whilst we wait for any news.' David took Thomas's arm and they strolled off to find her sitting outside her cave.

'I'm glad you've come I wanted someone to talk to,' she said, as soon as she saw them. 'It's nice to have some young company occasionally.'

The boys sat with her and asked questions about dragons, where they lived, what their likes and dislikes were and they wanted to know all about Shimmer.

They had been chatting together for about ten minutes when Rowena, came hurrying up to them.

'I've managed to find out about your sister. It's not good news. I'm afraid. She's been captured.'

'Oh no, now what are we going to do?' Thomas asked in despair turning to his brother.

'Where is she?' asked David.

'She's in the top turret of Morgana's quarters, she appears to be all right, at the moment, but I'm not sure why she's being held. No doubt we will hear from Morgana soon.'

'Meanwhile we must go back and rescue her,' David cried.

'You would never get past the guards outside the castle, never mind make it to the turret room. Even if you did get there you would still have to bring her back down the stairs with all Morgana's men against you,' Rowena interjected.

'We can't just sit about and do nothing,' David replied and Thomas nodded

'I could rescue her,' Shimmer said.

They all turned to her in surprise.

'How?'

'I could fly to the top of the turret and get her to climb out of the window onto my back and then bring her here.'

'I don't know. You make it sound so simple but it's so dangerous for all you dragons at the moment, also no one's ever flown on the back of a dragon before, how do you know you could manage it?' Rowena asked her.

'Just because it hasn't been done before, doesn't make it impossible,' she replied.

'She's right.' Greor came out of his cave closely followed by Shimmers mother, Sherna. 'She's the only dragon small enough to land on the roof and it would be very difficult for a dragon as big as me to fly in unseen.'

'I agree with your father,' Sherna added 'I'll be very proud to see you help in any way you can.'

Rowena looked from one face to another a look of relief covering her face.

'In that case I shall accept your kind offer. Especially as there is no other option open to us at the moment. I had better give you some directions for you to find Freya's prison.'

Rowena went and fetched pen and paper and proceeded to draw a map for the brave young dragon. Once Shimmer was satisfied that she understood the directions, she made her way out on to the cliff top. Everyone followed her where they gathered around her taking turns to wish her luck.

They were so engrossed in giving the little dragon last minute instruction that no one was looking upwards.

A voice called down to them. Up above, the sky appeared to be full of dragons as they came in low over the hill and circled around.

'Can we land here or should we go down on the beach?' the voice called down.

'You can land here, it should be fine,' Greor replied looking up.

They came down one after another, in fact there were only eight of them, all different shades of green. The last one to land was mottled with red. As he landed, Rowena broke away and ran towards the dragons, shouting as she went.

'Don't just stand there, go and fetch water and bandages from my cave, can't you see he's injured?'

Thomas rushed off to collect everything she had asked for, leaving all the others looking on in wonder.

Rowena put her hand gently on the back of the injured dragon and looked to see what damage had been caused.

'We'll have this cleaned up in no time and you'll be as right as rain. Can you tell us what happened?'

'The slaughter has been terrible; we are the only surviving dragons from England. The men have been coming in their droves and killing us. Why are they doing this? We don't understand. We have done nothing to them,' the leader of the flight spoke to them all.

'We don't know the reason yet, the only thing that we're fairly sure of is that Morgana is behind it somehow. We were just sending a dragon to see if she can learn more. She has to rescues my granddaughter from that evil woman's clutches,' Rowena replied looking over to where Shimmer was standing.

'This is worse than we thought and we can't afford to waste any more time. I'll leave immediately,' Shimmer said and walked away from everyone before she leapt into the air and swiftly flew off over the hill.

'Take care!' Rowena shouted to her as she looked up briefly from where she was tending to the bleeding dragon.

David stood watching her go, wishing her a safe journey and wondering what it would be like to ride on the back of a dragon. His daydreaming was ended as Thomas returned with water and bandages, which he handed to Rowena who immediately started to remove the blood and grime from the poor beast's scales.

'What is your name?' she asked

'Fredlie, but everyone calls me Fred.' he replied. 'The wound isn't too bad but there's a broken spear under one of my scales that's driving me mad, as I can't reach it,' he said turning his head to show where he meant.

Rowena immediately saw it; just behind the place his wing joined his body.

'Hold still,' Rowena said, as she wiped the blood from around its base.

'Ouch! That hurts,' Fred exclaimed.

'Sorry I'm being as gentle as I can. Now this is really going to hurt. I shall be as gentle as I can whilst I remove the spear, but you will feel better afterwards,' she replied.

'All right,' said Fred, closing his eyes.

She took hold of the broken shaft of the spear and with a quick pull it was out.

'You were right, it did hurt!' Fred cried.

Rowena did not look up from her work as she cleaned the wound and applied a liberal amount of salve making the bleeding stop.

'Oh that's better already, it's stopped hurting now.' Fred looked gratefully at her.

'Now perhaps someone can tell us everything that happened,' Rowena looked around as one of the other dragons came forward.

'My name is Jade, and I am Fred's partner' she said, 'and the others are Fraynor, Farled, Greylee, Grandie, Minter and Emerald.'

As Jade spoke each name the dragon it related to bowed their head.

'I'm Rowena and these are my grandsons, Thomas and David,' the lady replied. 'I just wish we could have met under different circumstances. Now tell us what happened to you all?'

Chapter Nine

Shimmer rose quickly into the sky leaving the incoming dragons in the safe hands of her friends. She now had one thought only, to find Freya as soon as she could.

Dragons have the power to fly very fast so the journey, that took three days for humans on horseback, took Shimmer only a few hours.

She arrived at the castle in the late afternoon. The drawing Rowena had shown her had been quite detailed so she had no trouble in finding the correct turret. She didn't want to draw attention to herself by flying around so, quickly; she landed gently on the roof and stood still listening carefully. She could hear someone laughing. It was not a nice sound. It sounded evil. If she had not been covered in scales she would have had goose pimples all over her body.

She climbed on to the parapet and looked down; there was light coming from the top window.

She took off again and landed quietly on the window ledge, perching dangerously on the edge, whilst looking around the corner into the room.

Morgana was there, luckily, with her back to the window as she paced up and down, addressing her prisoner, Freya, who sat tied in a chair facing her tormentor with a look of defiance on her face.

'My brothers know what you are planning and will defeat you.'

'I don't think so. If you had known my plans before they set off, they would not have left you behind. Now you are in no position to get in touch with them.' Morgana cackled once again. 'It does not matter what you think; we have killed the last of the dragons that were foolish enough to stay in England. Everyone is calling George "The Dragon Slayer" and calling him a hero. I wouldn't be surprised if they didn't make a saint of him. The only dragons left are so far away and so afraid of us now that we will not hear from them again. The Saxons and my army will kill Arthur and I shall become the new Queen,' Morgana said, full of confidence. 'I have sent word to your family telling them that you have agreed to come away with me as my servant. They will hear tomorrow and so stop thinking about you until it is too late and you, my dear, will be dead.'

Freya felt helpless, and glanced around the room trying to think of a way to escape. The only way with no bars was the window; she looked at it in despair, only to see Shimmer's face looking back at her. She let out an involuntary gasp, quickly changing it to sound like a sob as Morgana looked at her with suspicion then glanced over her shoulder at the window, but she saw nothing as Shimmer had withdrawn her head just in time.

'The thought of not seeing my family again is upsetting, I hadn't realised you were so clever,' Freya said, pretending to sob some more. 'How will they defeat the King, he has his army about him.'

'That is where you are wrong, His armies are being disbanded even as we speak and all his men will be going home for the winter. He will not even speak with his knights until Christmas. Aelle's army will join with mine and march on Camelot, where they will catch him with no defences and he will die,' Morgana gloated. 'Now I shall leave you to contemplate your fate, whilst I go and organise your funeral.'

She swept out of the room, locking the door behind her.

No sooner had her footsteps faded than Shimmer's face, again, appeared at the window. Putting her head right through, she said 'Can you move the chair to the window I'm not sure I can squeeze my body through this gap.'

'Excuse me for asking, but who are you?' Freya enquired.

'Oh sorry, I'm Shimmer, your grandmother sent me to rescue you.'

'But how did she know I needed rescuing? Oh never mind, you can tell me later.' She struggled to lean forwards and put her unbound feet, upon the ground and this way shuffled over to the window.

Shimmer stretched her front leg through the window and with her wickedly sharp claws hooked into the rope binding Freya to the chair. With a little pull, the claw cut the bindings, as if they were butter, and Freya was free.

'Thanks for that but now what? ' she asked. 'I don't think I shall be able to make it out of the door and past the guards, without being caught again. And it is much too high for me to climb down outside.' Freya looked miserable.

'You will not have to go out of the door or attempt to climb down the wall,' the little dragon replied, smiling.

'Then how am I to escape? It's alright for you, as you can fly.' Even as Freya said the words enlightenment dawned. 'You're going to carry me, aren't you?

'Of course, now climb onto the window ledge and then onto my back, so that I can take you back to Cornwall,' Shimmer replied.

'Have you ever carried anyone before?' asked Freya, as she hesitantly did as she was told.

'No, but I don't think I'll have any trouble.'

'Oh,' replied Freya, in a small voice, as she looked down and went very white.

'Don't look down.' Shimmer quickly said.

'Too late.' Freya clung to the window frame with her eyes tightly closed.

'Trust me, just climb onto my back and catch hold of the collar. I'm very strong,' she added.

Freya slowly managed to let go with one hand and reached for her rescuer. Once she had a firm hold on one of Shimmer's wings she let go with the other hand and managed to climb on to her back, careful not to look down this time.

It was only just in time because they heard footsteps coming back up the stairs and as the key grated in the lock Shimmer jumped off the ledge, down they spiralled, down and down. Freya held on tightly with her eyes closed tight, then with two beats of the little dragon's wings, the pair soared up and up until, they were high above the castle.

'I knew I could do it,' Shimmer cried gleefully.

Freya opened her eyes and took in the landscape below, now all shrouded in the gloom of the autumn night. 'What are those lights down below?' she asked

'They are the houses in your village, in the daylight you could see for miles; it's quite breath-taking.'

'I am happy to take your word for it,' replied Freya, really quite enjoying herself, sitting comfortably with the wind streaming through her hair. 'If we do this again I think I should wear warmer clothes. How long will it take to reach Cornwall?'

'Not very long, and if you snuggle down against my neck you will not feel as cold.'

'We'll need to get a warning to the King, telling him of his sister's treachery and stop him disbanding his armies. I'm sure my grandmother will have a plan to help,' Freya said as she snuggled tight into Shimmers neck. Every now and then she peeped out to gaze at the countryside as it changed beneath then.

Shimmer pushed hard with her wings and it seemed no time at all before they were over the moors of Bodmin where Rough Tor and Brown Willy, the two highest points, could be seen stark against the, now, moonlit sky.

Then below, they saw the rolling waves of the sea, sparkling and dancing their welcome to them as the two descended towards the little beach lit up in the silver light of the moon. The tide was now out far enough to allow them to land there.

Shimmer landed with a bump. 'I need a little practice at that,' she observed tiredly.

Freya slid off Shimmers back and flung her arms back around her neck.

'Thank you so much for rescuing me,' she said giving her a big hug. Then she turned to see her family hurrying across the sands to welcome them.

'We were a little bit concerned about you.' David said as he hugged his sister.

'We received a message from Morgana, telling us that you were going away with her. We were just praying that Shimmer reached you before you left,' Thomas added.

'You must send a message to King Arthur, telling him he is in great danger,' Freya cried. 'He must not disband his armies.'

Rowena came forward.

'First things first, you both had better come and have something to eat whilst you tell us your stories. Then when we have all the information I'll send one of the dragons to warn the King.'

'Before anyone does anything I have to say that Shimmer saved my life and if I can ever do anything to repay her I will.'

The little dragon blushed. 'It was nothing. I actually enjoyed having company as I flew home.'

They made their way towards the cave and Shimmer flew up to be with her own family, where they would all meet again shortly to make plans to help defeat Morgana.

Chapter Ten

Rowena led the way back to her cosy quarters followed by Thomas and David who each had an arm around Freya, in the middle.

Once they had had something to eat and Freya had told them her story they all made their way back to where the dragons were waiting. As they were walking David asked Freya.

'What was it like to fly?'

'It was great, once I overcame my fear of heights.'

'I wish I could have a go at it.' Thomas said.

'Why not!' David exclaimed. 'I've been thinking and I've come up with a great idea. Why don't we ask the other dragons to let us learn to sit on their backs when they fly? We could even learn to fight from their backs. That way we could be of help to King Arthur in defeating Morgana and her cronies. '

'You know it really could work, at least let's ask,' Thomas agreed.

The three of them set off to find Greor and put the idea to him.

They found him with the other dragons they had been talking.

Greor turned to David and the others as they arrived. 'I've sent one of the dragons to talk to King Arthur about his sister, so we don't have to worry about that at the moment. Now, Shimmer has told us how she flew back with Freya but we would all like to hear the full story.'

'Yes I agree, Freya please go right through your story again.'

Freya stood by the fire and Shimmer came and sat down beside her as she related the tale again. When she had finished there was a lot of mumbling from the dragons as they talked to each other, then Greor spoke for them all.

'We have discussed all this and we would like to help stop Morgana in any way we can.'

'Good,' David replied 'my brother and I have been talking too. We wondered if we could learn to ride and fight on your backs. Then we could attack the enemy from all sides at once.'

The dragons again talked amongst themselves for a short while before Fred turned to the boys and replied

'We think it would be a good idea, but we will need more people to ride on our backs.'

'We will have to put the word about in the local villages.'

Shimmer looked at her father. 'The trouble is we can do nothing except carry you. I wish there was something we dragons could really do to attack,' she put her head down on her front legs as she gazed sadly into the fire and breathed out a great sigh. The fire flared across from her.

'How did you do that?' David asked amazed.

'What? Oh making the flames blow, that's nothing, our breath always catches fire. I think it's all the wild garlic and herbs we eat. Why?'

'I'm not sure yet, but I think I have an idea.'

'What are you thinking?' asked Rowena, looking puzzled.

'I think we may be able to give the dragons a weapon, just let me work it through.'

Thomas grinned at his brother. 'I may be of assistance to you.' He went and collected his travel bag and removed his flint stone. 'I think we may need a few more of these.'

'Yes but I have not worked out how the dragons could strike the spark when they are flying.'

'You need a spark, will this do?' Sherna clicked her claws together and a spark flew off.

'Brilliant, now do that again and breathe out at the same time.'

Sherna did as she was told and her breath caught fire.

'Good gracious!' she exclaimed with flames billowing from her mouth. She snapped her jaws closed and the flames died.

'Do you think you could direct it where you wanted?'

'Probably, with some practice.'

'Well would you mind practicing outside?' Rowena said. 'Look what you have done to my lovely rug.'

She held up a slightly scorched article then started laughing. It was infectious; soon they were all rolling around holding their sides.

'You should have seen your face when you saw the rug. I've never seen anyone so surprised.'

'Well, I've never seen anyone breathing fire before;' Rowena replied as she wiped her eyes 'I can't wait until the others arrive.'

Just then there was a disturbance outside.

'Reinforcements I think.' She put her shawl around her shoulders and went out to meet the new arrivals. The others hurried after her.

Freya and the twins looked on in amazement at the newcomers. Their shape was the same as their English cousins but there the similarity ended. They were all shades of red! The colours ranged from the palest pink to a darkest red so dark that it was almost black.

'We'll not be able to surprise anyone with that colour, they will be seen for miles,' Freya murmured to Rowena.

'I had forgotten that they are all so beautifully different. This is going to be a bit of a problem,' the older lady replied 'What we could do with is the ring of invisibility or rather one for each person.'

Greor came across. 'May I introduce you to Caw, the leader of the Welsh dragons'?

He then turned to Caw and said

'This is Rowena, daughter of Cador, Duke of Cornwall and her grandchildren Freya, Thomas and David. They are friends of Arthur and the dragons and, with our help, are going to help stop Morgana and her evil.'

'Welcome Caw and your followers, may I ask how many of you there are?' Rowena asked as she walked forwards with a welcoming smile upon her face.

'I have brought nine of my relations, we are not a large band in the hills, most of our cousins stayed in the flatter country of England where it was easier to find food and now I fear they are no more.' The dragon looked sad.

'Some of us escaped,' Fred said as he came forwards. 'But it's all the more reason to overthrow the forces of darkness. Wait until you hear our ideas.'

'I don't suppose you have talked to Merlin have you?' Rowena asked.

'No, sorry,' Caw replied 'he left some time ago to join Arthur on his travels. We didn't expect him back at Camelot before Christmas. We heard the rumours of the slaughter of the dragons across the borders in England. But no one has been hurt in all of Wales. I suppose they think it is too far to bother with.' Caw turned to address Fred. 'Now do tell us of your ideas'

'Well I think David can explain it better than I could, after all it really was his idea.'

David stepped forwards and told them about how they had all discussed learning to fight whilst flying on the dragons' backs and how the dragons could set their breath on fire to help defeat Morgana's army.

The red dragons looked amazed, as they had never considered such a thing.

'We've never attacked humans before, I'm not sure that I could.' Caw spoke for them all.

'You could if you'd watched them kill your family and then turn on you,' a green dragon replied.

The green dragons told their red cousins what had happened to them when the men came to kill them all. The red dragons mumbled and roared when they heard the terrible things the men had done to their green cousins and every one of them agreed to start training themselves to fight with fire.

'What about the villagers you want to come and learn to fly on our backs, will we be able to trust them?' Caw asked.

'I, personally, will guarantee that no harm will come to you while you are here in Cornwall.' Rowena said, 'I've put a strong spell around this area to warn us if the shadows should try to infiltrate us.'

'I would think Morgana will not be bothering with the shadows anymore. Since Freya's escape she'll be intent on bringing her armies together as quickly as possible. She will want to kill her brother before we can warn him.' Thomas said.

'You're right, so we must start practicing our skills immediately,' Greor said.

There is only one thing we are going to have to solve now,' Freya said to Rowena. 'How do we camouflage them all to allow us to attack without being seen first?'

'Well, I have been thinking about that,' the older lady replied. 'You have heard of the thirteen treasures of Britain? Well one is a cloak called Pais Padarn, which is owned by Padarn Redcoat. It renders the wearer invisible. Now, what we really need is some thread from the cloak to take to the magic weavers in the caves of the welsh mountains. They'll be able to produce enough cloth to make into cloaks to cover us. This won't make everyone completely invisible, but enough to stop people being aware of them too soon.'

'What exactly do you mean, Rowena?' Freya asked her grandmother, puzzled.

'Well when the weavers make a cloth with a thread from the cloak on their magic looms, the result will make a cloth with a dream like quality, like something you see from the edge of your vision, not quite to be believed. You'll have to take Shimmer into the mountains and find Padarn to beg a thread, and then have it made up for all the dragons and their riders. No time must be lost; you'll have to start out immediately.'

Greor turned to Shimmer, 'You are too small to learn to fight, so your way of helping will be to have Freya as your companion and do all you can to help in other ways.'

'Yes Father,' Shimmer replied, then turned to Freya and said, 'I shall be honoured to be of any help to you all.'

'Great,' Freya replied, 'tomorrow we'll set out for our relations in the welsh mountains, they will surly know where Padarn can be found.'

'Well, we all have rather a lot to plan. I suggest we all go and make ourselves ready to start first thing tomorrow morning.' Rowena said, taking charge, then without waiting for a reply, she bustled off to start sorting out what Freya and Shimmer would need on their journey.

Chapter Eleven

Early the next morning, Freya put all her things into a small back pack, leaving her hands free to hold on to the collar Shimmer wore around her neck. Rowena, David, Thomas and all the dragons came out to see them go as they departed for Wales.

Rowena gave Freya a hug. 'Give our love to your aunt and uncle and take care.'

'I will, and don't worry I have Shimmer to look after me.' She turned to her brothers. 'Take extra care when you are learning to fly and fight with the dragons. I don't want to come back to find you with broken bones. That goes double for you Thomas; I know how reckless you can be sometimes.'

Thomas laughed and gave his sister a quick hug. 'I'll be fine, don't worry.'

David stepped forward and gave Freya a hug too. 'You just concentrate on your job in hand. I promise I'll keep a close eye on Thomas. Anyway the dragons will make sure we don't do anything too stupid.'

Freya nodded and then climbed on to Shimmers back and took a firm hold of the collar. 'Right, Shimmer, I'm ready.'

'Let's go then, good-by everyone enjoy your practices.' Shimmer called, as she sailed off into the sky.

With just a few strokes of her wings they were high in the air. Freya looked down at everyone and waved, then settled into Shimmers neck ready for her quest.

Below, her brothers and Rowena stood waving until they were a tiny dot in the distance.

'Come on,' Thomas said, 'it's time we started practicing.

The evening before, David and Thomas had talked to all the dragons and they had agreed to go out onto the beach area to see what could be achieved.

The time passed quickly and the tide started coming in. The dragons had great fun breathing fire at the click of their lethal looking claws, with the boys sitting on their backs as they flew around. But after a while of scorching each other they decided that the beach at Tregardock was too small and it was only available for a few hours while the tide is at its lowest.

'I think we are going to have to find somewhere more suitable,' David decided as he came in, yet again, to change his burned top.

'Well you could have a look down the coast.' Rowena replied, grinning at her grandson's smoke blackened face.

'Come on everyone lets go and find somewhere else,' he called as he went back to join everyone.

'There's a large stretch of beach a few miles down the coast,' Greor said.

'That would give us more room,' Caw agreed. 'Come on lets go,' he called as he took to the sky once more.

David climbed on to Sherna's back and Thomas went with Greor. They took off followed by all the other dragons and flew further down the coast to see what they could find.

A few minutes later they arrived at the neighbouring cove, to find it had a large amount of sand for use when flying in to attack targets. Even when the tide came in there was enough sand to enable some form of combat to be practiced. It was ideal.

They landed and quickly organised setting up of targets using driftwood.

By lunchtime the brothers were hitting the targets with their arrows from their positions on the dragons' backs. The dragons, too, were now quite adept at scorching their targets.

They all were beginning to enjoy themselves.

Rowena came with a pony and trap, to bring them some food, and watched for a while.

Everyone stopped for a while to gather their breath and have some lunch when they realised there was a large gathering of locals assembled on the cliffs overlooking the bay, watching with envy at the goings on.

They resumed their practice and one of the watchers left the crowd to make his way down to the sands. The next time David came around he saw the man waiting and signalled the others to land with him. Immediately the man approached.

'We've come to join you, we saw the notices in the local villages and we want to help.'

'What notices?' David asked.

'I put some up,' Rowena said coming forward. 'You are going to need more people to ride the other dragons. We'll need all the help we can get.'

David and Thomas looked up at the cliff top and saw that the other people had started to make their way down to join them.

The people on the beach watched and waited until they had all arrived. Then the first man spoke.

'May I introduce myself, I'm Marcus from St Teath and these good people are my followers and friends.' He made a sweeping gesture with his hand, indicating all the people.

There was a commotion at the back of the throng.

'Excuse me please, do make way. At once,' an imperious voice commanded. The men stepped back to let through a tall lad closely followed by two others.

Marcus laughed.

'Don't be fooled by the way they dress; I would like to introduce my daughters. This is my eldest, Faith.' The young woman inclined her head to the brothers. 'Next are Hope and my youngest Charity.'

They all smiled charmingly and went to stand next to each other. They were all very alike with large brown eyes and long dark hair tied up and tucked under hats. All were dressed similarly in the same fashion of all the local young men, with loose fitting tops and long trousers worn over boots.

'We don't want to stay at home with the other women, we want to help you and the dragons' making sure Arthur stays as our rightful King,' Faith said and her sisters murmured in agreement.

'I want to fly on the back of a dragon.' added Hope.

David smiled at her. 'Of course you can help. Our sister would be pleased to have you. She is away on a mission at the moment but as soon as she returns I know you'll get on famously.'

'I'm Edwin, Marcus's steward and I, too, would like to help' said a tall fair man and stepped forwards.

Marcus went on to introduce everyone else.

'You are, all, more than welcome to join us,' Thomas said, smiling broadly at the assembled people. David nodded his agreement from his position beside the girls.

They all moved over to the dragons and David and Thomas, with some input from the great beasts, explained to them what they were practicing.

The dragons agreed to take everyone up for a ride, one at a time. Before long, everyone had had a flight on the back of one or other of the dragons and were starting to practice just staying on their backs as the great beasts swooped and soared before diving to fire a great breath of flames at the targets.

One or two of the people found that they were no good at flying. They went to join Rowena collecting grasses and drift wood to build into bigger and better targets for practicing. Soon everyone had found something they were good at. But there were still more, would be, riders than dragons to carry them. Each one worked their hardest to become the best and outdo each other.

Thomas and David stood together and watched as the three sisters had a practice run they could see that they were very good riders and, being light, were easy for the dragons to carry as they swooped and soared over the golden sands and the sparkling sea.

Marcus and Edwin more than held their own as they overcame the novelty of flying around on the great beasts backs.

A break was called later when some of the village women brought bread, cheese and drinks for them all. A party atmosphere took over as they stood around chatting and laughing at some of the early spills.

To begin with it had been decided only to fly over the sea. This way the riders would only have a cold dip rather than landing on the hard sand. This meant that no one was really injured, unless you count the pride of some of the men as they realised the girls were as good, if not better, at riding on the dragons backs as any of them.

David and Thomas went over to them to congratulate them on their skills.

'I have to say you looked as if you had been stuck on with glue,' Thomas said to Faith.

'Thank you, you aren't bad yourself. I think being allowed to ride my father's spirited horses, from the time I could hardly walk, has a lot to do with it.'

'Hope and Charity were just as good,' David added.

'Oh, thank you but Faith and Hope were always better riders than I am. I think it's because I am a bit more timid,' Charity said, with downcast eyes.

'You mean you're more ladylike than your sisters.' Marcus had come up beside her and put his arm around her waist. His other two girls smiled at him.

'The trouble is I find it hard to say no to my daughters, as I've no son, it gives me great pleasure to be able to share things with the three of them.'

Edwin came and joined them. 'Sorry to interrupt you but I think I have an idea to make things easier for us when Dragon riding. Greor and I have been talking; he told me his daughter, Shimmer, wears a collar and this made it easier for Freya to hold on. So we thought if we made a collar for all the dragons' necks, we could attach a pouch or something to put our weapons in. Not to mention there would be something to catch hold of when quick manoeuvres are necessary.'

'That seems like a good idea, let's go and talk to the others,' David replied. 'Then perhaps I could be as good as Hope when we have to turn tight corners.'

They all laughed, earlier David had very nearly fallen in the sea when Sherna had swerved to avoid colliding with Greor, if she hadn't righted herself quickly and allowed him to gain his balance he would have been very wet.

Hope looked across at David and smiled, 'You are as good, I'm sure I'd have fallen in the sea if I'd to manage a manoeuvre like that.'

He grinned back at her and went over and putting his arm around her shoulders, he gave her a squeeze, 'You're as good as any boy,' he told her.

Hope's face lit up, she felt wonderful, but whether from the compliment or because David had put his arms around her, she was not too sure.

Everyone had agreed to the use of collars so Marcus sent his servants to measure the size of each of the dragons' necks and then to arrange for them to be made.

'I think everyone has done really well today. Now I think we should all go and get a good night's sleep. Hopefully we'll have the collars to help us tomorrow, so we need to be fresh and ready,' Rowena said, coming forward and putting her arms around the shoulders of her grandsons.

'I'm extremely proud of you two, you have been tireless in helping teach the others,' she added in a quiet voice.

The brothers both looked pleased as they wished goodnight to everyone, promising to meet up again at eight the next morning.

The following morning after everyone had a good night's sleep, probably the fresh air and extra exertion had helped. They were all there and waiting on the beach when the dragons arrived at eight.

The collars had been made and were soon fitted by the eager hands.

The riders sat just in front of the wings, and could hold on to the collars when a quick turn was needed. This made it easier to ride on the dragon backs and by the end of the day they were flying in and hitting the targets with their arrows more often than not. Whilst the riders learned their riding and shooting skills the dragons learned to breathe out as they passed over the targets and click their claws to make the spark to light the flame.

At the beginning they had to come in one at a time with everyone well away to avoid being burned. Luckily they were all fast learners and it did not take long before they all became quite expert, flying around, weaving in and out of each other and most importantly only scorching what was aimed at.

The newcomers were as full of fun as the brothers, everyone trying to be the best. They all knew there were only twenty dragons so only the very best would be picked to be dragon riders for the final battle. Quite a friendly rivalry grew between Thomas, Faith, Hope and David. While Charity tried equally hard to be as good as her two sisters. Although she enjoyed the thrill of riding on the Dragon's back, her heart was not in the thought of real fighting and worried that she would be a liability if she were chosen for the forthcoming battle. She decided to go and seek out Rowena to confide in her.

'I'm worried that I'll be chosen because I'm Marcus's daughter, not because I'm one of the best riders.'

'Don't worry yourself. The fairest way of choosing is to have a tournament,' Rowena decided. 'Tomorrow we'll have a match, everyone against everyone and the best twenty will be chosen. Afterwards we'll have a grand party. That way everyone will have something to look forwards to.'

'That sounds a fair way to decide who should ride,' Charity agreed, as the two of them went back to the riders as they assembled to discuss the day's practise.

Rowena went and stood on a handy rock to make herself seen by everyone.

'Listen everyone, I've thought of a way to decide who can fly with the dragons. We'll hold a tournament and then only the best will win a place to help defeat King Arthur's enemies.'

'That's a great idea,' David said, turning to Hope he added. 'That'll show I'm as good as you.'

'You are as good as me, probably better,' she replied shyly.

He smiled at her as she stood, catching the last of the afternoon sun shine on her face and his heart did a little summersault, he hadn't realised just how lovely she was. They stood looking deep into each other's eyes; their heads drew closer to each other. Then the moment passed as Thomas and Faith came over.

'I bet we can hit more targets then you two,' Thomas said.

David shook his head to clear the bemused look from his face and turning to his brother replied.

'You've a bet.' He turned back to Hope, 'what do you say? Shall we beat them?'

'We'll leave them standing,' she replied staring straight into his eyes. Then with a shy smile she turned to her sister took her arm and walked away.

The rest of the afternoon and evening was spent preparing for the forthcoming tournament. The rules had to be drawn up and it was decided that there would be a draw with everyone's name in a hat so that the running order could be decided. They also decided to have another draw as to the order that the dragons flew. That way the dragons would fly once, and then have a rest as the other nineteen flew before it was their turn again, that way none of them would get too tired.

Whilst the, would be, riders decided on the rules of the competition Rowena enlisted Charity's help to talk to the local women about making a banquet to celebrate afterwards.

It was late in the evening when everyone finally retired to their beds, all in a state of excitement with the thoughts of the coming day.

Chapter Twelve

Shimmer and Freya left North Cornwall and followed the coast going further north. By keeping the sea on their left and going as straight as they could towards their goal they found that within an hour they reached the Severn River estuary. Thy followed it east for a while before crossing at the narrowest point.

Freya looked down at the blue sparkling water. 'One day they'll build a bridge across there to make it easier for ordinary people to reach Wales,' she said.

The good weather held for them and the sunshine made their journey very pleasant as they flew on. Within another hour the land beneath the pair became mountainous with deep valleys in between each new mountain. Still they flew on, until, at last, they saw the valley that Freya remembered. She asked Shimmer to fly down lower so that as they followed the river Freya could look for places she remembered from her childhood. Eventually they came to a small town that was familiar.

'It's not very far now, below is the place our grandmother was born,' she said.

They over flew the house, and carried on over the forest behind it until they came to the centre of the woods, where there stood a beautiful little cottage.

'That's the place; can you land in the clearing?'

'Of course,' Shimmer replied circling down to land safely close to where the relatives of Freya and Rowena still lived.

Freya slid off Shimmer's back as the door of the cottage flew open and an old couple came out, their faces wreathed in smiles as they recognised the young woman striding towards them. Hurrying across to meet her they took it in turns to hug Freya.

'Freya, there's lovely to see you, how are the family? I couldn't believe my eyes when I looked out of the window and saw you on that little dragons back,' her uncle said, beaming all over his old face.

His wife pushed him out of the way and took both Freya's hands in hers and looked her up and down. 'My, you've grown into a beautiful woman; you do remind me of your mother.' She looked sad for a moment but once she had gathered herself together she went on. 'What brings you here?' She smiled at her niece. 'But where are my manners? You must both be in need of some refreshments.'

Taking Freya by the arm she led her into the cottage.

'You don't seem to be fazed by my arriving on a dragon,' Freya observed.

'Bless you, we see many dragons. They quite often come to the woods to collect nesting material, especially at this time of year,' her aunt replied.

They went through the door into a little kitchen.

Her uncle remained outside where he fetched some food and water for Shimmer. Then, when he was happy that he had seen to all her needs, he followed the other two into the cottage. The dragon, even though she was much smaller than a full grown one, was still too big to follow so was content to wait outside as she was able to look in through the window.

Her aunt had been busy preparing some tea for Freya and when her uncle came in she sat down to eat.

Freya told them of Morgana's plan to kill King Arthur and to take the crown, also about how the dragons had been attacked and so many killed.

She continued. 'We left Rowena and the twins, working with some of the dragons that are left. They are practicing ready to go to war to defeat the dark forces and help save the King. But the most important thing is; we need to find Padarn Redcoat and the magic weavers. Can you help us?'

Her aunt thought for a moment.

'Well, the weavers are easy. They live at the top of the mountain above this house. They're just under the rocking stone on the way to Merthyr Tydfil. They are three sisters with long grey hair and very serene, beautiful faces with piercing blue eyes. One sister does the spinning, the second the weaving and the third one cuts the cloth, to make their magic clothes. Once the cloth is ready they, all three, sew up the garments adding more spells as they make them. Good spells for good people, but be aware all their clothes can only be used for good, the spells will freeze you to the bone if you try to use them to do something that is bad or selfish.'

'What about Padarn?' Freya asked.

'I think you may be in luck,' her uncle interjected. 'I was only talking to Jones the pub this afternoon and he'd heard of a meeting in Cardiff for all the wizards here about. So we are expecting Padarn Redcoat to be passing through the valley in the next few days, on his way there.'

'Well you had better go down to see Jones again and ask him to pass the word to have Padarn come to Forest Cottage to meet with us. No need to say anything about Freya and Shimmer, just in case there are spies about,' his wife advised him.

'Right, I'll go straight away,' replied her uncle with a grin on his face.

'Now don't you be staying out to all hours. Remember you have guests.'

'All right, all right I'll just be long enough, so no one suspects anything.'

He went off, whistling, leaving his womenfolk to catch up on all the family news.

Freya and her aunt were in bed and asleep long before her uncle returned, a little the worst from wear.

The next morning Freya awoke early and went to the end of the track to see if she could see any visitors approaching.

After a short while she returned to the cottage and started pacing about picking up and putting down things, without taking any notice of what she was doing.

'For goodness sake sit down and have some breakfast, your pacing will not bring him any sooner.'

'What if he's already gone past and we can't find him? Everything will be finished before it's started.'

'Don't be so silly; your uncle said Padarn had not been through the valley yet. Just sit down and have a cup of tea.'

Freya did as her aunt said and she did feel better after a cup of tea.

The next two days passed uneventfully. Freya became more and more worried, convinced that they had missed the wizard and would have to try to follow him on the road to Cardiff.

The morning of the third day was the same and having been out, again, unfruitful in looking for Padarn. She had made up her mind that she would have to move on and went about packing up her things even though her aunt and uncle tried to tell her to have patience. In fact she had hardly finished her packing before there was a knock on the cottage door and on opening it there stood a very old man carrying a bundle over his shoulder.

'Hello, my name is Padarn and I understand someone needs to see me.'

'Oh do come in. I thought I'd missed you' cried Freya, nearly hugging him in her delight.

'We need your help!'

She led Padarn into the warm kitchen where her aunt made him sit by the fire and busied herself making him some tea and breakfast. Whilst he was eating Freya told him of their plight.

'You see we need a thread of your cloak,' she finished.

'My dear,' the old man replied 'If everyone had a thread of my cloak there would be none left and then where would I be?

'But we need to weave it into some cloth to make into cloaks for everyone it's for all the dragons and their riders.'

'Wouldn't it be better for the leader to borrow the cloak and lead your fighters into battle at least he would be invisible and safe?'

'No, that wouldn't work; there are only twenty of us and probably hundreds of the enemy. We need the covering to give us as much of an advantage as possible.'

The sage looked thoughtfully at Freya.

'You do realise that, if you only had one thread in all the cloth you would need, you would not be completely invisible. At best your shapes would not seem solid, 'he paused and thought for a moment. 'I suppose if you came at them with the sun behind you. You'd be upon them before they realised'

Freya looked at him with hope beginning to shine in her eyes.

'Please give us a chance. We are such a small army, we would not have a chance against Morgana's forces without some outside help,' Freya begged, and then she continued. 'I appreciate if you give a thread to us then the next time someone asked, you would have to say yes again and it would not be long before you had no cloak left. So, how would it be, that we promised to return all the material to you after the battle and then you would have it to lend to folks if they needed it.'

Padarn smiled. 'I've listened to everything you have said. Your cause is good and just, so I have decided to give you a thread, as you have asked, but with just one stipulation.'

'Yes anything you want.'

'You have to ask the weavers to include a very strong spell to stop anyone attempting to do anything evil whilst they are wearing the garments. Therefore they will be rendered powerless if any cloaks fall into the wrong hands.'

Freya threw her arms around the old man's neck. 'I promise to ask, 'she said.

Padarn smiled sheepishly as he disentangled himself from her embrace. Leaning down he picked up his bundle and took out his cape, which looked like nothing special, just an ordinary homespun warm cloak. He placed it on his shoulders … and he was gone…. It really did work! The old man removed his cape again

'Just for effect,' he laughed as he sat down and pulled a long thread from the hem and handed it to Freya.

'I don't know how we can thank you enough, but now I must go and find the weavers for them to start their job, time runs short and the need is great.'

'Just save our land from Morgana's black magic and that will be thanks enough.'

The old man gathered his possessions together thanked Freya's aunt for her hospitality and left them.

Freya immediately made ready to follow him but first she went over to her aunt and uncle and gave them a big hug each and picked up her bag.

'Thank you for helping me, or rather us, we must go and arrange for the cloth to be woven. I hope we'll see each other again, soon, in better times.'

Freya kissed them both on their cheeks and went out to join Shimmer who had been listening at the window. She mounted the little dragon and they flew off to find the weavers cave.

Her aunt and uncle came out to wish her god speed and wave her away.

The old ladies, with their magic, had overseen Freya's exchange with Padarn and knowing of the urgency of the mission had their loom ready for the thread as soon as Freya arrived.

In no time at all, it had been added to the other threads and spun. They worked all day and into the night, until all the cloth was woven. This they quickly cut into various sizes and made it into the cloaks. The finished garments had the appearance of clouds because the thread had been spun into their wool from their own flock of Welsh mountain sheep Some cloaks were very large, to cover the dragons, and the rest just right for the riders. Every one of them was made with a magic spell added.

'If any of these cloaks fall into the hands of anyone evil they will not work. They will just become ordinary cloaks but with one difference they will not warm the wearer, in fact it will make them freeze completely if they carry on wearing it,' one of the old ladies told Freya and she laughed.

At last all was ready. The bundles were securely tied before Freya took them and fastened them on to Shimmer's back. Freya thanked the three sisters for their work and offered a bag of gold.

'We don't require payment for helping rid the land of the evil that Morgana would bring, if she were allowed to overthrow her brother. Quickly go back to Cornwall because we can feel the darkness spreading.'

Freya acknowledging the warning, kissed each of the old women, climbed onto Shimmers back. With a mighty leap, for such a small dragon, they were once again airborne and away on their flight back to Cornwall to catch up on all that had happened in their absence.

Chapter Thirteen

Freya and Shimmer arrived back in the middle of the preparations for the match.

There were great bonfires on the beach with pigs and sheep roasting over them, plus the people from the surrounding villages, were busy making bread, cakes, bowls of vegetables and fruit and not forgetting the Cornish Pasties.

As many eager hands took the bundles of cloaks from Shimmer's back, the boys told their sister of the latest developments.

'So we are all going to have a chance, but the twenty best will become the Dragon Riders and earn a cloak for the forthcoming battle.'

By now the sun had begun to set.

'Come on everyone, to bed, we have a full day tomorrow,' Rowena went around shooing everyone off. Then when all was quiet she made sure the roasts were taken care of by the villagers, who took the meat and wrapping it in clay before placing it back into the dying embers, to allow it to finish cooking, slowly, through the night. Then she, too, went to bed.

The next morning dawned fair, with a little bite in the air, which soon disappeared as the sun came up. They had been lucky with the weather as it had been unseasonably warm for the time of year. It was now the first week of December, time was running out.

The first event was the archery. There were two targets and each man had three arrows, for each shoot off, the best were to go on to the next round. There were forty-eight competitors so this took most of the morning. Competition was fierce, all of them wanted to be the ones chosen. Greor had already decided that

Shimmer would not actually be in the battle. She was too small to carry a full-grown person, with armour, for a long period of time. Freya was going to ride her and stay out of harm's way, ready to bring news to and from home if, and when necessary.

The twenty-four winners, from the morning's competitions, then had to mount the dragons and as the beasts came flying in shoot at the targets again. This part was arranged to start after a light lunch. No one wanted to eat very much as they were all anxious to finish. The, normal leisurely, break lasted only fifteen minutes before the dragons and the riders were lined up ready to see who would gain the honour of going to battle to save their King.

First to go was David and Sherna. Up they flew in a tight circle to come flashing back down towards the target.

'Steady,' muttered David to himself as the target came into range and he pulled back his bow and let loose the arrow. It flew straight and true right to the centre of the target.

'Yes!' he exclaimed and punched his fist into the air. He indicated to Sherna to land.

'Congratulations,' Thomas said as he patted his brother on his back before he went over to Greor to have his try and told the dragon 'We'd better be as good or we'll never hear the last of it.'

Thomas proved himself to be just as good as his twin and when he ran across to join him and their sister he hugged her and said, 'I must admit to being rather pleased with our performances.'

Freya looked at them both with mixed emotions, on one hand she was proud of their achievements and on the other she was worried for their safety, as she thought of the dangers of being involved in the mission against the forces of evil. Nothing of her thoughts showed on her face as she smiled at her two brothers

The rest of the competitors were just as dedicated and all of them hit their targets. It was difficult to bring them down to the final twenty but it had to be done, so the ones that had their arrows nearest the centre had to be chosen.

The final line up was, Thomas with Greor, David with Sherna, Marcus with Fredlie, Edward with Caw, Faith with Cawson, Hope with Jade and the other fourteen paired up with the remaining dragons. Charity was not chosen and she stood in Rowena's arms trying to look pleased for her elder sisters.

'Try not to be too disappointed,' the older lady said, 'someone has to be here as backup and ready to treat the wounded and that is just as important a job.'

The young girl looked up at her gratefully.

'I'm better at cooking than fighting anyway,' she said, resigning herself to being left behind.

Once all the places had been filled they went on to enjoy the wonderful feast that had been prepared. When most of them had eaten their fill and the mead was being passed around, Thomas stood up.

'I would like to propose a toast to my sister Freya, who is just as good a rider as my brother and I, but did not have the opportunity to compete for a place in the Dragon Flight because she was off doing important business elsewhere... To Freya!' He raised his glass and everyone else did the same.

'To Freya,' they called as they held their glasses aloft before taking a sip.

'Whilst on the subject of toasts,' David added. 'Here's to all the other people who weren't lucky enough to join the Dragon Flight and who now will join the main army and fight with King Arthur on foot…. To the gallant losers.'

He raised his glass and took a sip.

Many more toasts were made before the party finished but that did not stop the riders all being back on the beach early the next morning.

They practiced all day, flying in formation, going for the targets one after the other, weaving in and out of each other as the dragons flew as fast as they could, until they all knew the capabilities of everyone else.

There was not much time left. Already the foot soldiers had left, in secret, to join up with the King and his army, so everyone was starting to think of the coming battle.

David called everyone together.

'We're no longer doing this for fun and I just wanted to say to you that I am proud of you all. When we go into battle it's going to be a case of every one of you will have to look out for yourselves but we must not lose sight of each other and try to watch each other's backs. I promise you all; I'll do all I can to keep you safe.'

Marcos reached over and grabbed his hand, and shaking it said, 'Well said, David and I, too, promise to watch out for each and every one of you.'

All the other riders came over and as they shook David's hand, they too, vowed the same. They drifted off in their ones and twos until, only Thomas, Faith and Hope remained with David.

'That was a good speech. You always think of the right thing to say. You are a natural leader and I'm proud to be your brother.' Thomas said.

'Thank you,' David replied quietly. He patted Thomas on the shoulder and taking Hope's hand moved off leaving the other two to their own devices.

Hope looked at David with shining eyes.

'You'll take care of yourself too, won't you?'

'Don't worry; life is too good to let anything happen to me, if I can help it.'

They made their way back to the dragons and rode them back to Rowena's cave where they parted to get good night's sleep.

Chapter Fourteen

Merlin had received a warning from Rowena about the intended attack on Camelot and had quickly sought an audience with his King

'Come in my friend, come and sit by the fire, this castle must be a draughty place for your old bones.' Arthur indicated a chair on the other side of the fireplace from him.

Merlin walked over to the offered chair and sat down.

'Thank you for your concern but I do not suffer from the cold any more than anyone else.' He smiled at his ruler. 'This is no time for pleasantries. I have some very grave news from the West Country. I am reliably informed that your half sister and her accomplices, Aelle the Saxon, are planning to attack you, here, over the festive season. We have a traitor in our midst. They know that our army is very under strength at the moment.'

Arthur looked aghast. He rose from his chair and started pacing the room with his head down. Suddenly he stopped and faced Merlin.

'We are going to have to trust to our instincts on this one. Who has been spending time with Morgana during her times at court? And who lives over to the east of our county?'

'There are two names that spring to mind on both counts,' the sage replied 'one is the young Knight, Edward, who succeeded to his father's castle, but not the land. It so happens that his father was a gambler and lost everything, other than the building, to Lord Alon, your grandnephew. I remember that night well. It was late summer and we were all relaxing after your last campaign. There were the three of them, Edward's father, Alon and Morgana, they had had a lot to drink and, if I remember correctly, it was Morgana who showed them a new game of chance! She must have been planning something all that time ago. Alon has much land of his own, plus, what he shall inherit from his own father, but he was always one for a beautiful face.'

'Why Edward?' Arthur asked. 'He is waiting to be made a full knight of the round table. Surly he would not jeopardise his chances. Against that, Alon has already taken the oath of allegiance, I am sure he would not break his word.'

'We will not be certain for a while but everything points to it being one of these two. We can at least start to contact the rest of our men. May I suggest we call each of your Knights to you and explain the situation to them? We could then send them back to their homes to allow them to gather whatever armies they can, in the short time we have. If we gave out the excuse that they should join their families at this time of year, I'm sure we would be believed.'

Arthur looked relieved that the answer had been given to him. He immediately sent a page to call his Knights in and, one by one, he warned them of a traitor in their midst. They, each in turn, fell to their knees in front of their monarch and reaffirmed their oath of allegiance. Swearing they would be back to protect him, with their men as soon as possible.

The knights were further told not to bring their men back to Camelot but to meet at Badbury Rings by the middle of December, where they would wait for the invading army. They knew Aelle must come that way to reach the intended battlefield of Camelot.

Sir Belvedere and Sir Lancelot remained with their King until all the other knights had left. They wanted to challenge both Edward and Alon.

'Sire, we would soon make them tell us which of them the traitor is and then we would put him to the sword,' Sir Lancelot cried.

'We don't like leaving traitors around while we're away from you,' Sir Belvedere added, 'who would protect you?'

'I have all the protection I shall need, knowing you will go and do my bidding. I'm sure the enemy will not change their plans at this late date. If you killed the informer, they would know we are aware of the plot. Also, my sister is a very persuasive person, with a little bit of her magic; she could make most people do anything. We must not judge the poor misguided person too harshly.'

King Arthur smiled kindly at his two most loyal knights

Sir Lancelot came forward and again kneeled before Arthur.

'My Liege, you shame me. You are good and fair. I'll go and bring as many men as I can find to meet you at the appointed time.' He took his King's hand and kissed the ring before rising and bowing out of the room.

Sir Belvedere did likewise and promised that he, too, would have his army ready for the forthcoming battle.

When Arthur and Merlin were once more alone, the king turned to the older man and said, 'I am, indeed, blessed with many good men. With their help we will overcome the invading armies and keep the evil out of our lands.'

'It won't be from want of trying, by your knights, they all love you as a father. Also I am reliably informed you have others preparing to fight at your side.'

'Of whom are you referring?' Arthur looked at Merlin with a puzzled look.

'I am referring to the grandchildren of Rowena, daughter of your friend Cador, Duke of Cornwall. They have raised a small army of Dragon Riders and are even now preparing to come to your assistance.'

Merlin went on to explain what he had learned.

'They're so young, and so many people will die in the coming battle. We can't let Morgana's evil take over my kingdom.' The king stood with a sad look on his face as he contemplated all the sacrifices his people were prepared to make to keep their homelands free.

Chapter Fifteen

Morgana had not been idle, even though she knew nothing of all the preparation being made in Cornwall. She was not hurrying unduly as she had not yet been informed of Freya's escape.

As Morgana had no more use for Freya, she had simply sent the hobgoblins to kill her but when they discovered her missing they were disappointed but did nothing. They had just assumed someone else had done their work for them.

Using her powers, Morgana called on the king of the Twilight Kingdom to send his Death Riders to come to join her army. These riders had no fear in battle because they were already dead but had been brought back to a, kind of, life destined to do whatever was wanted of them. They were shrouded in black flowing robes from head to toe, even the horses, with only slits for eyeholes where the glazed eyes of the living dead could be seen. Invincible against swords or arrows there were only two things that could destroy then, one was strong magic and the other fire.

Not relying on these alone, Morgana had also cast her spells to bring more of her shadow men and hobgoblins to join her army of evil. She felt certain that her army plus all the men Aelle would have at his command they would have no trouble in annihilating Arthur and his men.

Edward, her informant from Arthur's court, had had been completely fooled by the King and Merlin. He sent a message to Morgana, reassuring her that all was going according to the plan. He went on to tell her that there were actually fewer knights at the court than there had been as Arthur had told them to go home to their families to prepare for the festive season.

While Morgana was gathering her demonic forces together, her partner, Aelle, had been busy too. He had sent, to all his neighbours, calling up favours, to make them bring their armies to his aid. He was not popular, and did not receive as many offers of help as he would have liked, but even so with the numbers he had managed to raise, he had made a formidable army, ready to join forces with Morgana and overthrow Arthur and his knights.

The men started to come together, in the South Downs, during the second week in November and by the twentieth of the month they were ready to move.

The weekend of twenty-second of November in the year five hundred and ten, the Saxon army set off, keeping fairly near the south coast to come to the south side of Winchester, as they relentlessly pushed forwards towards their goal of Camelot. .

From her stronghold, Morgana and her army moved out and the two forces joined a few days later.

By the beginning of December the entire army was to the west of Ringwood. Now the total force pushed on towards Blandford on the road to Sherborne, which was to the east of Camelot.

The Saxon forces were not happy with Morgana's army. The hobgoblins were unruly and liked to pick fights with everyone. The Death Riders with their horses gave off a cold feeling of dread to all who went near, whilst the shadow men just made everyone uneasy. When the time came to make camp, the Saxons went as far from Morgana's forces as was possible.

This unrest made the men moody and they grumbled amongst themselves.

Moving a great number of men took time, even with a happy band of people. This uneasy army did not pass Wimborne until nearly the middle of December. Winter had set in and the mild weather, that had been such a boon of the early months, was no more. The mornings were cold but bright, making the men happier to push on and warm themselves with the exertion of the march. The real advantage of the weather was the hard ground, with hundreds of men moving across the countryside, soft ground would have soon bogged them down.

They pushed on across the bleak countryside taking supplies, as and when, they wanted, robbing and pillaging from the local farmers. They did not even care if they left those poor people with nothing for themselves.

The leaders crested a hill out of Wimborne as the afternoon drew on.

'We will stop by the village over there for the night,' Aelle commanded.

The troop started to set up camp at Badon, a few miles short of Badbury Rings. The outriders scouted on a little way, searching for farms to raid, and anything else to report back to the leaders.

One, who had gone farther than the rest, came to the edge of a copse of trees, bare now of their foliage. He paused a moment before turning back, when a sound came over the still air. He stood undecided what to do when the sound came again; it was the sound of someone chopping wood, even then he nearly ignored it and returned, but he decided it may be a peasant farmer with supplies that would be very welcome for his supper. He moved forward, up a short rise, to a swath of fur trees. He edged his horse forwards through the undergrowth and stopped in amazement.

There below him spread out across the grass was an army encampment. And what an army, there were knights, with all their men around them, and then a group of dragons with men and women beside them. Then he saw, in the centre, the royal standard fluttering from a flagpole, next to it the King's tent.

Gathering his wits, he turned his horse around and kicked him to make a getaway. Even as he turned, he realised he was too late, for there in front of him was a dragon. A small one admittedly, but his horse was having none of it and reared in fright throwing its rider. The horse would have immediately taken off at full speed if a hand hadn't grabbed the reins and hung on, whilst talking in a soothing voice. The animal steadied. The scout had not noticed Freya and Shimmer standing in the woods because they had been wearing their cloaks of invisibility.

He looked at the dragon with fear in his eyes. Then his gaze flickered across to Freya. He glanced behind her and to each side as he tried to decide which way to go to escape.

'Don't think of trying,' Freya said, in as menacing a voice as she could manage. 'One step and my friend,' she indicated Shimmer, 'will burn you up.'

Shimmer breathed out and clicked her claws to send a small flame shooting across towards the man.

'Don't set me on fire,' the man pleaded. 'I'll come quietly.'

'Right, get up and we'll go straight down towards the army,' Freya instructed and moved forward pushing the man in the direction she wanted. He fell over and let out a shout of alarm.

'Don't hurt me...Don't hurt me,' he repeated.

Hearing the commotion, Marcus had come running up from the encampment. Quickly taking in the situation, he caught hold of the scout and hauled him to his feet before pushing him forwards, down the hill towards the tents, leaving Freya to follow with the horse.

Shimmer, meanwhile, had taken to the air to see if there was any other danger near at hand. She circled the area a few times, each time making a larger sweep. On the third turn she saw the other army. She took in all the details before she dived back towards her friends and landed in the centre, right beside the King's tent.

Arthur, Merlin and a few of the Knights were gathered around Freya and Marcus, who were still holding on to their captive.

A servant came over and took the horse from Freya and led it to the picket line. Shimmer removed her cloak.

'What have you to report?' asked Arthur on seeing the young dragon. 'This man refused to say anything.'

'There is a great army just the other side of a small wood, a few miles over there,' she indicated the direction she had flown from.

'Did they see you?'

'No, I had my cloak over me' she replied. 'They were busy putting up their tents and bedding down for the night. They are not expecting anyone to see them.'

'Take the prisoner and make him safe. He must not be able to return to warn of our presence. We must be ready for them,' Arthur said and turned to his knights.

'Arrange for your squires to run to all the different sections to have each of the leaders come to my tent immediately to plan our campaign.'

This was done quickly and all his knights came to him. The light in Arthur's tent burned late into the night as they discussed their plans for the next day's battle.

Chapter Sixteen

The morning dawned bright and sunny, with cotton wool clouds floating in a deep blue sky. The ground was rock hard and all the grasses, trees and bushes were white with hoarfrost. How it sparkled in the rising winter sunshine. It was breathtakingly beautiful and so peaceful. Merlin looked out at it and thought no one would know there was going to be a major battle today. He shivered and pulled his coat tighter around his shoulders.

His thoughts went out to all the young men and women who had brought the dragons from Cornwall to help stop the plot by Morgana to kill King Arthur. Although Merlin knew he was not to play a major part in the forthcoming conflict, he could not help but worry about Freya and her two brothers without whom the plot would not have been discovered. He prayed nothing would befall any of the family today, as they meant the whole world to each other. Ever since their parents had disappeared, and later, when they had been presumed dead, Freya had been just ten and the twins only eight, she had looked after her two brothers and had devoted her life to them.

Merlin shook himself; thinking he should not spend time worrying about one family when there were so many brave warriors risking their lives for King Arthur.

He moved over to the king's tent.

'Are you up my liege?' he asked.

'Yes Merlin,' Arthur replied pushing the tent flap aside as he came out. 'I have been up since dawn, preparing for today.'

'I expect the Dragon Riders to be making their way over to the dragon camp now.' Merlin walked with his king to where the army was lined up ready to go.

David and Thomas with their sister Freya were indeed walking over to the little hollow where the dragons had made their camp using lots of bracken from the surrounding area for bedding.

As they crested the ridge David looked down at all the dragons and the other Dragon Riders making their way to join them. A feeling of excitement ran through him and then it was immediately replaced with one of fear, not for him but for all the brave people that were going to risk their lives to defeat the Saxon and Morgana's armies. His blond hair blew into his eyes; impatiently he raised his hand and brushed it back. He would have to have a haircut when all this was over. He turned to look at his twin, his blue eyes squinting in the bright morning sunlight.

Thomas smiled back at him. 'I can see you are worrying. We will be all right; we three have been through so much together, so we are not going to let a silly thing like Morgana's army separate us now,' Thomas said. He turned to their sister. 'Tell him we will be okay.'

'For twins you could not be more different, oh you look very similar but David, you must try not to take on all the worries and Thomas, you could do with being a bit more serious,' she said and wrapped her arms around each of her brothers in turn, her long dark hair blowing with their golden tresses.

'Seriously, David, you don't need to worry about me as I'll not be in any danger. Shimmer and I will be keeping well back, just watching everything going on. You will be close enough to Thomas to keep an eye on him, and actually you are the one who is always in the thick of any danger. Take a leaf out of your brother's book and hold back a little. There are a lot of you doing the same thing you don't have to protect everyone all the time. Remember I worry about you both too.'

David smiled at his sister and pulled back out of her embrace.

'I'll do my best. Now we had better join everyone else,' he replied and they all went down into the hollow.

By this time everyone else had gathered there, including Faith and Hope, the two dark haired sisters from Cornwall, who had proved they were as good as any man when it came to fighting. Everyone looked the same, they all were wearing breaches and doublets and all carried what looked like a bundle of fluff, but when Faith shook hers out it turned out to be a cloak of fine wool made in the mountains of Wales where the owner of the cloak of Invisibility, Padarn, had given a thread from his cloak to weave into the material for the Dragon Riders

Freya put hers around her shoulders and her outline was no longer defined and her appearance became hazy.

'Wow!' exclaimed Thomas. 'I haven't seen anyone put one on in daylight '

David laughed as he fully realised the advantages of wearing the cloaks. 'If we approach the enemy with the sun behind us, as Arthur said, no one will see us coming.'

Freya felt much happier now, she, too, had not seen the effect of the cloaks before and now felt they had at least an even chance of winning.

All the riders helped put the cloaks on the dragons. It would not do to have anyone properly visible for the forthcoming fight.

'Is everyone ready?' Marcus, the leader of the Cornish people and Faith and Hope's father, asked as he gathered his bow and arrows together and placed them in the special holder on the saddles that Rowena had made for each of the riders.

Each Dragon Rider strapped on a harness, with special clips, to fasten to the dragon's collars. This had been at Greor's, the leader of the dragons, suggestion this way the riders would not need to hold on with their hands when the dragons swerved and swooped through the sky.

Dragons do not like hurting humans, for this reason Arthur had decided to send the dragon flight in from the east. This would bring them behind the enemy. They were to seek out and destroy Morgana's dark forces and therefore would not have to start by killing humans. This move meant the morning sun would be behind them, and as they would be wrapped in their cloaks, hopefully, this would make them almost invisible.

The riders were ready and before they all mounted, Thomas and David went over to Faith and Hope

'Be careful you don't get yourselves hurt,' David said to them both whilst looking at Hope. He took her hand and smiled at her.

'You take care too. When this is all over I want to prove to you that I'm a better rider than you.' She smiled back.

'In your dreams!' he replied laughing and returned to his dragon, Sherna.

Thomas just held Faith's hand for a moment before he too turned and went to Greor.

They all climbed in to their saddles and Freya came over to adjust the capes and give her encouragement to each and every one.

'The rest of the Kings men left before first light. You had better get going. You'll have to make a wide sweep to come in behind the enemy when Arthur signals for the attack.'

Freya went over to stand by Shimmer. She put her arms around the little dragon's neck and they stood silently as they watched Greor leap into the air, closely followed by all the others. Freya placed her cloak around her shoulders and climbed into the saddle, she felt a ripple run through Shimmer's body as they set off after the departing dragons.

As Freya had told her brother, she was not going to be in the final battle as it had been felt that Shimmer was too small to fight. They were only going as observers.

They quickly flew over the copse of trees where they had captured the enemy scout such a short while before; this had led to them finding the oppositions camp without them knowing their danger. She flew on, until below there was line after line of Arthur's army. The pair flew down and landed near to Merlin, who stood to one side of the soldiers.

'The dragons have left on time,' she reported.

'Good, the order to advance has just been given,' the sage replied.

They watched as King Arthur joined his knights at the head of the column and they moved forward.

From their position, the bowmen ran quickly through the trees and stopped. They were just out of sight of the enemy. The front rank dropped to their knees, with another rank standing behind they fitted arrows into their bows and were ready. They did not have to wait for long. A horn blew and a cacophony of sound ensued as the enemy realised they were going to be under attack.

There was a 'whoosh' of arrows as they flew to find their marks, first the front rank and then the second, then the first again. This was kept going for, what seemed, an eternity.

Even as the arrows were being fired, the knights on horses came thundering into view from the north, and simultaneously the foot soldiers attacked from the south.

The Saxons were caught off guard, as King Arthur had hoped. They had just been getting ready for another days march. No one had been expecting to meet for a fight until they reached Camelot. There were shouts and screams as the arrows found their marks and the enemy were sent scurrying around, in confusion, as they tried to find their own weapons.

Aelle, the Saxon leader, came out of his tent where he had been conferring with his scouts. They had just reported to him, that one of their comrades had not returned. Now he had a fairly good idea what had befallen the scout.

Calling for his squire to bring his horse, he quickly finished putting on his armour and mounted his steed. He looked around at all the confusion and seeing his other knights mounting their horses he shouted to them to get the men into ranks and stem the advance of the attacking army.

Morgana was at the rear with her army and when she realised what must have happened she was incensed. She roused her Death Riders and ordered them to attack.

'Who could have warned Arthur of our intended attack?' she raged, even as she spoke, she heard a new sound. She whirled around and tried to see what was coming. The clouds appeared to be raining arrows and missiles at her troops, bringing them down, even as they surged forwards to attack. Then there were flames belching out of ... dragons. Yes they were dragons, even though they couldn't be seen properly.

The Death Riders and their steeds just shrivelled into nothing as the flames from the mighty creatures caught them. Rows upon rows of them were consumed in just a few minutes. Her army was going to be wiped out at this rate, she realised. Not wishing to be caught herself she ran across to where her own horse was tethered and, flung herself into the saddle, immediately she urged the horse into a gallop fleeing from the scene of destruction, leaving her comrades to their fate. As she rode she cursed the dragons and whoever was riding on them, swearing she would get even with them someday.

Chapter Seventeen

The battle continued with Arthur's men succeeding in accounting for over nine hundred and fifty of their enemy in one attack.

Once Morgana left the battleground the spell to keep the hobgoblins and the shadow men began to fade but not before Faith on her dragon Cawson flew in from the flank with her sword at the ready, she cut into the nearest dark shape, which just disappeared.

Hope followed on her dragon, Jade, and they flamed five hobgoblins in one pass, but they left no remains.

Thomas on Greor, Marcus on Fredlie and Edwin on Caw dispersed the shadow men, while David on Sherna led the remaining men to hound the Death Riders and destroy them.

The battle was not going to be won too easily and the dragons with their riders had to keep up their speed and positions. At times it looked as if there would be a mid-air collision as they weaved and flew to attack the enemy, but the dragons had a fast reaction and could swerve or dive to avoid hitting each other and also the flames that they sent so effectually to the destruction of the dark forces.

David and Sherna flew high to see how the battle was going and were pleased to see Morgana's army seemed to have been completely wiped out.

'We've done it!' he shouted to Thomas with glee.

Thomas was making a low pass and he turned to reply to his brother not seeing the last two Death Riders on his blind side but David did. He urged Sherna into a dive and she responded sending out a column of flames as she went. One veered away to the left, in an attempt to avoid the flames, and as he went, he let fly his spear, it caught David a glancing blow on the leg. Sherna quickly swung around and blew out another great gust of air as she clicked her claws, the resulting flame shot across and the last Death Rider was gone.

Thomas let out a cheer, which the other riders took up.

'Good shot Sherna and David,' he called across. 'Now let's go help wipe out the others.'

The Dragon Riders all turned as one and flew over to where Arthur's army was still engaged in fighting the Saxons. They started firing their arrows at them and the dragons once again blew out their flames.

This was enough for Aelle and his followers. The order to retreat was given before a second wave could be brought against them.

Freya hugged Shimmer as she looked on from their safe place by the trees.

'Look they are going!' she exclaimed as they watched the rabble disperse from the battlefield, picking up their wounded as they left.

Below her Arthur called to his knights.

'Lancelot and Belvedere you will go after the lady Morgana and bring her to me. We can't let her stay free to plot against us again. The rest of you take some of the troops after the retreating army and make sure they leave the area completely.'

When the troops returned they reported that the army had gone they were sent to bury the dead. The foot soldiers were told they could take any articles that the enemy had left; therefore ensuring the field would be left clean.

The Dragon Flight came in to land where Freya and Shimmer were waiting for them.

David and Thomas dismounted closely followed by Faith and Hope. They stood in a group laughing and hugging each other. All talking at once as they recalled the details of the battle.

Remembering their friends, the four of them thanked their dragons then made their way across to where Freya waited.

She smiled in relief to see them all alive, then glanced down and saw David's leg.

'Are you hurt?' she asked with concern.

He looked down. 'Bother my trousers are ripped,' he laughed. 'No, it's only a tiny scratch, and it will heal in no time.'

The rest of the riders came over with all the cloaks, which they gave to Freya. These were placed in a pile ready to take back to Wales as promised where they would always be available whenever anyone needed them.

'Was anyone hurt?' asked Merlin, as he came over to congratulate all of the riders on a job well done.

'Only David, his trouser leg was ripped by a spear,' Faith volunteered.

'Let me look,' the old man ordered as he walked over to David and told him to sit down on a nearby rock, then he ripped the trouser leg a little more to look at the wound. He inhaled sharply.

'This needs a little treatment,' he said turning to Faith.

'Go and get my bag from my tent. My servant will know which one if you tell him it's for dark dressings.'

Thomas had been listening closely. 'Don't worry Faith, I'll go and fetch the bag.'

He went off at a fast jog. Something in the way Merlin had looked when he saw the wound had alarmed

Thomas and he wanted to be sure the treatment for his brother was fetched as soon as possible.

Merlin's manservant did, indeed, know which bag his master needed and the look of surprise and concern on the serf's face redoubled Thomas's fears. He grabbed the bag and ran all the way back.

Merlin took it and opened the top to take out a flask. Taking a piece of cloth from a bundle he poured some of the liquid on the cloth and proceeded to clean the wound on David's leg.

Freya, who had been talking to some of the other riders, realised something was going on, so she had come over, watching Merlin. When he had finished she had a good view of the cut and what she saw made her go cold inside. The flesh around the wound had taken on a silver sheen.

Taking the old man by the arm, she moved him away from the injured boy.

'What is it?' she asked in a whisper, when they were away from the others.

'He has been wounded with a weapon from the Death Riders. I don't know what will happen. It depends what spell was put on the weapons,' he replied.

Freya looked stricken. 'What do we do?'

'The best thing is to take him to Summerdale,' Merlin said. 'First go back to Cornwall and talk to your grandmother, she will help you arrange everything, as she and Gwendolyn the Empress of Summerdale are old friends.'

The old man patted Freya on the arm then returned to where he had left David.

'I have told your sister to take you away,' he said as he picked up his bag and made his way back to where Arthur stood.

Freya went with him leaving Hope with David.

'What is all this fuss about, it's only a scratch after all,' David said mystified.

'Better safe than sorry,' Hope replied trying hard not to look worried. She had overheard Freya's exchange with Merlin.

Merlin and Freya stood waiting until the King had finished talking to Sir Lancelot and Sir Belvedere who had just arrived back from his quest to capture the king's sister.

'We have captured Morgana, my liege, she is presently bound and being guarded by some of your men,' Lancelot reported.

'You brought her back very quickly. How did you manage that?' the king asked.

'We knew she would be heading back to Camelot, and she would not have thought we would go after her so quickly. Luckily for us I know the countryside around here and had knowledge of a short cut across to the main road. We were able to arrive at a point in advance of her,' Sir Belvedere told the king.

Lancelot took up the tale,

'We hid in amongst the trees on the side of the road and when Morgana came cantering up, I went out in front of her, she tried to turn away but Belvedere was behind her and caught her reigns, therefore she could not ride away. We immediately tied her hands behind her back and brought her straight back to you,' he paused then added. 'What will you have us do with her?'

'I shall banish my half sister and her son to the Orkney Islands, where she can do no more harm. The king there is a good friend and he will guard her well,' the king said.

He looked over to Freya and Merlin who were waiting. Smiling at them he asked 'Did you wish to speak with me?'

'Yes, Sire, I have come to beg for leave for all the Dragon Riders to return to Cornwall,' Freya said.

'As there is no further need of your help at the moment, of course you can leave. When did you think of going?'

'As soon as possible, the dragons will take us as we have urgent need of help for David; he has been injured by one of the Death Riders.'

The King, concerned, turned to Merlin, he asked him to explain.

'They need to go to Summerdale to find the cure for what ails David. The longer he leaves it the more the poison will affect him until eventually he would die and become a Death Rider himself.'

The king turned back to Freya and taking her by the arm walked back to where the boys were waiting. He addressed them all.

'You have all been of great service to your King this day. It will not go un-rewarded. I will give each of you land to build homes. When you come back from your journey we will discuss where you want it and how it will be built. As for you dragons,' he turned to the mighty beasts and continued. 'I will do everything in my power to keep you safe in future. He paused thoughtfully before continuing. 'To show how much I am in your debt I shall have a banner made with a picture of a dragon on it and I shall call myself Arthur Pendragon in your honour.'

The King turned, brushing off their thanks and left the band to pack up for their journey.

This did not take long as they had brought very little with them. Greor and Sherna talked to the other dragons and they all said they would go and live in the mountains after they had taken their riders back to Cornwall.

Caw turned to David and said, 'If ever any of you should need our assistance again, please call on us, we will come at any time.'

'Thank you so much for all you have done,' David said to them. He was then still unaware of the danger he was in and how soon he would need the dragons help himself.

Once again, they all mounted the dragons and set off back to Cornwall.

Merlin and Arthur stood and watched them go until they became too small to make out. The king turned to Merlin.

'I think you had better go to Summerdale yourself. I want to know the boy has the best chance to recover.'

'I will make my preparations immediately after I have seen to all the injured men and seen them setting off safely back to their homes,' Merlin replied. 'I still have a feeling of doom coming again.'

'I don't like the sound of that, the last time you had one of those feelings it was before we knew of this plot to kill me. I'll inform my knights and have them on standby to come to your aid immediately whenever you may have need of it. I wonder what new evil there is coming.'

The king and Merlin parted, each going their own way, but both with a worried frown on their faces.

Chapter Eighteen

Once again, they all mounted the dragons and set off back to Cornwall, leaving the battle grounds far below the dragons flew back as fast as they could towards the West Country. They had heard the urgency in Merlin's voice when he had treated David's injuries and knew they had to reach Rowena as soon as they could.

Greor shouted out to all the riders, warning them to hold on extra tightly and to close their eyes for a few moments as the dragons entered their extra speed as they past time. The cold burned and then they were over the cliffs above Tregardock. They circled down and landed to be greeted by Rowena.

'What has happened? Who has been hurt? I have had the most terrible feeling of dread all day.'

Freya hugged her grandmother and told her what had happened as they went across to help Marcus and Thomas lift David off Sherna's back

'Carry him gently,' she ordered, seeing how weak he had become in just the short time of the flight back to Cornwall.

'Merlin told us you could help us to get in touch with the Empress of Summerdale, He said she was the only one who could help him,' Freya said.

'Yes, of course, I haven't been in touch with Gwendolyn since I was young; we were both studying magic in the valleys of Wales,' Rowena told her as she led the way forward. 'She married Godwin the Emperor of Summerdale and went to live in his lands on the borders of the Twilight Kingdom,' she continued as she and Freya stood to one side and let the injured boy past. The two women followed the procession of helpers as they took David and his belongings down into the cave,

Hope walked alongside David holding his hand to comfort him.

'What is the Twilight Kingdom, Grandmother? I have never heard of it before,' Freya asked in a low voice, not wanting the others to hear her question.

'You wouldn't have, unless you were under a black spell, then you would feel its pull. That's what's happening to David. The wound must have been made by a Death Rider, and now it is pulling him back to them.'

'What are Death Riders?'

'They are people who have been poisoned the same way as David and if they go untreated they turn into the living-dead that you saw. It is a powerful magic and then they are put to work for the powers of darkness. They are usually clothed from head to toe in long black cloaks with hoods so that you do not see that they are all but skeletons. They only have limited power in our world and are much stronger in their own kingdom, but have no power at all in Summerdale.'

They went over to David and his grandmother checked that he was as comfortable as possible.

'How are you feeling now?' she asked him.

'I am so tired and weak at the moment. It was only a little cut but I feel as if all my blood has been drained out of my body. Everything's hazy and unreal as if I'm a long way away. Am I going to die Grandmother?'

'Definitely not! We'll get you to Summerdale and you'll immediately feel better. Now all you need to do is rest and leave everything to me,' she replied. Turning to the others she continued. 'I'll go and contact Gwendolyn. Once I've spoken to her I'll come and find you all to let you know what she advises.'

'Hope, you can stay quietly with David, in case he needs anything, we will be back as soon as we find out anything' Freya said.

Everyone else left the room.

David looked up at Hope and seeing her worried face, smiled at her.

'I don't understand what's happened. It was only a scratch and I felt all right when Merlin looked at me. Then as I came here on the back of Sherna, I felt worse and worse. I think I would have fallen off if I hadn't had the harness on and Sherna hadn't been so good and smooth when she flew. Don't look so worried, I'll be fine, once Grandmother has spoken to her friend. They will know what herbs to give me to make me as fit as a fiddle.'

'You look so pale and ill, I would hate anything more to happen to you,' Hope replied.

'Don't say you actually care for me" David teased.

'You know I do. Now you must rest they'll be back in a moment to make you well again. I'll just sit quietly here while you sleep.'

"Thank you, I do feel a little sleepy.' He closed his eyes and at once fell into a deep and troubled sleep. Hope sat and watched his dear face as he tossed and turned fretfully.

Rowena returned to her room, going over to the fireplace she reached up to the mantelpiece and lifted down a large brown jar. She took this and put it on a table next to her chair. She took the stopper out and poured a little of the golden liquid into a goblet. Sitting down in her chair she picked up the goblet and drained the contents. She put the goblet back on the table she waited. Soon a glazed look passed over her face. After a few moments more Rowena's inner being rose out of her body and floated away up the chimney, like a wisp of smoke. The wisp went up into the sky until it disappeared into the clouds.

The lands below sped past as Rowena's image flew upwards, up through the clouds and on for only a few minutes before she began to descend again. She came back down through the clouds; and there below she saw the beautiful land of Summerdale. She landed in a meadow, filled with flowers, and listened to the beautiful bird song from within the trees.

Over to the left a river flowed gently and a pair of unicorns drank from the water. Everywhere there was a feeling of tranquillity. She walked past the trees and up a roadway to a white castle set in a lovely garden and guarded by a tall wall and a pair of iron gates.

As she neared the gates a young man came out to meet her.

'Welcome Rowena, my lady awaits you in her drawing room. Please follow me.'

They proceeded, through large double doors, into a cool entrance hall with the floor of marble tiling set in a black and white chequered pattern. From there they went across to the next door and through there to a, large comfortable furnished, room where Gwendolyn, the Empress of Summerdale awaited her.

'Rowena it is so nice to see you after all these years. It is such a shame that it has to be in the time of troubles.'

'How did you know I was coming for help?

'There have been many disturbances on our borders. We knew Morgana had been up to something so we have been expecting someone to come to us. What has happened?'

Rowena told her old friend everything. In her present form she could not take any of the refreshments brought in by the servants.

The tale came to the end as Rowena told of David's injury by the spear of one of the Death Riders. Gwendolyn sat up straight in her chair.

'How long since he received the wound?'

'Only earlier today,' she replied.

'Good, the earlier we can catch it the fuller the recovery. You had better bring him here to get better. We can give him a mixture to combat the dark spell '

'How will I manage to bring him here quickly?'

'The dragons can fly here in no time at all. You do realise he'll always have a slight pull to the Twilight Kingdom unless he can go there and receive the antidote to the poison? But that will have to wait until he is properly fit again.'

Rowena rose, went over to her friend and she embraced her.

'Thank you so much I'll return and organise his departure immediately. Oh, there may be some companions who may wish to accompany him. Will that be all right?'

'It would probably aid his recovery if he had company, so yes, it will be fine.'

Five minutes later Rowena was back in her chair by her fireplace. She quickly rose and went out to find Freya, Thomas and the others, to inform them of the developments and explained the need for speed.

After hearing everything Rowena had to tell, Faith immediately went to ask the dragons for their help again, whilst the others went to break the news to David and Hope.

'What is happening?' David asked weakly.

'Grandmother has been speaking to her friend in Summerdale and the outcome is we are to go there,' Freya told him. '

'You should feel much better as soon as we land,' Thomas added, 'and whilst we are there we will be able to find the cure and make you completely well.'

Faith returned from speaking to the dragons and joined everyone.

'I have spoken to Greor and he and all the other dragons will be pleased to take you to Summerdale as they like it there. I have also been to see my father and he agreed that Hope and I can go with you, as long as Edwin, his steward, accompanies us.'

'I'm pleased,' said Freya. 'It'll be nice to have female company for a change.'

'I had assumed that Thomas would go, to keep his brother company, but I hadn't thought of the rest of you going. Will you be safe?' Rowena pondered.

'We'll be as safe there as anywhere, in fact probably safer, as I'm sure Morgana is not going to forget what we did to foil her attempt of becoming the Queen,' Freya replied.

Edwin came into the room.

'The dragons are ready, so we had better make haste.'

Thomas and he went over to David and lifted him gently between them to carry him out to the waiting dragons. They carefully helped him on to Sherna's back and attached him and his bundle of clothes to the collar before they both joined Greor and Caw respectively.

The other three had mounted their dragons after giving Rowena and Marcus a hug and wishing them farewell.

'Right everyone' Greor said, 'hold on tight and we'll be off.'

'' Bye Grandmother,' Freya and Thomas called, David just waved. Then the dragons leapt into the sky and flew fast upwards before turning south and heading towards the Empire of Summerdale, on the borders of the Twilight Kingdom.

Their grandmother stood and watched them go. She wondered how they would cure David and what adventures they would have where they were going. Would she see them again? Would they be safe?

Chapter Nineteen

The dragons flew south to Summerdale carrying their riders. It was cold as they passed through time to arrive almost before they had taken off. Normally people would only travel that way in dreams because people had forgotten how to believe.

The riders looked down eagerly, taking in the beauty of the land with the lush green meadows filled with line after line of almond trees all covered in their snowy white blossom and giving off a delicate perfume to fill the spring like air. The lemon and orange trees, in the other fields, were covered in fruit and the birds could be heard singing as they flew around, busily making their nests. Over on the left a sparkling river flowed past some cattle as they grazed quietly on the bank. On the other side of the river was a great cliff with many caves cut into its sides with the land beyond rising gently and turning into tall green mountains. Whilst over to the right was another meadow and at the edge of that stood a beautiful white castle set in a lovely garden and guarded by a high wall and a pair of iron gates.

The six dragons circled around as they looked for a place to land, once they had decided they alighted in a meadow making the cows stop their grazing for a moment to see what the commotion was all about, then, unconcerned they returned to their meal.

The air was warm and a feeling of tranquillity washed over the new arrivals.

'I shouldn't think it will take you long to get better here, David,' Thomas remarked as he slid off Greor's back and walked over to Sherna as David struggled to climb down.

Hope and Freya quickly dismounted from their dragons, Jade and Shimmer.

Edwin patted Caw's neck as he alighted before holding a hand to bring Faith safely to the ground from Cawson.

It was difficult to believe that only yesterday, in the cold of winter, they had been fighting a battle with King Arthur and his armies against his evil half-sister Morgana and her partner Aelle.

David shuddered, his mind going back to the battle. Once again he was back on Sherna as she made a final pass towards the last two Death Riders, one veered away to the left, in an attempt to avoid the flames, and as he turned, he let fly his spear, this caught David a glancing blow on the leg. Sherna quickly swung around and blew out a great gust of air as she clicked her claws, the resulting flame shot across and the last Dark Rider was gone.

David's thoughts came back to the present time and he looked down at his leg, now tightly bandaged and again he shuddered. The familiar feeling of darkness and tiredness swept over him. He staggered and would have fallen if Thomas hadn't been there to catch him.

Quickly recovered himself he called. 'Thank you, Sherna, Greor and all of you for getting us here so quickly.'

'Yes our thanks to all you dragons from all of us. Without you I shudder to think what might have happened,' Thomas said and the others murmured their agreement.

'It was our pleasure to be of service to you, and anyway we like coming to Summerdale for the winter as it is much warmer here than at home,' Greor replied. 'Now if you don't need us further we will go and settle ourselves in our caves.'

'We're expected at the castle, so we'll not need you again today,' Freya said and they all watched as the dragons flew off over the river. They gathered around David and helped him walk the short distance across the grass.

The Emperor Godwin and his wife Gwendolyn came out of the massive front door and down the steps to meet them.

'Welcome, welcome,' the emperor cried, catching hold of Thomas's hand and shaking it enthusiastically

Gwendolyn went straight to David.

'How are you my dear?' she enquired gently putting her hand on his brow. 'You appear to still have a slight fever but you'll be feeling better in no time,' she said then turned to her servants who had followed down the steps.

'Take Master David to his room and make sure he is fed and has everything he needs.'

She turned back to David she said in a softer voice.

'You must go and rest now and I shall be up to see in a short while, to make sure you are comfortable, after I've seen to your companions. Meanwhile don't hesitate to ask for anything you may need'

The servants took hold of David's arms and helped him up the steps into the castle leaving everyone else to follow behind.

'Right, now let's see, I expect everyone would like something to eat and drink after that journey,' Emperor Godwin declared, turning to address them all as they came to the large front door.

Nodding in agreement they followed him into the hallway. Immodestly in front of them was a sweeping staircase leading to the upper levels. On each side of the hallway were many doors, one of which led them into a large banqueting hall where they found a table laden with every conceivable delight. There was roast lamb and pork and duck and chicken, peas, carrots, and other vegetables that they did not recognize; also roast potatoes all golden straight from the oven. There were apples, oranges and pineapples not to mention the cakes and jellies. They sat down and all set to with healthy appetites.

The servants hurried from one to another making sure that everyone had exactly what they wanted to eat and drink.

When, at last they had all eaten their fill, and they sat back to finish their drinks Gwendolyn asked them to tell their story.

Thomas began.

'We discovered a plot by Morgana, King Arthur's half-sister, to use her magic powers to kill all the dragons and then, with the aid of her co-conspirator Aelle, a Saxon king, to kill her brother to become Queen.'

He went on to tell the story of how the dragons learned to make fire, and how they had all helped King Arthur defeat Morgana in the battle that led to David becoming injured.

'Well that was quite a story, it sounded quite terrifying but I'm so glad you were able to help King Arthur,' the emperor beamed at them all. 'Now I think you deserve a rest so we need to allow you to go to your rooms.'

'Yes, I think you'll need a long lie-in in the morning. Come with me and I'll show you the way. ' Gwendolyn interjected. 'I said I'd look in on David to see if he's all right,' she added.

Thanking their host for the marvellous meal they pushed back their chairs and arose to follow

Gwendolyn across the hall and up the staircase to their rooms.

Thomas was next door to David, with Edwin on the other side whilst the three girls were put in their own rooms across the hallway. Gwendolyn checked they had everything they could possibly need, and then wished them good night. Once the last door closed on her guests she went back along the corridor to look in on her patient.

Thomas stuck his head around his door and called.

'Would you mind if I came with you? I'd like to know David was all right before I turn in for the night.'

'Of course you may.'

He followed her in to the room. One of her servants was sitting by the fire waiting for her arrival. He looked from one to the other and reported.

'He didn't eat a good meal, my Lady; he said he was a little tired so I helped him to get ready for bed. No sooner did his head touch the pillow than he fell asleep.'

The servant left the room and they both went over to the bed and looked down at David's sleeping face.

'I think his sleep will be untroubled by dreams,' she whispered, 'I've put an enchantment in his room to keep all dark thoughts at bay. He will sleep like a baby.'

Thomas looked at his brother's face and nodded.

'Thank you for letting us come here, I'm sure he will be back to his old self in no time at all.'

'Yes you mustn't worry. The healing properties of Summerdale are quite strong and I will make enquiries to find exactly where you'll have to go for the fruit that is the antidote to the Death Riders blow. In the meantime we'll keep him out of further danger. You should all take this opportunity to try to rest.'

'It will be nice to spend some fun time with the dragons too. All we have ever done with them is learn how to fly together and fight,' Thomas yawned. 'I am tired, so I'll go to bed. You are sure that David will be safe for the moment?'

Empress Gwendolyn smiled. 'Yes he will be quite safe for now.'

With one more look down at David they left him to his sleep.

Chapter Twenty

David awoke with a start. He looked around in puzzlement; he did not know where he was. He noted the deep blue bed curtains on his four-poster bed and the matching ones that were drawn across the two large windows. It was still quite dark in the room. He climbed out of bed and went over to the windows where he flung back the curtains and let the sunlight stream in. Below was a tranquil courtyard where a groom was slowly leading a large horse across to the steps where the Lady Gwendolyn waited. He watched as she mounted the animal and cantered out into the surrounding countryside.

The feeling of peace left him as his mind took him, once again, back to the battlefield. Again he saw the Death Rider as it veered away from him and his dragon mount, Sherna, even as it turned it let fly his spear. David closed his eyes and he could almost feel the tip of the spear as it ripped through his trousers and cut into his leg. He turned and sat on the edge of his bed as the feeling of weakness once again engulfed him. Even as it did, he realized that the feeling was not as strong as it had been on his journey to Summerdale. He had slept right through the night without dreaming and so he did feel rested. He thought he would make the most of it, he looked for his clothes to dress ready to go out and explore, but where were they?

Even as he looked around him, the door opened.

'Good morning Master David,' the servant from last night said as he came in carrying his bags and his clothes from the day before, now all clean and nicely pressed.

'How are you feeling this morning?' he asked.

'I'm well…Emrys, isn't it?'

'Yes sir, if you would like to dress, breakfast is being served down stairs.'

'Thank you, I really feel hungry this morning.'

He allowed Emrys to help him dress and it was only a few minutes before he was leaving his room in search of his breakfast. He had only taken two steps before Thomas came out of the next-door room.

'I don't have to ask if you slept well, I can see it in your eyes but how's your leg?' he asked coming over and putting his arm around his twin's shoulders.

'It is still a little strange, but I'm sure it'll not be long before it heals properly,' David replied. 'What sort of night did you have?'

'I slept like a top, and so did Edwin by the state of him, he's still dead to the world. I couldn't stay in bed any longer I'm dying to explore.'

'Me too but can we eat first, I'm starving.'

Thomas laughed and the two of them went clattering down the stairs to the dining room.

While they were eating the girls joined them then Edwin came in only a few minutes later. They chatted to each other and described their beautiful rooms. The servants came and served their breakfasts. Then when everyone had eaten enough they wandered outside.

'I can't believe how mild the weather is at this time of the year,' Freya remarked as they walked through the open gates and into the countryside.

'We must have travelled quite a long way south to reach this warmer climate,' Edwin observed.

'Let's go and see how the dragons have settled in,' Thomas said.

'I don't think I can walk that far at the moment,' David replied sitting down on a convenient tree trunk.

They gathered around him with looks of concern on their faces as Lady Gwendolyn cantered across the grass towards them.

'Good morning,' she called, taking in the situation at a glance. 'I have made arrangements for you all to have mounts to allow you to explore the country side at your leisure.'

As she spoke, three grooms appeared leading six ponies between them.

Gwendolyn slid off her horse and went over to the brothers. She took them aside as the others went over to choose which of the animal they would ride.

'I have just been to a meeting with some of our men. They have been patrolling the borders of Summerdale, where they join with King Golgog's land, he rules the Twilight Kingdom. The men reported that all the animals and birds are very restless. There is definitely something wrong, but they don't know what. The animals have been like this for some weeks, but I thought it was just the problems you had been having with Morgana asking for assistance from the Death Riders. Today I expected to hear that it was starting to get back to normal.'

'What would you like us to do to help?'

'If you're going to see the dragons, perhaps you could ask them to fly over our borders, now and then, to keep a lookout for any trouble.'

'I'm sure they'll do that, but surely there is something more we can do?'

'Well, yes, there is. I hate to ask this of you, David, but if you could just let your mind open to the poison in your body, you may get an insight into what is happening, especially if it is to do with the Death Riders.'

'Will it be dangerous for him?' Thomas asked anxiously.

'I don't think it will be dangerous, more unpleasant as the pull of the darkness takes hold. This mean that you may have nightmares again, though I think my magic is enough to keep those at bay.'

'Of course I'll do it if it'll help' David replied immediately.

'It will not be for long. When we have the cure for you all the images will completely disappear.'

'When will we have the cure?' David asked.

'I have sent a message to my friend, Queen Josephine, asking her for the information and I am expecting a reply in the next few days. In the meantime whatever you can learn will be a great help.'

'We'll see what we can do. Now I intend to join the others and go and explore a little,' David stood up and walked over to the ponies, selecting a gentle looking one he mounted with a little help from the groom.

The others followed his lead and calling goodbye to Gwendolyn mounted and turned their ponies in the direction of the river.

Ten minutes later they arrived at the foot of the cliffs. The dragons were watching from their lofty perches and on seeing them arrive flew down to enquire after David's health.

David reassured them 'I'm a lot better but we have just been told that there is still some unrest over the border in the Twilight Kingdom. We were wondering if you would keep an eye on it and overfly the area every so often.'

Greor did not look worried. 'I expect everything will settle down in the next few days so don't worry. Just go and enjoy yourselves. It will be no trouble for us to fly around and see what is happening if anything.'

They all chatted together for a few more minutes before the friends said goodbye and went off to explore. Left on their own the dragons flew back up to their caves.

For three months they enjoyed their time as David grew stronger and everyone became quite carefree. Nothing more was heard of any unrest on the borders of the Empire and the friends spent their time visiting the local villages and meeting the people.

Not wishing to spoil things for the rest of them David did not tell them that he could not shake off the pull he felt from the direction of the Twilight Kingdom.

He wondered what it meant and decided that at the first opportunity he would go and visit the place that was calling to him. He knew the others would try to stop him so he decided not say anything.

The opportunity to steal away presented itself much earlier than he had thought.

At lunchtime, the next day, they visited one of the remote white-housed towns where they were made very welcome and asked to join the headman's family for lunch. After the meal they were all sitting around talking and David seized the opportunity to slip away unnoticed by everyone, except his sister.

Freya had been fetching something from her saddlebag when David mounted his pony and left. She immediately mounted her pony and followed.

The others carried on talking to their host family, unaware that their numbers had been reduced until there was a lull in the conversation.

Edwin turned to make a comment to David and realized that he was not there. He looked around and saw Freya was missing too.

'Has anyone seen Freya and David lately?' he asked.

'Two of your companions left a short while ago,' a villager said.

'I expect David got tired and decided to go back, he'll be there when we return,' Thomas said, quite unconcerned. 'We had better make our own way back to make sure they are all right.' He turned to his host and shook his hand. 'Thank you for your hospitality you have made us all most welcome.'

'It was our pleasure,' replied the headman. 'It has been good to hear tales of different lands. We look forward to seeing you all again.'

One by one they thanked their hosts and collected their ponies, mounted, and left the village waving to the villagers as they went.

Laughing and joking between themselves they made their merry way back to the castle, little realizing the danger David and his sister were facing as they headed away from the safety of the villages and nearer to the evil radiating from the Twilight Kingdom.

Chapter Twenty One

David urged his horse into a fast canter as soon as he was out of the village. He made straight for a wooded area. Such was the pull he did not consider he would be followed so did not look back if he had he would have seen his sister riding fast behind him. He was heading due north, directly for the border with the Twilight Kingdom; he did not stop to think why he felt he had to travel there. He just felt someone or something calling him, drawing him onwards.

There were not very many miles to go, as all morning the party had been gradually edging closer to the northern part of Summerdale. The nearer they went to the border the stronger the pull had been getting in David's head, until now, he could not ignore it anymore he had to go to the Twilight Kingdom.

It was not long before Freya realized where David was heading. She urged her pony into a gallop to catch up. She, suddenly, was terribly afraid that if David went over the border on his own he might not come back.

As he drew nearer to his goal David was certain that he heard a voice, but he still could not quite make out the words being spoken. He pulled up his mount to listen better and as he sat there, trying to make out the meaning of the words being said, he heard the thunder of Freya's pony's hooves. Alarmed he spun around in his saddle but was relieved to see it was only his sister.

'Where do you think you're going?' she shouted at him as she pulled up beside him. 'You must realize you are not well enough to do anything on your own.'

'Something is calling me, Freya, I don't know what it is but I think I can hear a voice,' he replied.

'I can't hear anything,' she said, straining to hear any sound other than the birds twittering in the trees.

'You wouldn't, it's just in my head, and I think I will be able to hear more as I get nearer the border'

'Well if you think I'm letting you go alone, you have another thought coming,' she retorted and urged her mount forward again.

David moved off too and they proceeded at a more leisurely pace until they were just a few hundred metres from the edge of the Twilight Kingdom.

They again halted and David sat with his head on one side as he listened.

'There is a voice… It's calling all the Death Riders to a meeting at midnight the day after tomorrow.'

'Well in that case we had better go back to the castle and tell everyone that something is definitely going to happen.'

'I want to go on and try to find out some more.'

'David, please don't be silly, it'll not tell you anything more yet. You can use the next two days to talk with everyone to come up with some sort of plan before coming back here to listen to the meeting.'

'Yes, I suppose you're right, the voice does seem to have stopped for now and the feeling, that I had to come this way, has faded too.'

Relived Freya followed as David turned his pony's head and set off at a gentle trot back towards the castle and the others.

Deep in the interior of the Twilight Kingdom the caller had stopped, she looked thoughtfully at her spell book. She was sure she had felt something as she had called the last time, but if she had, it was gone now. She would be more alert next time she sent her thoughts out.

Morgana picked up her book and returned it to the shelf of the room she was staying in, at the top of King Golgog's castle.

She was completely unconcerned as she chuckled to herself at the thought of how she had fooled everyone in the Orkney Islands, where she had been banished by her brother. It had been so easy to persuade a serving girl to come into her cell, and once there it had been even easier to cast a spell on the girl and they changed places.

Now everyone thought the girl in the cell was Morgana, whilst in reality, she had left and made her way to King Golgog and his Twilight Kingdom.

She laughed again; Freya and her two brothers would be so surprised when they received their punishment for meddling in her plans.

She left the room as she went to report her progress to the King.

Thomas was getting a little concerned about his brother. He had looked everywhere but he had been unable to find David or Freya. Now, when he had persuaded everyone to go out to search for them, there was a shout heard from the guards at the gateway.

Edwin came running across. 'It's all right they've been seen coming over the rise.'

Giving a sigh of relief, Thomas went, with the others, to meet them at the gate.

David and Freya urged the ponies into a canter when they saw the reception committee. Eager hands caught hold of the bridles as they slipped off their mounts.

'Where have you been?' Thomas shouted, giving in to his fears. 'We thought something terrible had happened to you, well I did anyway.'

'We'll explain everything, just come with us to see Lord Godwin and Lady Gwendolyn, and then we can tell you all together.'

David led everyone into the castle in search of their hosts who were found relaxing in the sitting room overlooking the central gardens.

They entered the room and all sat down to listen to David as he told them what he had heard.

Everyone was speechless. Emperor Godwin stood up and walked over to the mantelpiece and leaned on the marble top staring down into the empty hearth for a moment before turning to face everyone. 'Now, before anyone gets in a panic, we have to remember that the Death Riders have never been able to enter our lands, so I am not unduly worried. We are just going to have to wait until we hear from David after the meeting. Only then will we know what is being planned.'

'I don't like the idea of David going to the meeting,' Hope said, looking concerned. 'What if he is captured?'

'I don't have to go and join the others to hear what's being said, all I need is to go to the same place I was today and I should be able to listen in,' David reassured her. 'Anyway I don't think I will be allowed to go on my own.'

'You are quite right. Thomas and I shall accompany you,' Edwin said.

'We want to come too,' Hope said indicating herself, Faith and Freya.

'I don't think all of us going would be a good idea. We don't want to draw too much attention to ourselves.'

'I think that the best plan would be to leave it all to you boys,' Lady Gwendolyn agreed smiling at the girls. 'I'm sure we will find plenty to do while we wait.'

Reluctantly agreeing, the girls left the meeting, leaving the boys to finalise everything with the emperor before they all went back to their rooms to wash and change ready for their dinner.

Gwendolyn also left the room but she did not go to her quarters, instead she went back to the cliffs where the dragons were staying.

'Greor, please come down to talk to me,' she called.

'The green dragon flew down to her. 'How can I help you?' he asked.

She told him what had been planned, then added. 'I am not happy with the situation and I think we need someone else to give us some advice.'

'Whom did you have in mind?'

'I wondered if one of you could go and fetch Merlin.'

'That would be no trouble, I will send Jade immediately.'

'Thank you, I hope I'm fussing over nothing, but it's better to be safe than sorry,' she said and turned to go back to her room before she was missed.

For the companions, the next day and a half passed much as the rest of their time had gone, riding out in the mornings and meeting new people, involving themselves in the local pastimes and generally trying to enjoy themselves without thinking too much about what the coming meeting could mean to them all.

The one thing they did was to make sure that they never left David by himself. He had a habit of drifting off in the general direction of the borders if they did not keep him occupied at all times. They took it in turns to guard him so that he would not feel as if they were unduly worried.

In all this time, because David had become stronger, so no one had thought to ask why the reply from Queen

Josephine was so long in coming. Even on the evening of the meeting Emperor Godwin was still not concerned.

'If you would like to go to see if you can find out what is being plotted, then by all means go, I shall not stop you. In fact I shall be quite interested to know what my neighbour is planning,' he laughed. 'You never know it may be useful.'

Gwendolyn was not quite as happy about it, but thought that there was nothing that the inhabitants of the Twilight Kingdom could do to Summerdale. All the same she was much relived to see two dragons, landing in the meadows. Jade had brought Fredlie with Merlin on his back.

Gwendolyn hurried out to meet them.

'I do hope you didn't mind me sending for you?' she asked Merlin as soon as she was within talking distance.

'Not at all,' he replied, 'I was actually ready to come when Jade arrived, King Arthur was worried and he had asked me to come to visit you and find out what is happening.'

Gwendolyn filled him in with all the news as they walked over to where the boys were getting ready for David's spying trip.

'Please all stay together, we don't want David wandering off alone, and do not, on any account, cross over the border because you will be vulnerable then and we will not be able to protect you.'

They all agreed that they would do as she advised. They wanted to be in position, near the border, well before the time of the meeting at midnight and, as there was quite a way to go, they decided it would be best if they set off right away

-----

The three boys made good time and arrived where they wanted to be well away from the borders. There was a small thicket of trees which was perfect to hide their ponies. Once they were satisfied there was no way they could be seen they set off to finish the journey on foot.

The evening light faded and it became a little more difficult to see where they were going but even in the dark there was no mistaking where Summerdale ended and the Twilight Kingdom started. The darkness became thicker and even though a full moon had risen, very little of its light penetrated the other side.

'Right, this is far enough,' Edwin said.

They just sat down and waited, with the occasional whispered remark thrown in from either Thomas or Edwin, David just sat there staring with his head on one side listening.

Edwin suddenly noticed David was moving; he was shuffling towards the boundary.

'Where are you going David?' he said quietly getting up and moving over to him, he bent down and put his hands on his shoulders looking straight into his troubled eyes.

David blinked as he brought himself back to the present.

'Sorry I didn't hear what you said.'

'I asked where you were going.'

'Nowhere, I haven't moved.'

'Yes you have. Look at the marks in the grass; you were slowly going towards the border. Can you hear the voices again?'

'Yes they are calling again.'

'It won't be much longer until the meeting should start. It's nearly midnight now,'

Thomas came over and sat closely on the other side of David.

'The pull is almost unbearable; I don't know how much longer I can fight against it. Perhaps you had better tie me to something because I feel as if I have got to get there, and I didn't realise I'd moved before.'

Edwin quickly ran back to where they had left the ponies and retrieved a rope from his saddlebag before hurrying back to the others.

'Sorry David,' he said as he bound his arms behind him and tied the other end of the rope to a small tree. 'We have to do all we can to stop you getting in danger.'

David struggled for a short while then once midnight arrived he became calmer. He appeared to go into a trance.

His eyes suddenly sprang open.

'The meeting has started,' he reported, 'the leader of the Death Riders is talking, her name is Marwolaeth, and she said they have the stone of the Forest people. This gives them the power to cross over in to Summerdale and that they are going to start sending out raids from tomorrow. They are to kill the people and take their possessions for themselves. She told them that no one would expect them so they were sure of victory.' David paused with his head on one side, listening intently. 'She is introducing someone, someone who had been waiting in the shadows, she says her name is Morgana,' he whispered, a look of alarm spreading across his face. 'We must go and warn the people. They must prepare themselves.'

He tried to get up but the ropes held him.

'Let me go, let me go, we must warn them, 'he begged.

Thomas put his arms around his brother as Edwin undid his hands.

'Quiet David, calm down, we don't want to draw attention to ourselves.'

'Sorry, it's hearing her name again. How has she escaped? '

'I can't think how because she was to be well guarded. Are you really sure that is the name you heard? No one is going to believe us,' Thomas remarked.

They hurried back to the ponies where they mounted and kicked them into a gallop to return to the castle, as fast as they could, to warn of the coming danger.

In the forest of the Twilight Kingdom, the lady of darkness had felt David's presence, and laughed.

Chapter Twenty Two

David set off like a person possessed with Thomas and Edwin close behind. They thundered on through the moonlit countryside, not caring if they disturbed the people in their houses as they passed through the villages on the way back to the castle. Any people who did put their noses out to see what was happening heard the cry from David.

'Prepare to defend yourselves. The Death Riders are coming.'

The warning fell on deaf ears. The people laughed at them telling them to go home and sleep it off. They thought David was drunk. The land had been safe for so long no one believed that there could be any danger.

At last they reached the castle and clattered into the courtyard and slid off their rides throwing the reins to the sleepy grooms who had been told to wait for their return.

The three of them swept in through the front door, through the hall to the reception chamber where they had been received on their arrival.

The guard who had been sleeping at his post by the door immediately ran to alert Emperor Godwin and Empress Gwendolyn. They, in turn, sent the guard on to fetch Merlin.

David paced back and forth whilst the other two lounged on the chairs as they waited impatiently for the others to arrive. At last they heard the ponderous footsteps of Emperor Godwin and the quick light tread of Gwendolyn. The door opened.

'Now then, now then, what on earth is all this fuss?' Emperor Godwin asked as he entered still tying his sash to his dressing gown around his corpulent figure. He was followed into the room by his wife and almost immediately behind her, Merlin.

'The Death Riders are going to attack tomorrow,' David blurted out as Freya, Hope and Faith burst into the room.

'Now how are they going to do that?' Emperor Godwin asked.

'I don't know exactly, they said something about having stone to give them more power, if that makes sense, and Morgana was there,' David said.

'Now I know you are wrong,' Gwendolyn said quietly. 'I had a message from your grandmother earlier today and she said she had just received a report that Morgana was turning into a model prisoner. She had even stopped promising to cast a spell on her guard. She was seen in prison, on the Orkney Islands only yesterday. So even if she had escaped after the last visitor had left, it would take at least three months to arrive here. That is unless you have dragon power.'

'I don't care what Grandmother wrote, I know she is here,' David replied in frustration. 'When I was listening I could see the people there in my mind's eye. The one who was talking, the leader, was just a skeleton covered with a film of skin, there appeared to be no eyes in her sockets and she had a little grey wispy hair clinging to her scalp. She was a figure from nightmares. Then she turned and introduced the other person as Morgana.'

'What did she look like?' Merlin asked quietly.

'She was fairly tall with a very pale face and long black hair and I suppose beautiful in a strange way. She was a real person.'

'It sounds like Morgana, I must admit, but the report said she was still being held in the Orkney Islands yesterday. It is a mystery.'

'Well whoever it was, there is no way that the Death Riders can come onto our land and do any damage,' Emperor Godwin replied stubbornly. 'Today we had planned to have a tournament to celebrate the end of winter, so most of my people will be already making their way here and we will not disappoint them,' so saying he started for the door. 'May I suggest that we all go back to our beds and make the most of what time is left of the night?' He left the room and reluctantly the others started to follow.

'Are you sure you did not dream everything?' Thomas asked his twin as they climbed the stairs to their bedchambers.

'Are you starting to doubt me too? It was real; it was like they were in my head. It is going to happen. We must make the people understand this.'

'OK, brother, I believe you. Best we try to get a little sleep now and start again in the morning.'

'Yes you are right; there is nothing to be done until its light. We had better all meet for an early breakfast and think of some plan to make them listen,' Freya said as she opened her door. 'Goodnight everyone see you, say seven o clock.'

The rest agreed and each went to get what rest they could before starting again to try to warn the people of Summerdale of the dangers to come.

Merlin watched them all go to their rooms before he walked down the corridor to where he had been given a room. Once he was inside he did not retire to his bed, instead he went to his bags and pulled out a large book bound in heavy leather. This he set down on the table where a lamp burned to illuminate the area. He pulled up a chair and started turning the pages, looking for inspiration. He had believed David and knew they would need some strong magic to get the better of Morgana.

Chapter Twenty Three

The next morning dawned, bringing a beautiful day. The sky was a bright clear blue with not a cloud in the sky; the river sparkled as it made its way past the erected tents on its banks.

The six companions had not slept much and had no trouble arriving for their first meal before the appointed hour of seven. None of them had much of an appetite and neither did they come up with any ideas to make the people believe what David had seen.

'Why won't they believe me,' David murmured for the umpteenth time.

Dejected, they made their way to the river where Shimmer; the little green dragon that Freya always rode, met them.

'I was wondering if you wanted to enter any of the competitions,' she said, 'or perhaps we could give a demonstration of how we fly and burn things while you shoot arrows into a target.'

'Oh Shimmer, I hadn't even thought about doing anything like that,' Freya said. 'We have a problem.'

David then told her about the happenings of the previous night.

'Let me call the others,' Shimmer said. 'Many minds will make it easier.'

'Why didn't we think of calling for the dragons help?' Thomas exclaimed.

'I don't know, I think we were too close to the problem to see,' Freya replied.

Within a few moments the rest of the dragons were standing in the meadow. They were told what David had overheard and they discussed it between themselves taking no notice of the activity of the locals as the people of Summerdale prepared the arena for their tournaments.

'What did they mean by a stone to give them power?' Greor asked.

'The stone of the Forest People I think that is what you said,' Edwin replied

'Yes, that's right, there is so much going on in my head I forgot the details,' David said. 'What is it?'

'Well I am not a hundred per cent sure, but the Forest People live in the forest area to the west, the name literally means "little people" in your language but you usually call them fairies. They are good people and would not help anyone from King Golgog's kingdom,' Greor said.

'Perhaps we had better go and see if there is a problem with Queen Josephine,' Caw said.

'I think that would be a good idea,' Thomas agreed. 'I suggest three of us go with the dragons and three wait here to try and make someone take notice of what's going to happen'.

It was agreed that Edwin, Faith and Hope would go with Caw, Cawson and Jade to find out if anything had happened to the forest, while Greor, Sherna and Shimmer would do what they could with Thomas, David and Freya.

Freya and Shimmer flew to the nearby villages to try and make people listen while David and Thomas accompanied Greor and Sherna back to the castle to try to see the emperor again. Leaving the dragons outside they hurried to the emperor's room only to be met by his servant. He told them Emperor Godwin was too busy to see them at the moment as he was preparing his speech for the opening of the tournament, but as soon as he had finished he would come to the reception room and see them.

David and Thomas went back to the hallway and decided to wait there, as they would see him as soon as he came down the main stairs.

David went over to the nearest chair and sank down into it. He leaned forward and put his head into his hands.

'Why will no one take me seriously? They sent me to listen to the Death Riders and then they take no notice of what I heard.'

Thomas looked over to his brother and seeing his despair went over to him and put his hand onto his shoulder.

'I think the emperor doesn't want to believe that any bad could come to Summerdale. That's why he doesn't listen.'

They waited and waited, but still the emperor did not come. Eventually Merlin came down the stairs.

'What are you two doing here?' he asked.

'We're waiting to see Emperor Godwin,' David replied.

'He left some time ago, he went out the back way and by now he will be down at the festivities.'

'This is ridiculous. The time is marching on, it is nearly the middle of the day and we are getting nowhere,' David fumed.

I'll go and find Gwendolyn for you,' Merlin soothed and went off to return shortly with the lady in tow,

'I am so sorry we have been so busy today. You are not still worried about the Death Riders are you? Emperor Godwin says there is no way they can attack us.'

'Have you heard of the stone of the Forest People?' Thomas asked.

'Well, yes,' Empress Gwendolyn said looking puzzled. 'The stone has magical powers; it belongs to the Queen Josephine. She is whom we are waiting to hear from,' she added. 'Oh no! That was not the stone you meant last night, was it?'

'Yes it was actually,' David said looking more worried. 'What does it do?'

'It gives a great deal of power to the person who possesses it. It would make the Death Riders strong enough to attack,' Merlin said from the doorway.

'If they've captured the stone from Queen Josephine it's no wonder I haven't heard from her,' Gwendolyn said with a look of horror on her face. 'I must send to find out what has happened. Also we must tell Emperor Godwin and let the people in the outlying parts of our land know what is going to happen.'

'Edwin, Faith and Hope have already gone with the dragons to the forest so it should not be too long before we hear something,' David told her. 'I'll go and tell Greor and Sherna what's happening and then I'll come back here.'

The rest of them went in to the reception room to wait for news.

David soon returned and reported.

'Greor and Sherna have gone off to meet the others and bring them here as quickly as possible, so we should not have too long to wait.'

No one, except Merlin, could sit still; he just sat slowly turning the pages of his book whilst Thomas kept going to the window to see if anyone had returned. David went around the room picking up objects and putting them down again, whilst Gwendolyn paced backwards and forwards in front of the fireplace.

At last the dragons and their riders returned. When Thomas saw them land, they rushed out to meet them.

'You had better send for the emperor. Things are looking worse and worse,' Faith exclaimed.

Chapter Twenty Four

When Emperor Godwin returned, he was not in a very good mood.

'I thought I had made it clear that there was no danger,' he puffed.

'I think we must listen to the news that Edwin, Faith, Hope and the dragons have to relate,' Gwendolyn said soothingly.

'Humph,' he replied crossly but he sat down to listen.

'We can't find any sign of the Forest People and the trees of the forest were all confused,' Faith reported.

'Something must have happened to the Queen because she keeps the trees all calm,' Gwendolyn looked very worried. 'King Golgog must have captured her, which is the only way that the Death Riders could have the 'Stone of Power'

'You didn't tell us that they had the 'Stone of Power',' Emperor Godwin said sitting up straighter. 'We had better send warnings to our people in the North, telling them to look out for any disturbances on the boundary with the Twilight Kingdom.'

He sent for the captain of his men and organized a small force to ride out to be ready to protect the people from any attacks.

'We will be quite all right, my men will protect the people, and even if the Death Riders have the 'Stone of Power' we will still defeat them,' the emperor looked quite confident. 'Now I must return to my people and I suggest you come too. You can watch the games and take your mind off all your worries.'

'I shall stay in the castle and carry on looking for a spell to stop Morgana,' Merlin told the emperor.

'I still don't know if I really believe that Morgana is here,' the emperor said.

'It won't do any harm to prepare something in case,' the sage replied. 'I shall ask one of the dragons to fly to the Orkney Islands and find out the truth.'

'That's a good idea,' the emperor agreed.

'Now come on everybody back to the games.'

Reluctantly the companions took leave of the dragons. But no one really had much enthusiasm for watching the games and after a short while David spoke to Thomas.

'I think I should be of more use if I went back north to see if I can pick up any more from Marwolaeth and her Death Riders.'

Edwin overheard them talking. 'I agree with David it would be better than sitting around waiting for something to happen. Perhaps on the way we could come up with some sort of plan.'

The others crowded around and all agreed anything was better than just waiting.

They went back to the dragons and asked for their help again. A short while later they could be seen flying off to the north.

Dragons can fly faster than horses can gallop, so they arrived at the outlying village long before the emperor's men. A scene of devastation greeted them.

Most of the houses were burned out shells; the dead lay all around with the few survivors just standing looking lost, not knowing what to do.

Freya, Faith and Hope wasted no time and took the poor shocked people, who were mainly women and children, away from the carnage to one of the relatively untouched houses on the outskirts of the village. Once they had them settled inside, the women were organised into groups to look after the children

There were a few minor injuries which were soon treated then they lit a fire in the grate and made some hot sweet tea, as this was one of the best things for shock. They all gave what comfort they could to the children who had lost their parents and gradually the crying calmed a little. One of the women told them what had happened.

'We had all risen very early as most of us were going to the emperor's castle to watch the tournament. Some of the villagers had left the night before so they did not suffer the fate of the rest of us. It was just after breakfast, we heard a thundering sound coming from the north and on looking out we saw a horde of riders wearing black robes streaming out behind them as they came towards the village at full gallop. Many of them had hoods over their heads, but one or two hoods had fallen back revealing the skeleton like features with the black empty eye sockets and the wispy long grey hair blowing back in the wind. They were truly a nightmare to behold, everyone who saw them was afraid. I just grabbed my children and bundled them out of the back window, then my husband and I followed,' she paused. 'Some of the children had been playing in the woods near the village as they waited for their parents to finish preparations for their day out. They were the lucky ones. Others were on the way to meet their playmates, but when they saw the riders coming they ran crying back to their mothers' they were slaughtered by the first of the invaders,' the woman started to cry and another took up her tale.

'The riders swept through the village, throwing burning torches on to the thatched roofs and cutting down the people as they tried to escape they showed them no mercy. Some of us had managed to climb out of the back of the houses and had fled to the woods, undercover of the smoke that was now billowing everywhere. The attack did not last very long, once there were no more people running about, the riders pulled up to look at their handiwork before they turned their horses and galloped off back the way they had come.' She took a breath and continued. 'Once we saw the coast was clear we went back and put out the fires that were still raging. When we had done this we just stood around in little groups' trying to comfort the children but not really knowing what to do next. That's when you and the dragons arrived,' the woman finished her tale and just stood there with tears streaming down her face making trails through the soot on her cheeks.

'We will arrange for help to be sent to rebuild your village' David said and turned to the others. 'Come on let's get things moving.'

The few men survivors from being slaughtered came forward and, with Thomas, they organised the collection of the bodies. These were taken to the church, which was roofless but still standing.

David and Edwin called the dragons over to come to help with the digging of a pit for a mass grave. With the use of their powerful front legs, they soon had the hole ready.

One of the villagers started the job of recording the names of the dead and organising the tending of the injured. This left the comrades free to leave the village and head, once more, to the boundaries of Summerdale.

They soon were standing on the grassland just before the start of the trees that marked King Golgog's kingdom.

'What are we going to do?' Thomas asked.

'We will take it in turns to stay and guard the borders,' Greor volunteered.

'Will six of us be enough to cover the entire border?' Sherna asked.

'I don't know but we must try.'

They all looked worried.

'There is something different,' Edwin said at last.

'I was just thinking that,' Freya agreed, 'but what is it?'

'It's just as gloomy here as over there. The darkness is spreading,' David said. 'I can hear them in my head; they are celebrating what they have done to the village. They are also starting to plan their next attack…Its going to be to the east of here at dawn tomorrow.'

'Right we had better go and warn the people. This time we will be able to set up a reception committee for the invaders. We will send for men from the other villages then with the dragons we will be here to repulse the attack.'

'Freya you go with Shimmer and tell the emperor that we need more help here. We shall wait here and David can "listen" in case there are any changes to their plans,' Thomas said.

Within an hour Freya and Shimmer had returned.

'The first of the men are nearly here, we have just flown over them and the emperor has sent some more on the way,' she reported. 'Have you heard anything else, David?'

'No, in fact it has been strange since we planned what to do, everything has become hazy, there was a lot of mumbling and talks, but I couldn't make out what was being said. It's like someone is muffling the voices.'

'That is strange but I expect you'll pick up anything important,' Thomas reassured him.

'We had better go to the village, where the attack is planned, to make them leave and decide where we are going to hide while we wait for tomorrow,' Greor said.

Having all agreed they made their way to the east. Once there they soon had the villagers packed and then sent them off to join the others at the tournament to take them out of any danger.

The emperor's men arrived in good time and they were all sent into the various houses to conceal themselves then set a watch whilst those off duty tried to get some sleep before the battle.

Long before dawn they were all up and waiting and as the sun made its appearance in the east they listened for the sound of the attack. The sun rose higher and still nothing happened. When full daylight arrived and still they had seen no enemy, they realised no one was coming.

'What can have happened?' Thomas asked.

'I think I know,' Freya replied turning to David. 'You know you said the talking went fuzzy after we had made our plans?'

'Yes,' David replied.

'Well, if you could hear their plans, why could they not hear ours?'

'Oh my goodness, why hadn't we thought of that before? They'll have known we were here. Let's just hope they haven't attacked anywhere else.'

'We'll fly along the boundaries and check the villages,' Caw said and all the dragons took off to go and check for any smoke or other sign of battle.

It was not long before they returned with the terrible news that two more villages, this time on the western side, had been completely wiped out. Luckily they were relatively empty as again the people had gone to the tournament and had not returned yet.

'You had better make some plans without me in your hearing,' David said sadly. 'It's all my fault that the people have been killed.'

'You mustn't blame yourself, we all knew what you had said, we just did not think properly,' Thomas put his arm around his twin's shoulder.

The leader of the emperor's force asked the comrades to go back and report what had happened while he and his men started to clean up the villages.

'Tell my Lord that we will patrol the borders as best we can but we will need many more men to help us.'

'We will,' David assured him as they all climbed on the dragons back and set off to carry the bad news to the emperor and his wife.

Chapter Twenty Five

As soon as the dragons landed, David and Thomas left the others and went to report to Emperor Godwin, Empress Gwendolyn and Merlin.

'We have some very bad news,' David blurted out. 'Because of me the Death Riders must have been able to overhear us. They knew what we had planned. They had no intention of attacking the village that I had heard them talk about; they went and attacked two other villages. We have to find the cure for me to make sure they do not know what we are going to plan in the future.'

'This is terrible news,' Emperor Godwin exclaimed. 'What are we to do?'

'Whatever it is don't say anything whilst I am here,' David said quickly.

'I have some news,' Merlin stepped forward 'While you have been away I have discovered there is a tree that grows deep in the Twilight Kingdom that has golden fruit. If David eats one of these it will cure him. All I will say for the moment is; go and prepare for a journey whilst I talk to Edwin, Thomas and the dragons.'

David left as he was asked and made his way up to his room. Thomas went to fetch the others to come to the meeting.

Once they had all reassembled Merlin said, 'To reach the place to find the cure for David, you will need to go through the little people's forest, then make your way north across the grass lands and over the mountains to come in at the northern most side of the Twilight Kingdom. This is where the tree can be found. It is on an island in the middle of a lake, which is full of terrible creatures that will kill you if they can. I suggest plans should be made for the journey and you all leave as soon as possible,' Merlin finished.

'I will go to David and see he is all right,' Freya said, 'you can let me know all the arrangements when I come back.' She left the room.

'Why can't we just fly there on the Dagon's backs?' Thomas asked.

'Two reasons; the first is, as soon as a dragon flew over the border the enemy would know and the second, there would be nowhere to land on the island as it is very small,' Merlin answered.

'There is a third reason,' Edwin said. 'We will need their help to keep the attacks at bay whilst you are away.'

'We? Are you going to remain here?' Gwendolyn asked.

'Yes, I became quite an expert at killing the Death Riders and I think you need as much help as possible. Also I would recommend a small group only go to find the tree as small numbers travel faster,'

'I agree,' Merlin said. 'I think Thomas and Freya should accompany David and the rest of you stay here.'

'No!' Hope said. 'David is my friend and I want to help him as much as I can,' she stood, with her hands on her hips, glaring at them.

'OK,' Thomas laughed. 'One more won't make much difference.'

'What won't make much difference?' Freya asked as she re-entered the room. 'I came to ask who we pack for.'

'Just David, Hope, yourself and me,' Thomas replied 'We were just coming to find you and David to start to get ready.'

'The rest of us will go and talk with the dragons to see if we can come up with some plan to protect the empire,' Emperor Godwin said as he led his wife and Merlin out of the room, Faith and Edwin followed close behind. 'We will see you when you are all ready to go,' Faith said as they left.

'Well come on we may as well go and pack,' Hope said and led the way upstairs to their rooms where Freya organised the packing in readiness of their coming departure

It was very difficulty keeping the details of their intended journey from David but he helped by not asking any questions

When the four at last came down stairs to say goodbye to the ones they were leaving behind. Their meeting was finished and they were all waiting for them.

Faith came over and hugged her sister.

'Take care of yourself and try not to get into any danger,' she said.

'I think you will be in more danger staying here than I shall be going away,' Hope replied moving on to give Edwin a hug. 'Look after her for me,' she whispered.

'I shall do, have no fear,' Edwin replied.

Then it was Gwendolyn's turn to give them each a hug.

'Take care of each other and return soon,' she said then turned to Thomas and drawing him aside asked. 'Try to find out what happened to Queen Josephine, I fear for her safety and with her all her people.'

'We will, don't worry and as soon as we have found the cure for David we will return here to add our help to the others.'

Emperor Godwin shook everyone's hands before he wished them 'God speed and return to us safely,'

Merlin came back just in time to wish them a safe journey.

'I have something for you,' he said and handed Freya a necklace it was in two halves. 'These are each half of a calling charm.'

He handed one half to Freya and went across to hang the other half on Shimmer's collar.

'If you need each other all you have to do is touch it and think of the other one, you will immediately feel the call'

'Does that mean if I am needed I shall feel Freya's thoughts?' Shimmer asked.

'Yes, but don't use it except in an emergency. With this you will be able to find each other no matter where you are.'

'Thank you Merlin, I feel much safer now,' Freya said and kissed his cheek.

They climbed on to the waiting dragons' backs and soon were soaring away to the west and the start of their journey.

They waved down to those left behind until they were too small to see any longer and then they just snuggled down against the great beasts' necks and enjoyed the sights as they flew towards the forest.

Once there each rider took a little time to goodbye before the great beasts were to head back in the direction they had come to help with the protection of the borders of Summerdale.

'I am pleased to hear that we will be able to find you if you are in danger,' Greor said. 'We know we are needed to protect Summerdale's borders but that does not stop us worrying about you on your journey into the darkness that covers the Twilight Kingdom.'

'You must take care of each other as well, whilst we are away. Come on we had all better be on our way,'

Freya replied, giving Shimmer an extra hug. 'Goodbye for now, my friends,' she called as the dragons took to the sky once more.

'I suppose we are going into the forest?' David asked.

'Yes it was decided we will go around and enter the Twilight Kingdom in the north western corner, therefore keeping you as far away from the Death Riders and their leader Marwolaeth, so they will not be able to detect you and make it safer for us all to find the tree with the fruit to cure you,'

'I can't hear any voices or see anything myself so you are probably correct, we are safe here,' David agreed.

Facing the green forest the companions put their packs on their backs and set off for the journey onwards to all sorts of new adventures.

Chapter Twenty Six

David led the way Freya and Hope were close behind and Thomas brought up the rear. They gazed around as the sun peeped through the new green leaves on the branches gave a dappled shade to the forest floor where a few spring flowers had started to open. There should have been a sense of tranquillity with the quietness, but they all immediately felt an air of unrest. The main thing they noticed was the silence; there were no birds' song, the only noise being the sound of the four of them walking over the leaf carpet. They followed each other steadily forward between the thickly crowded trunks. As they went deeper, towards the centre of the forest, the trees started to sway and sigh as if from a gentle breeze. But not a breath stirred!

'Oh,' said Hope, 'did you see that?'

'What?' Thomas asked.

'I could have sworn the tree up ahead moved slightly.'

'I didn't see anything,' David replied.

'I think you are right,' Freya said worriedly, 'the one just ahead seemed to move a few inches across, making the path a little easier to follow.'

'I think you girls are imagining things,' Thomas said from the rear, 'but if they were to make the pathway easier to follow, then I am all for it.'

The two girls moved into the lead as they kept looking around and commenting on the trees whilst the boys laughed at them and chatted amongst themselves about sport and other things.

After they had been walking for about fifteen minutes they walked out of the trees and into the open.

They were back where they had started.

'You have led us in a complete circle,' Thomas said laughing.

'We'd better show them how it is done,' David replied joining in his brother's merriment.

They set off again this time with the girls at the rear but after the same time they again emerged into the field they had started from.

'I told you the trees moved,' Hope declared.

'Perhaps there may be something in what you say,' David agreed.

'I think you're right,' Thomas said, 'they don't seem to want us to get to the other side of the forest.'

'How are we going to get through if this keeps happening?'

'I have a compass somewhere in here,' Hope said diving into her bag. After emptying nearly all her things out on the ground, she found the item she required; this of course, had been right at the bottom of her pack.

'I think if we just follow this straight north, not taking notice of where the trees are trying to make us go, we should make it through.'

'Well it's worth a try anyway.'

Hope repacked her bag and hoisted it back on her shoulder.

Thomas took the compass from her and set off with everyone following behind. It was not long before there were trees right in the middle of their path, but by going around them and returning to their course they seemed to be making progress. They began to think they would succeed, until they came up against an enormous tree with thick bushes stretching each way from its base.

They looked at this obstacle in dismay.

'There is only one way we can get through,' Freya said sadly, 'we are going to have to cut our way through the bushes.'

The leaves started rustling and a sighing as if there was a strong wind in the branches.

'They sound as if they are crying,' Hope said. 'We can't hurt them.'

'I'm glad you said that,' a voice from behind the trees said.

'Who said that?'

'I'm one of the Forest people. We look after the trees and they look after us. Normally they would not behave like this but our Queen Josephine has been captured along with her 'Stone of Power'. Now the trees no longer trust strangers and try to keep them away from us.'

'We're not here to harm you or your people. In fact we could help you.'

'How could you help us?' the voice asked.

'We're going into the Twilight Kingdom to find a cure for a cut from a Death Rider's spear and after that we are going to try to rescue your Queen because Merlin says the 'Stone of Power' is allowing King Golgog to come into Summerdale and kill all the people.'

A little person came around the trunk of the large tree and the bushes moved aside with a sigh. He was followed by others of his kind. They were all very beautiful with blond hair and green eyes and all were dressed in clothes of gossamer that gleamed like silver. On their backs were little wings.

'Why; you are Fairies!' Hope exclaimed and clapped her hands in delight. 'I have always wanted to meet some of your people.'

Their leader looked at her and smiled. 'Normally we are invisible but now the 'Stone of Power' has gone we can't fade properly, otherwise you would not have seen us. May I introduce myself, I am Prince Owen and this is my sister Princess Poppy, Queen Josephine is our mother.'

A young girl stepped forwards and smiled.

'We will help you to the other side of the forest if you are going to help us and we will point your way to you.'

'Thank you,' David replied for everyone. 'We were beginning to despair at ever getting through to the other side.'

'I thought we had been defeated before we really started,' Hope added.

The Forest people came and took each of the hands of Freya, Thomas, David and Hope then they pulled them forward towards the trees, as they walked along the fairies started to sing in sweet light voices. The trees swayed in time to the music and drew back to let everyone pass. Some of the fairies flew up through the branches and soon birds were appearing, joining in with their sweet songs to make the music swell.

The band of travellers moved forwards through the forest until they arrived at a very big clearing and saw a little village. The tiny houses stood in a circle around a courtyard with a larger dwelling in the centre; this one clearly was the royal house. All of the buildings looked as if they were in need of some repairs.

Just beyond the village there was a little stream where a few of the little people who had stayed behind were going about their business washing clothes and other linen which they then hung on a line fastened between the trees where it was left, to blow dry, in the slight breeze that now blew.

They realised they needed to plan the next part of their journey very carefully, so were pleased when Prince Owen asked them to stay for the night. He promised to give them as much information as they needed for the next stage of their quest. Because of the trouble finding their way through the trees the evening had advanced far more than they had hoped and the journey onwards was into unknown dangers.

Chapter Twenty Seven

The houses were too small for the four to stay inside so David and Thomas unpacked and erected their travelling tents while the host organised a meal to be prepared for their guests. Freya and Hope went to help setting up a long table which the busy fairies soon had piled high with all sorts of food.

When everyone had eaten and drunk their fill, Thomas turned to Prince Owen and enquired.

'You said that your mother, Queen Josephine, had been captured, along with the 'Stone of Power', perhaps you could tell us what happened?'

The prince looked sad as he replied.

'Not so long ago we used to live on the edge of the Forest next to Summerdale. One day my mother and her maid went for a walk through the trees, as they did every day, but this time King Golgog had sent some of his men to capture them. They tied my mother's hands and threw her in to the back of a cart. Then they released her maid, who they sent back with a message telling us to all come to this place and bring the 'Stone of Power' with us. They said when they had the Stone they would release the queen,' Prince Owen paused. 'We did everything they had asked, but once we had handed over the Stone, instead of releasing our mother, the king used the Stone to make the forest keep us here. Now we can only go out on the Twilight Kingdom side, whilst anyone coming in from Summerdale would be sent back, as you found out,' Prince Owen finished.

Everyone was quiet for a moment then Princess Poppy asked.

'You said earlier that you could help us. What did you mean?'

'Summerdale has been suffering from attacks from the Death Riders of the Twilight Kingdom and this has led to the death of many of the villagers, also the darkness is spreading. This is going to affect the lives of everyone because all the plants will fade as the darkness brings winter to the land. If we cannot stop this it will slowly spread everywhere, bringing the dark and the cold with it and this will eventually cause all the crops to fail,' David paused and looked around at all the little faces looking at him.

He continued. 'We have left the dragons to help defend the borders, to try and stop the riders killing the people and the cold spreading further. Meanwhile we are going to go in to the Twilight Kingdom, by the back door, so to speak. Hopefully they will be concentrating on the attacks against the dragons and will not look to the northern borders, enabling us to cross over in search of the cure for my condition.'

David finished and turned to Thomas who told them the rest.

'Whilst we are far away from the Death Riders they will be unable to oversee David and therefore they should not know what we are doing or where we are. Unfortunately this means we will no longer be able to listen to their plans either. Once we've found the fruit of the tree that will cure David, we'll go and rescue Queen Josephine and restore her and the 'Stone of Power' to you all.'

'We'll help you all we can and show you the way to go once you are through to the other side of the forest.'

'How did we manage to come here then?' Freya asked.

'You probably noticed there are a lot of our people, so by taking hold of your hands and surrounding you whilst we sang to the trees. They forgot that you were amongst us and let you come here.'

'Very clever,' David said. 'Is that how we will be able to go to the other side tomorrow?'

'Yes,' Princess Poppy replied. 'Now we need to make you as safe as possible, so I intend to give you this picture of our home in Summerdale. The picture is enchanted and anyone who looks at it feels a sense of peace and tranquillity. When you near to the Twilight Kingdom, David, you may feel you are being overlooked. All you need to do is gaze into the picture; this will calm your mind. This in turn will confuse anyone trying to see your thoughts; it will appear that you are still in Summerdale and not going anywhere near to their kingdom.'

'Thank you that will make our journey a little safer.'

'Now I suggest we all go and have a good night's sleep before the start of your long trek to find the tree to cure all ills' Princess Poppy finished.

Prince Owen advised the boys on their journey as he walked them to their tent.

'Once you cross the scrub plains you will come to the mountains. There you must seek out the elves. They will be able to send you on your way. I must warn you that it will not be easy. There are beasts on the grass plain and they will try to kill and eat you. You will have to go very carefully; you must not draw attention to yourselves.'

With this warning ringing in their ears they all went to their sleeping quarters to rest in comparative safety for the last time.

The companions lay down on their beds but found it hard to go to sleep. Each of them had their own thoughts and fears of what they were going to have to face and each one was glad they were not going to be alone for the start of their journey over the rolling scrubland and the danger that they were going to have to face along the way.

Chapter Twenty Eight

The next morning, after an early breakfast, the travellers packed up their belongings and let the fairies lead them through to the edge of the forest, where they came out into an empty meadow with evidence of the poor crop harvested stacked in one corner.

Pointing to the little hayrick the Prince commented, 'our crops started failing here ever since my mother was captured, we would like to go back to Summerdale but we have been told we have to stay here if we want the queen to live. Also the trees will not let us back that way. So what choice do we have?'

'Don't worry, we will bring your queen back to you and everything will be fine again,' David replied sounding more sure than he was feeling.

The others nodded their agreement as they followed their hosts over a slight rise in the ground. From the top they could see the start of vast open grasslands. Here they saw small scrubby bushes growing in small areas and far away in the distance they could see a large mountain.

'Wow! Just look at that, it goes on for ever!' Hope exclaimed.

'It is not as far across as it looks. To be as safe as possible the best path for you would be to follow the hill tops, the route is slightly longer but you will be high enough to see if there is any danger lurking about,' Prince Owen advised them.

'What danger? Do you mean the creatures the Princess told us about?' Freya asked.

'Yes. The plains are the home of some cat like creatures. They are not as big as lions or tigers, in fact they look like very large domestic cats, all fluffy and cuddly, but they aren't!'

Princess Poppy filled in, 'They are very good hunters and once they see their prey they keep on following, they may not be as fast as some animals but they do not give up. So if you are on the high ground you will see signs of them before they can see you and you can lie low until they have passed.'

'Won't they smell us?' David asked.

'Not unless they cross your trail, they hunt by sight mainly, not smell, but they are like most animals, and they do have good hearing.'

'How long should it take us to cross to the mountain?' Thomas asked

'It shouldn't take much more than a day. I expect you will come to the foothills of the mountains before lunchtime tomorrow. And then you have only to find the Elves to help you on the rest of your journey.'

'You make it sound so easy,' Hope said.

'It should be if you go quickly and do not make too much noise. But remember do stay alert and on the higher ground.'

'I think I can speak for us all when I say a heartfelt thanks to you for all your help and guidance,' David said and the other three nodded their agreement.

They four of them went around giving everyone a hug before they moved off on to the next stage of their journey.

The sounds of the little people voices followed them through the early morning air as they called after them with their good wishes as the four made their way into the unknown.

Moving over the ground was easy as it was dry and by keeping to the top of the rises they could walk at an even pace. This meant there was no running up and down the slopes and, although it actually was further than going in a straight line, they probably covered the distance quicker.

Every now and again they looked back and could see the fairies standing watching them go. Gradually they became smaller and smaller until they disappeared from view as the hilltop took a slight downward slope.

'Do you think we should go downhill?' Hope asked fearfully as she looked around.

'We're just heading for the next rise over there,' Freya replied as they all turned slightly and made their way up again.

'We can see a good distance so we should be all right, so do try not to worry.'

'Thank you David, did I say I was worried,' Hope retorted annoyed that they had seen that she was a little concerned.

'Sorry, I didn't mean anything by it,' David replied.

'Ok, everyone let's keep the chat to the minimum. It would be best to keep our wits about us in case there is any danger around,' Thomas retorted.

They travelled on for the rest of the day, occasionally catching sight of some deer like creatures in the distance but no sign of anything to worry about.

After four hours of walking Freya called a halt.

'I think it's about time we had a rest and something for refreshment, I don't know about you all but I'm quite thirsty after all the walking.'

'I could do with something to eat as well,' replied Thomas and slid his pack off his back and flopped on the ground beside it.

With sighs of relief the others followed his example.

For a while they all sat or lay quietly, having a few mouthfuls of food or drink. David even started to nod off to sleep.

'This will never do,' Hope groaned as she repacked her rucksack. 'We really must continue on our journey otherwise we will not reach the other side by tomorrow morning, also no one is on lookout, we could have some of those cat creatures near at hand and not know about it.'

'She's right,' Thomas agreed and he too began repacking the few items he had removed from his pack.

'All right, slave driver,' David retorted as he opened his eyes. He stretched and slowly stood up; he did not want them to see that the journey was taking more out of him than he had thought. To give himself a little more time to pull himself together he stared out at the horizon and then slowly turned a full three hundred and sixty degrees to take in the whole of the view.

'There isn't much to see is there? Just small bushes interspersed with wild thyme and cotton lavenders but mainly just tufts of grasses growing out of the dusty stony earth. Though there are the occasional few olive trees around,' he paused whilst he studied the landscape. 'I wonder if there is any water in the valleys.'

'There must be water somewhere otherwise the wild animals could not live here,' Hope replied, getting up to follow his gaze around.

'Well other than the few deer we saw early on, we haven't seen any sign of life have we? Perhaps the cat creatures are no longer around and we have been worrying for nothing.'

'Well I, for one, am not prepared to take the risk,' David said. 'Come on everyone let's get on with it.'

He shouldered his pack and started off again in the direction of the mountains. The others slowly followed. It was not long before they were back into their stride and were making good inroads into their journey.

The afternoon passed peacefully, but the sun beat down on them relentlessly, making them all thirsty and just before the sun sank into the horizon behind them. Freya again called a halt.

'We are going to have to find a stream tomorrow as I'm nearly out of water. How's everyone else doing?

'I have a little left,' Thomas said, 'but I could do with topping up.'

'Well I have just a mouthful left, so the sooner we find water the better,' Hope answered.

David agreed adding, 'I think we should make camp for tonight and set off early tomorrow before the sun is completely up to conserve what we do have left. We are going to have to go down into the valley to see if we can find traces of a stream or any other sign of water.'

'I agree, David, but perhaps we had better take turns at being a lookout tonight, just in case there is anything on the prowl around here.'

'Thomas, I think you are being over cautious, but anything for a quiet life,' Freya retorted.

They had their evening meal then drew straws for the order of the watches.

'If everyone does two hours, we will all have six hours sleep and we will still be off after breakfast before it is fully light,' Thomas said as he settled down under his blanket using his backpack as his pillow. They packed away the remainder of the food and placed it all together by some rocks, ready for their breakfast.

'Wake me in two hours, Hope,' Thomas said and pulled his blanket right over his head, almost immediately he was asleep.

The others followed his example, leaving Hope staring into the night sky, and listening for any sounds. After about an hour of listening to the breeze through the undergrowth, Hope's eyelids began to droop. Realizing she was in danger of falling asleep whilst she should be keeping watch, she got up to walk around for a short while.

'What is the problem? Nothing had appeared all day,' she muttered to herself as she sat back down, and let herself drift into sleep.

She woke with a jerk, glancing up at the position of the moon, she realised she had been asleep for the best part of an hour. She looked around wondering what had awoken her. She was just in time to see a low shape backing around the rocks, with its teeth it was pulling the remains of their food

She jumped to her feet and rushed across to try to save the package but she was not fast enough, the small jackal like creature now had the food firmly in his jaw and he took off with it. Far too fast for Hope, who could only stare in disbelief as she watched their breakfast disappeared into the gloom.

The disturbance had woken Thomas. 'Is it time for me to take over yet,' he whispered to Hope.

'Just about,' she replied, 'although there is not much to watch over as a dog of some sort has just stolen the food.'

'What! How did that happen?'

'I'm sorry, I only dozed off for a moment and the animal stole the food in a flash. I hadn't seen anything around. I really don't know where it came from.'

'Well we'll just have to hope we can contact the elves early tomorrow and that they can let us have some food, as I haven't seen anything to hunt to enable us to catch our own food. Now, just turn in you must be exhausted,' Thomas replied, trying not to let her see how annoyed he was.

The rest of the night passed without any further incidents, Thomas passed the watch on to David after explaining about the food theft, and he in turn passed on to Freya.

When Freya woke them all in the morning, nothing was said about the loss of the food. They just packed up and set off, this time they went downhill in search of water. They were all keeping a good lookout, as they now knew there were creatures around. Every rustle had Hope jumping as they steadily moved down to the valley below. Here they became aware of more trees that, hopefully, meant water but also probably the existence of wild life and maybe the cat creatures.

Chapter Twenty Nine

The going was harder as the undergrowth became thicker. The grasses were greener now with the occasional bush of Oleander with its pink flowers to brighten up the view. When they reached the bottom they were delighted to see a small stream trickling amongst some rocks. Following it along its course they soon found a small pool where they could set about filling their empty water bottles, which luckily had not been in with the stolen food package.

'I think it would be wise to make our way back up to the top of the next rise, then we can see where we are going better also we would have a better chance of seeing anything following us,' Thomas proposed.

'I think you're right,' David agreed. He looked with dismay at the steep side of the valley they would have to climb up to regain the higher ground.

'Well come on then,' said Freya as she started out, climbing back up the hill.

Hope just nodded and followed behind the rest of them, still feeling very down about allowing the food to be taken.

Once they reached the top of the hill, the walking became easier and even David soon regained his breath after the hard scramble up. They were all feeling much more positive, now that they at least had water. They set off at a good pace towards the mountains that were much nearer now with the sun just peeping over the top of them.

Before they went over the next rise, David took one last look down into the valley. It would not be in view once they crested the ridge.

'Oh my goodness, look back there!' he exclaimed, stopping to stare.

The others turned to see what he was making such a fuss about.

'Look, down there, he pointed with a shaky hand, 'there are cats back down there and they are sniffing around on our trail.'

'We had better make tracks, fast, before they look up and see us,' Freya said quietly. She turned and moved onwards at a far faster pace than before.

The others followed as quickly as they could, each one checking that their bows and arrows were easy to get to in the case of an emergency.

At the top of each rise they glanced back fearfully, hoping that they would not see what they were dreading.

The pace they set became a jog as they moved nearer to the welcoming mountains.

The sun rose higher in the sky and the heat of the day began to take a toll on the travellers. Thomas was in the lead at this time, so he held up his hand to call a halt.

'We must have a little rest or we will exhaust ourselves, just time for a drink then we will start off again. This time we will walk for sixty paces then jog for sixty paces and so on. That way we will cover the ground without draining our energy as much.'

They did as suggested and no one spoke, each keeping their thoughts and fears to themselves also they had to concentrate on counting the number of steps. The reward was that they covered the ground with far less effort than jogging all the way. It was comforting to see the mountains getting closer by the minute.

David, as usual, glanced over his shoulder at the top of a ridge and this time his worst fears were realised.

There, just two ridges behind them, was the first sign that they were being followed. A cat like creature was sat on its haunches looking forward, searching for its prey. Even as David looked the cat dropped down and started running towards them followed by others.

'Here they come,' he called in a low voice and started to run down off the top of the ridge.

'How many are there?' Thomas asked as he picked up his pace to keep up with his brother.

'I didn't stop to count, but more than three.'

The girls, too, were now running, as fast as they could, towards the base of the mountain that, thankfully, was now very close.

The last ridge had flattened out into a plateau leading up into the foothills of the mountain. On their right and left the sides were steep cliffs. These formed a natural valley to lead them to the gentler slopes on the way up to the peaks that towered above them.

As they tore across the ground looking for a place of safety they heard a sound that made the hair on the back of their necks rise in fear. It was like nothing that they had heard before, a cross between a meow and a roar.

Glancing over her shoulder Freya saw one of the feline creatures standing, and calling, it was telling the others that it had them in its sights.

'They've seen us,' she shouted. She upped her pace again and ran on as fast as she could.

'I can see a place in the cliff that we could climb, follow me,' Thomas called and took off to his right.

The others quickly followed, running as fast as they could, towards a fall of rocks. They realised that when they reached the rocks they would be able to start climbing up, this would allow them to reach the cliff face and, if they could only move fast enough, out of reach of the cats.

Thomas, reached the rocks first, he quickly climbed to the top, before he turned to help Hope up and showed her where to start climbing to a shelf a short way up on the side of the cliff. Seeing her start off he gave his hand to Freya as she scrambled up in her turn. He glanced at David as he arrived at the foot of the boulders then across at the pursuers.

The cats were coming fast.

Thomas un-slung his bow, fitted an arrow and fired in one fluid motion. He hit the lead cat as it reached for David's leg and sent it bowling over into the path of its followers. This allowed David those extra few seconds that he needed to scramble up the rocks and then on up the face of the cliff.

Thomas let fly two more arrows and both found their mark. The rest of the pride of cats stopped for the moment, allowing him the time to sling his bow over his shoulder and follow his brother up to the ledge.

Once there everyone was safe out of reach and looking down at the cats. Not wanting to lose their prey, the cats were taking running jumps at the side of the cliff. They were obviously trying to gain some footholds to follow the travellers to their perch. After a while they realised the futility of their efforts and just settled down in the shade afforded by the cliff side and patiently waited for the group to come back down. The injured cats pulled out the arrows and licked their wounds.

Freya walked the length of the ledge, looking all around to see if she could find another way, either up or down.

'Well I can't see any way out of this, we have no food and the cats look as if they are set for a long wait,' she said gloomily.

'Perhaps they will give up eventually. At least we are in the shade so we shouldn't burn up,' Hope observed hopefully.

'We are in the shade at the moment but when the sun moves around, later this afternoon, we will be in full sun,' David replied.

'Well so shall the cats perhaps they will go away then.'

'Let's hope you are right. Now may I suggest that we all get some rest so that when the opportunity presents itself we shall be ready for every eventuality,' Thomas sat with his back against the cliff face and closed his eyes.

David, too, closed his eyes. No one had noticed the greyness of his features, they had all been concentrating on avoiding the cats, and for this he was grateful. He did not want them seeing how his wound was still affecting him. Although they were some way from the Twilight Kingdom and the call of the Death Riders he still felt the pull of the poison in his system. There were times when he felt as if he was not with everyone but in a swirling mist, with strange shapes flitting past him at these times the sound of someone speaking to him was muffled and far away. He fell into an uneasy doze.

The others sat and settled down for what looked like a long and hungry wait.

'What will we do if the cats don't go?' Hope asked after a few minutes.

'We'll have to hope we can kill all of them,' Thomas replied without opening his eyes.

'The only trouble is they are not going to stay within range of our arrows are they?' Freya observed.

'I know,' her brother replied, 'all we can do is hope for a miracle.'

On that depressing note they all fell quiet as they settled down to wait to see what fate would have in store for them.

The four of them relaxed as best they could, leant against the steep cliff face they each tried to think of a way out of their predicament.

The day moved on and the sun came around the end of the mountain making the shaded area became smaller and smaller until there was non-left and they were bathed in the full warmth of the sun.

It was quite pleasant for the first half hour, as they had all become a little chilled from sitting in the shade after the exertion of their run to safety, but as the afternoon progressed they began to suffer from the heat.

'We're going to have to do something soon or we'll run out of water as well and then we will be in real trouble,' Freya voiced all their thoughts.

'I wish I knew what to suggest,' Thomas replied.

Chapter Thirty

David had awoken and now he stood up.

'None of you would be in this predicament if it wasn't for me,' he said, 'first I go and get myself injured in a way to make you all come away from your homes.'

'But I put the final touch when I went and lost all our food,' Hope interrupted.

'Yes, that's as maybe, but you would not be here if it wasn't for me. I feel it's up to me to rescue you all, so I have been thinking. If I go down and lead the cats off you could all come down and make your way safely into the foothills without the animals realising you have gone.'

'It's good of you to offer to sacrifice yourself for us all, but there are one or two flaws in your thinking. One, you rightly say you have an injury, well that will just make you too slow to draw the cats far enough away for us to make an escape, and two, if you are not with us what's the point of going into the mountains anyway,' Thomas answered his twin.

'Don't be silly you have got to go on to rescue the little Queen,' he replied.

'Will you two stop that and come here, I think I can hear something,' Freya said from her position leaning with her ear against the rock face.

'What is it sis?' Thomas asked

'I'm surprised anyone can hear anything with the noise you two were making' Hope added smiling at them.

'Please be quiet!' Freya said crossly. 'I can hear something and it is inside the mountain.'

They all crowded around her and put their ears to the rock face to listen.

'I can hear something too,' Hope said with a look of wonder on her face.

'I'm sure it sounds like people talking,' David said excitedly and banged on the wall. 'Where are you?' he shouted and banged again, this time with the hilt of his sword.

The voices stopped and a crack appeared in the face of the cliff and a door opened inwards. A face appeared in the gap, then another.

'Who are you?' the first person asked.

David quickly introduced everyone and explained about the cats down below.

'It's very lucky that we decided to come down to these storerooms today, normally, no one has much call to come here at this time of the year' The first person replied.

'But where are my manners, let me introduce my companion, Heddwch, that means "Peace" in your language and I am Adain, which means, "Wing" to you. We are some of the elves that live in the Blue Mountains.'

Heddwch and Adain came out on to the ledge and shook hands with everyone.

David spoke for them all. 'We are so pleased to see you, we have been sent to find your King Brenin to ask for assistance to rescue Queen Josephine. She has been captured by King Golgog of the Twilight Kingdom.'

'If you come with us we will take you to our king and you can tell him your story,' Heddwch said and ushered them in through the doorway. Adain closed it behind the last of them. The two elves picked up their lanterns, from where they had left them just inside the door, and led everyone up the slope, back towards where the rest of the elves lived, deep inside the mountain.

They climbed upwards for some time, before they started to hear the noises associated with a large group of people living together. At last the passageway became lighter as they drew nearer to a large well-lit cavernous area. Then, as they stepped out of the side passageway, the hubbub of many voices met them.

Adain motioned them to remain where they were, as she and Heddwch went over towards a crowd in the middle of the hallway. The people stood aside to let the two elves through allowing the four travellers to catch a glimpse of a rotund gentleman, richly dressed, with a golden crown upon his head

'That must be King Brenin,' Freya whispered to Hope.

Heddwch dropped to one knee and addressed his king, he told him of finding David and the others outside the lower passageway. On hearing this everyone stopped talking and all eyes turned to look at the four. The King pushed past his subjects and walked over to them.

'May I bid you welcome?' He greeted them, as his red jovial face broke out into a beaming smile.

David and Thomas gave a little bow and the girls dipped a curtsy.

'Come over to the tables and join me in some light refreshments, whilst you tell me your story.'

Everyone hurried across to join the King and the newcomers' once they were seated around the table.

To the travellers delight food and drink was put in front of them and they ate it with hearty appetites.

The king and the other elves watched them with some amusement as they quickly finished their meal.

'Oh you don't know how good that all tasted,' Thomas said with a contented sigh.

'Have you had enough to eat,' the king asked.

'Yes, thank you, David said sitting back, looking far more healthy now.

'Then perhaps you wouldn't mind telling us your tale now,' the king said.

An expectant hush fell over the gathered company.

David started telling the story of their adventures; starting with the time they first saw the shadow men, the flight to Cornwall whilst being chased by the Hobgoblins. How they met up with the dragons who then learned to make fire with their breath. He told them all about learning to fight whilst flying on the back of the dragons and how they joined forces with King Arthur to defeat his sister, Morgana, and the Saxon army that was helping her. He went on to explain how the Death Rider threw a spear, at him, in the final stages of the battle.

'Unfortunately the spear had something on its blade so, when it managed to cut me, the poison quickly worked its way into my blood stream and made me feel the pull to the dark forces in the Twilight Kingdom,' David finished.

Freya continued. 'That is why we have come this way to find the tree to heal him. If we had gone straight over the borders from Summerdale the Death Riders would have felt David's presence immediately and they would have found and captured us.'

Thomas now took up the tale.

'The troubles are spreading. Queen Josephine was kidnapped and the 'Stone of Power' taken, this has given the Death Riders more power and they are now able to send raiding parties into Summerdale.'

'But we have left two of our companions with the dragons back in Summerdale to help try to stop the raids, while we find the cure for David before we rescue Queen Josephine and her stone,' Hope finished looking around at their audience.

There was a pause as the elves took in all that they had been told.

'That is some tale. For some time now we have known that there was trouble brewing but we could not find out what form it would take,' King Brenin told them.

'If we can be of any assistance to you on your quest, you only have to ask,' he added.

'Well we could do with a little assistance in finding the tree to cure David as we don't know exactly where it is,' Freya said.

'That is easy enough,' the king replied, 'we have a wonderful view from the top of our mountain where "The Tree of Healing", as it is called can be seen in the distance. If you would like to come with us we will show you then we can discuss the easiest way for you to reach it in safety.'

The king rose from the table and called across to four of his elves to join them. The king led the way out of the dinning chamber, with the others following.

The four elves were Adain and Heddwch, who they had already met, and Llawenydd (Joy) and Enfys (Rainbow) who introduced themselves as they walked after the king.

The way led up a wide passageway. To the left and right doors led off to different rooms, but they just walked on upwards. The slope was quite hard going and in the steeper places, wide steps had to replace it. By the time they had reached the top they were all quite breathless and what breath they had left was quite taken away when they stepped outside and looked at the view. They were looking to the west across the grasslands with its hills and valleys. They could see the deer like creatures grazing amongst the low trees and bushes. Looking over to the very far distance, they could see the darker trees that made the Forest.

They turned to look to the east and the view was different. They were now looking at the Twilight Kingdom and realised that the name described it well. The land below was dark. The grass was blackish green and then there were gloomy forests and swamps. There did not appear to be any flowers or lighter plants to brighten up the drabness. Then, in the far distance a big lake, even that water looked grey, but there in middle of the lake was an island and in the centre of the island stood a huge tree. Even from this distance the sight was wonderful. The tree was covered with beautiful white blossom that seemed to glow in the otherwise miserable land.

'That is where you have to go,' the king said pointing towards the tree, 'it is not a long journey but here are many dangers on the way. The hardest part will be crossing the lake to the island, as the waters are full of serpents that have six tongues with barbed hooks on the end of each tongue. They would rip you to pieces, if they caught you. They can climb the sides of boats; they use the hooks on their tongues to pull themselves up the sides. You are going to have to find a way to outwit them.

'I think you will need our help to find your way through the forests and swamps below,' Heddwch said, 'my companions and I would be honoured if you would let us be your guides. We often go into the forests when we are out hunting for meat and all of us know the secret pathways across the swamp to the lake beyond.'

'Thank you, any help will be gratefully received,' David replied. 'When do we start?'

'I think it would be as well to stay here and rest for today and start first thing tomorrow morning,' Adain replied. She had seen how tired David looked.

'We need to pack a few items to take with us and it would do no harm for us to put our heads together to try to find a solution as to how we are going to cross the water to actually reach the island.'

The king left the eight of them whilst they each put some ideas to the others as to how they would get past the serpents. Some of the ideas were so ridicules that they fell about laughing some of the time. They talked and talked but could not come up with any sensible idea that they thought would work.

'Don't worry, something will present itself once we are there,' Freya said, as the day drew on and they returned to have some supper before turning in for the night.

Sleep was slow in coming to them all, as their thoughts turned to the dangers that they would have to face on the next part of their quest.

Chapter Thirty One

The next morning David was up before it was properly light, he felt much more like his old self. The rest, in a proper bed, had helped and also the knowledge that they were entering the last stage of their quest to reach the 'Healing Tree" and the cure to his problem.

He went and woke the others. They were all eager to set off feeling much happier knowing they were to be escorted by the elves. They went to the dining hall and after a decent breakfast they thanked their host, King Brenin, and set off.

The first part of the journey was fairly easy as they were just walking down the side of the mountain until they reached the start of the forest where the land flattened out. The way was a little harder going then as the trees were quite close together but the pathway was fairly well defined.

'We must make good time through the trees as I would like to be well into the swamp land before dark,' Heddwch said.

'Why?' Hope asked looking a little nervous.

'There are wolves and wild boar not to mention other, not so normal, creatures roaming through the trees at night, but don't worry they are all asleep during the day.'

Hope smiled at him. 'I'm not worried,' she lied, moving closer to David.

The elves knew the way and so they did make good time and came out at the edge of the swamp in the early afternoon.

'I think we could stop now and have a little rest and something to eat and drink,' Thomas said.

'I would prefer not to stop at the moment. If we just go on a little further, there is a fairly dry area where we could set up camp for the night. Then we will be well away from the trees,' Adain said.

'You really don't like the tree area, do you?' David said thoughtfully.

'We would prefer to have an all-round vision of anything that may be trying to hunt us, that's all,' Llawenydd replied.

'Some of the creatures are Trolls and they will try to catch you as they like to eat humans. The other reason we are wary of them is that just a bite from one of them would cause an infection which can change you into a Troll too,' Enfys explained. 'Even we elves are not immune to the venom from the bite of these creatures.'

David saw Hope's face go white so he gently reached to take her hand before they started forwards again, the others followed without a word but none of them could help themselves from looking back over their shoulders with fearful glances.

Adain led the way over the marshy ground, stepping easily from one grass tussock to another. The other elves were equally fleet of foot. The rest followed as best they could. Only once did Thomas step the wrong way when a frog, jumping back into the water, took his attention. Luckily Heddwch was only a few feet in front of him, so was able to quickly pull him back to the firmer ground before he had sunk more than to his knees in the stinking mire. By this time they had been going for another hour and were all relieved when Adain said

'This is the little dry spot, I told you about,' she hopped over to a little island of solid grassland in the middle of marsh.

'There is even some wood to make a fire,' Heddwch said.

He went over to a dead tree and picked up some of the broken branches that lay on the ground.

Putting their backpacks down they each took out the items they would need for their short stay.

'We will make our meal now. I suggest we put out the fire before dark so that we do not draw any unwanted attention to ourselves,' Adain said

Some of the food was set out for the hungry travellers.

'We'll be guided by you, as you know what dangers there are here,' David agreed.

'Would it be a good idea if we set up a rota for keeping watch?' Freya asked.

'Could we do it in pairs this time?' Hope said thinking about the last time she had kept watch and all the food had been stolen because she had fallen asleep.

'Good idea, but even a full moon does not give much light here in the Twilight Kingdom. We may not see very much but we should be able to hear anything coming as it is not easy to stay on the dry bits in the dark,' Enfys reassured them.

It did not take very long to set up their camp and they had eaten a good meal well before the darkness overtook them. As the shadows lengthened Heddwch brought water from the bog to put out the fire.

The watches had been set, there was going to be one elf and one human in each round, starting with Hope and Heddwch, then Freya with Llawenydd, David with Adain and finally Enfys with Thomas. The first watch passed uneventfully and Hope felt much more at ease when they handed over to Freya and Llawenydd. It was not long before she was rolled in her blanket and fast asleep.

It was just before midnight when Llawenydd, with his sharp eyes and acute hearing, pointed out some movement in the marshes.

'What do you think it is?' Freya whispered.

'I'm not sure at the moment, but I think it may be a Troll. It is too tall for a wolf or wild hog.'

'I'm a fool; I should have made a spell to protect us and ward off all the creatures that could do us harm. You keep a watch on what is happening and I'll try to find something suitable,' Freya pulled her bag towards her and took out some herbs and other things. 'For a start I have some of my magic oil for keeping evil out of our homes, with any luck that will dissuade them, but I don't have enough to keep them away completely.'

'We have our swords to protect ourselves if they can find the path across to us. Llawenydd said, then added, 'I could cut some sticks into short lengths with points on the end and if we place them around the edge of this little island, perhaps the Trolls would be put off if they walked into the end of the sticks.'

He soon had the sticks cut ready and he stuck them into the ground all around their little island. He pushed the blunt end into the earth leaving the pointed end sticking out at an angle. Freya followed behind him sprinkling the oil to keep all evil things at bay. This done all they could do was sit and listen to, whatever it was, bumbling away in the darkness trying to find the way across to them.

Eventually their watch time finished,

Freya said to Llawenydd 'I don't think I could go to sleep knowing something was out there. So I suggest we stay on watch a little longer and let the others rest.'

'I agree with you. When the creature goes away we can hand over to David and Adain.'

The splashing and other noises went on getting gradually closer and closer so the pair drew their swords and waited, ready, to call out an alarm to the others.

Then what they had been dreading happened. The Troll found its way to the edge of their 'island'. It let out a low screech, as it must have come in contact with one of the sticks. Freya held her breath, as the Troll tried to come forwards, but as it put its foot into the gap between the sticks, sparks flew in the air. The Troll jumped back and fell into the water with a splash. Whimpering to itself, it started back the way it had come. Splashing noisily across to the next hummock of grass, then the sounds became more distanced as it made its way back to the relative safety of the forest.

'Did you see the sparks?' Freya asked. 'It must have been the magic oil, working better than I expected.'

'At least it seemed to do the trick. I think we could probably sleep a little now. So I shall wake David and you wake Adain,' Llawenydd replied.

When they were properly awake Freya explained to David and Adain what had happened.

'You should have woken me,' David said crossly, 'I could have helped.'

'There was no need for help, Freya's magic was quite enough,' Llawenydd answered him. 'We would have woken you if there was any real danger.'

'I suppose so,' David said begrudgingly.

'The trouble with you, David, is you want to protect everyone from everything. You must start to think about yourself first,' Freya said kindly and patted her brother on his arm.

David grinned at her. 'Get some rest now, bossy.'

Taking his advice Freya and Llawenydd rolled themselves in to their blankets laying for a while listening to the night sounds, but as nothing happened to unduly worry them they soon fell asleep.

During the remaining two watches, sounds from the forest were heard but nothing ventured out into the marshes towards them. Even so everyone was glad when the dawn came and they could make their way, onward, over the rest of the marshes to more solid ground. The water from the bog land fed into a stream, this in turn became a river.

Following the water they came to the edge of the large lake that housed the island in the middle. On this island there stood the Tree of Healing. They could see it clothed in blossom of white flowers.

David approached the edge of the water and looked across at their goal. Even as he looked, several large eel shaped heads came out of the water and started swimming towards the shore. As they swam, they opened their mouths and out shot their tongues with the lethal barbs on the ends. He backed away from the water and re-joined the others where they stood a safe distance from the water.

One by one they sat down and watched as the creatures swam around on the edge of the lake, all of them still wondering how were they going to cross to the island.

Chapter Thirty Two

David rolled over on to his stomach and stared at the eel like creatures.

'They don't appear to be interested in following us out of the water, so we should be safe on dry land.'

'But how are we going to reach to the island?' Hope asked.

'We'll just have to build a boat,' Thomas replied.

'That's all very well, but the eel creatures can climb the side of wooden boats, also they would be able to catch hold of paddles to make their way up to us,' Adain replied.

While the others had been talking Freya and Enfys had wandered off towards a small copse of trees, as they walked under the branches they looked around at the vegetation.

'I think I have an idea. Let's go back to the others,' said Enfys.

Freya looked down at where Enfys had been looking and smiled, then hurried after the elf to tell the others.

'There is enough wood over there, to make a boat,' Freya began.

'And there are lots of lovely thorny briars that could be attached to the sides to stop the eels climbing up,' Enfys finished.

'How would we propel ourselves over the water?' Thomas asked.

'That's easy, we make a sail from our blankets, we can make the rope to attach it by platting the reeds together into lengths,' Adain added.

'Well we're going to have a lot of work to do so we'd better start straight away. Are any of you good at designing boats? I have to admit to never having tried to build one before.' David looked at the elves as he spoke.

'You are in luck, both Heddwch and Llawenydd are expert at making canoes out of the trunks of trees,' Enfys told them.

'Will it take long to hollow out a tree trunk?' David enquired.

'It would normally, but we have special tools, a great magician made them especially for us when he came to visit us some years ago. You may have heard of him, his name is Merlin,' Llawenydd explained.

Freya laughed, 'Yes we have heard of him, it was he who suggested that we came here. He taught Rowena all her magic and she has started to teach me.'

'Why hasn't she taught David and Thomas?' Hope asked.

'Some people can't learn magic,' Thomas replied. 'David and I have no talent for it at all. We have to leave all that sort of thing to Freya and Rowena.'

'Well we have been standing around long enough, we must get to work,' Heddwch said walking off towards the trees. Everyone else followed and watched as Heddwch and Llawenydd talked together until finally they decided which tree to use. The two elves then set to with their axes to cut it down.

The girls moved off back to the swampy ground and collected reeds until they had gathered a large pile. Sitting down in the shade of the trees they began platting small bundles of them together. Each time they joined on a new bundle Freya put a binding spell on them to keep from pulling apart.

As soon as the tree was cut down Thomas and David helped the elves as they dragged it out into a clearing where they started to make cuts into its length. Into each cut they hammered sharp edged stones. This was to aid in splitting the sides open. It was very hot work and when Freya realized what they were trying to do she walked over and just said a splitting spell and the trunk fell in half.

'Thanks, that saved a lot of hard work,' David said gratefully.

'If you think that's magic, just watch this,' Llawenydd said proudly. He and Heddwch set to work at hollowing it out. They only had to start cutting into the wood and then they whispered a few words and stood back. The tools, which looked like half cups just, went on cutting at a very fast rate. There were chippings flying everywhere, as the tools cut further and further into the trunk.

'Won't they cut through the bottom?' Thomas asked.

'No, Merlin taught us the different instructions to make it only cut the amount we want.'

By the time the girls had finished the reed ropes the boats were nearly finished. The boys used that time to fetch as many bundles of the briars as they could manage. These they piled beside the now hollowed out trunks. Llawenydd and Heddwch collected their tools from where they lay, quietly, at the bottom of the boats and stowed them safely in their packs.

David and Thomas went back into the woods and selected three long, straight, branches for the mast and cross sections. These were cut and brought back to be secured into the boat. All that remained was the sail. They tied the blankets to the cross sections and the boats were ready.

Adain and Enfys had not been idle; they had gathered some long grasses to plat into thinner ropes. They needed these to tie the brambles to the side of the boats. Llawenydd cut grooves in the top of the sides to wrap the ropes around to stop everything slipping down into the water.

They all gave a hand in dragging everything nearer to the water's edge before they finally assembled them. The two trunks were lashed to each other side by side and the brambles were hung all the way round, making sure that there were some spiky bits in-between the hulls as they did not quite touch in places. They did not want to leave any areas that the eels could use to climb up.

The mast was firmly wedged between the two hulls and the cross bars attached top and bottom with a blanket firmly tied on.

'Well we are now ready to try to cross to reach the island,' David said, 'but one thing puzzles me. I was told to eat some of the fruit of the tree to make me completely better.'

'Yes, what's the problem?' Thomas asked.

'I don't see any fruit on the tree, it's all blossom. Will we have to wait months for the blossom to turn to fruit?'

'Sorry I hadn't realized that you hadn't been told all about the tree,' Adain laughed, 'When you touch a flower, if you are in need of healing, the flower immediately turns into a small fruit for you to eat. This will cure you.'

'What happens if someone else touches the flowers?'

'Nothing, the tree knows if you need a cure for any illnesses from dark magic.'

'So the blossom is quite safe really?'

'Yes, I have been told that the perfume from it is wonderful and it makes everyone who smells it feel really fantastic.'

'Well then we had better try out this boat and get to it.'

They pushed the boat into the water and quickly jumped in, four in each side of the log boat. Thomas and Heddwch pushed off with long branches, which they had brought for the job, until they could no longer reach the bottom with them. The eel creatures put their heads out of the water and seeing the boats bobbing about on the slight well they came swimming towards them.

'What are we going to do now?' Hope asked nervously.

'Just a moment,' Freya replied, 'while I call up a breeze to push us towards the island,' she stood up with her arms held upright and called for the wind, in a few moments they felt the breeze stir, then it became stronger filling the sales making the boat move quickly towards the island, but the eels were close behind.

Chapter Thirty Three

There were at least a dozen eels following them and it was only a short while before they caught up with the boat. Immediately their barbed tongues flashed out towards the sides, the barbs caught in the briars and the eels started to pull themselves up. As soon as the creatures' bodies connected with the thorns, they gave a squealing sound and dropped back into the water. One after another they tried to reach the occupants of the vessel, only to be met with the thorns and drop off, only to immediately return for another try.

'You have to admit they are persistent,' David observed.

'Will they harm us if they manage to get in?' Thomas inquired.

'Oh yes,' Heddwch replied, 'they would love to eat us if they could.'

'We'll just have to hope the briars stay on all the time,' Hope said anxiously.

'Don't worry we're nearly there,' Freya cried as the boat came alongside the island.

'Give me the rope and I will jump ashore to pull the boat right in,' Llawenydd said as he stood up on the bow.

'Look, the eels are turning away,' Adain pointed out. 'They left us as soon as the boat touched land. Do you think the tree is protecting us?'

'I don't know but whatever it is I am thankful.'

They jumped out and all helped to pull the boat well on to the shore, to make sure it could not float away and leave them stranded. Once it was secure they set off for the interior of the island. It was quite hard going as the undergrowth was very thick on the route to the tree.

Even as they started forward they noticed the smell from the blossom. It was very delicate and pleasing, giving everyone a feeling of happiness and tranquillity.

David was in the lead and made his way straight up to the tree. He reached up to gently touch one of its many white flowers. The moment that his hand came in contact with the flower the petals fell away leaving a small golden coloured fruit about the size of a cherry. He picked it and turned to look at the others who were now standing watching him. No one said a word

'Well here goes,' he said and took a small bite of the fruit. 'Oh! it tastes wonderful, a bit like a strawberry and cherry together.'

'Look!' Hope exclaimed pointing at David's leg. 'It's glowing.'

David looked down in amazement, the whole length of his injured leg had a warm golden glow rippling up and down and a lovely warm feeling crept over him. He reached down and pulled up the leg of his trousers. They all looked in amazement. The scar from the thrust of the poisoned sword had been all black and silvery, now a golden light washed over it, and even as they watched, the darkness of the scar faded until it was only a faint white line. The glow faded too until it completely disappeared.

'How do you feel?' Thomas asked.

'Wonderful1' David replied, 'I hadn't realised how ill the cut had made me feel, but now I feel fantastic. I am ready to face anything.'

'That is brilliant, the best news I have had in ages,' Freya said going to her brother and giving him a quick hug. 'Now if you really are better we had better set off on the next part of our mission. Our first obstacle is going to be re-crossing the lake.'

'As we want to go southwards now, it would make more sense to pull the boat right around the island and set out for the shore on the other side of the lake from where we started,' Llawenydd said thoughtfully.

'That's a good idea, that would save us walking right around the lake,' Heddwch agreed.

Pulling the boat back into the shallow waters on the edge of the island, they set about pulling it around to the other side. They kept a close watch on the eels as they waded around in the shallow water but they did not have to worry, the eels did not even stick their heads out of the water to watch them.

Once they were on the other side of the island they all boarded again, Thomas and David pushed off and jumped in the back of the craft. The breeze that Freya had conjured up was still blowing so the sail immediately filled and they started to sail off in the direction of the far shore.

They had not travelled more than a few metres before the evil eel creatures' heads showed above the surface and they started to swim towards the boat. Freya called a few words to the wind and it blew harder sending the boat skimming forwards over the water. The eels also moved faster and began, slowly to gain on their intended prey.

The boat had almost reached the shore when the leading creature's tongues shot out and the barbs caught in the briar, it squealed in pain from the thorns, but did not let go this time. It was using its weight to try to pull the briar off the side of the boat and leave a clear way for its companions. Thomas went to push it back into the water, only to have one of the other eels tongue lash out at him. He only just pulled back in time before the barb hit the place where is hand had been.

Slowly the briar was unravelling! Then with a rush the thin branches broke, falling into the water. Luckily the eel was still attached and it disappeared under the water. There were plenty of others to take its place and three surged forwards for the now clear side of the boat. One eel started to pull itself up over the side and immediately there were dozens more joining it. Hope moved towards the bows, looking wildly from one side to the other as the creatures started over the sides. The others followed her example and crowded away from the barbed tongues. The leading eel slid over the side and into the bottom of the boat.

Hope screamed and turned around looking for a way of escape. Relief flooded her whole being as she saw there was an escape route.

'Hold on! she called and the boat hit the beach.

Thomas cut the binding to save the blanket, and everyone else grabbed any bundle they could reach and almost flew over the side on to the dry land. They ran to the edge of the vegetation before they stopped to look back at the boat. It was swarming with the eels as they looked for something to eat. A few had even started to follow them. They moved quite quickly over the muddy sand but once they reached the sharp stones, where the beach met the land, they paused and looked around for an easier way.

The friends decided to wait no longer and set off at a run into the trees. Once they had covered a few hundred metres Faith called a halt.

'Wow that was a little bit too close for comfort!' David exclaimed.

'At least we managed to reach the tree and heal you David, it's a pity we couldn't bring some of the fruit with us, just in case we needed something in the future,' Hope said wistfully.

'I know,' Freya agreed, 'but I touched the petals in the hope of collecting some fruit and nothing happened.'

'You didn't need any healing, that's why they didn't change,' David said laughing. 'I did need help, so when I touched more of the flowers they all changed into fruit, and I collected quite a handful,' he opened his pack to show them.

'Brilliant,' Enfys said, 'they may be useful. We'll have to brave more evil when we travel to rescue Queen Josephine.'

'Well I think we had better repack and make our way onwards,' Llawenydd said to bring them all back to the task in hand.

'How far do you think it is to King Golgog's palace?' Hope asked.

'I would say another day's walk, at least. Do you agree?' Adain replied and turned to the other elves for confirmation.

'That would be about right' Heddwch agreed and the other two nodded.

'Right, we don't know what dangers we may come across, but at least they'll not be able to see my thoughts anymore,' David said. 'If we go now and only stop when it starts to become too dark to see, then we should be within striking distance of the enemy tomorrow morning.'

Everyone agreed, repacked their bags and hitched them on to their backs before they once more set off into the unknown.

Chapter Thirty Four

After the dragons had left their friends by the Forest, they had flown straight back to where the latest attacks between the Death Riders and the citizens of Summerdale had been. They joined up with Edwin and Faith riding Caw and Cawson respectively.

'What happened here?' Greor asked.

'The attack was on two villages simultaneously this morning. They came in just before dawn. The villagers were still in their beds, they didn't have a chance, they were slaughtered where they lay,' Faith replied.

'By the time we arrived they were leaving,' Caw reported, 'but they didn't expect us and we managed to kill a few before they went back over the border.'

'What are we going to do to help the poor people?' Sherna asked.

'Emperor Godwin has gathered a small army, but they are all untried warriors. They have never had to fight in anger before. He is moving them up to be as near the border as they can manage, with the idea of engaging the enemy before they can reach the villages. The only trouble is there is such a long boundary and no one knows where they are going to strike next,' Caw replied.

'I think we could help them find out,' Greor said. 'We could each patrol a small part of the border and report back to the emperor when we see signs of movement. As we can move so fast no time would be lost in arranging for the army to go to the best places.'

'I think that would be a great help. Now, before you take Faith and me back to Emperor Godwin, how are the others? I gather they set off on their travels with no problems,' Edwin asked.

'They were just starting their journey into the Forest when we left them. We did not stay longer as we were worried that we would be needed here,' Sherna told him.

'I don't like letting them go off on their own,' Sherna said.

'I know, but we can help them by keeping the Death Riders busy so that they don't realise that David has gone from their senses,' Greor reassured her.

'Now we must take Edwin and Faith to the emperor and come back here,' Cawson interrupted.

'Good,' Faith said as she mounted on to his back, 'we can tell them what you are going to do. This will leave you free to go and find the best places to patrol.'

Edwin climbed on to Caw's back and the two dragons took off. They flew back to the main army and left their riders on the edge, while they hurried back to the other dragons.

'Come on Edwin let's find the emperor and report to him. I don't think we'll have any problems until tomorrow,' Faith said.

They made her way through the gathered soldiers until they found Emperor Godwin with his captains.

'We have some news for you,' she said as soon as she was near enough, 'the dragons are going to patrol the borders and report any movement so you can keep your force all together ready to march on any attack.'

'That is good news; I was just instructing my captains on where to take their patrols. Now they can just wait here with us,' Emperor Godwin said and then turned to his men. 'You heard the news; you can go back to your men and rest this evening. Make sure you are all ready to move at a moment's notice, whenever we receive any news from the dragons.'

The captains went back to their men leaving Edwin and Faith looking around wondering where to go.

'I feel a little restless,' Edwin said, 'I think I'll go for a walk before we eat.'

'Would you like some company?' Faith asked. 'I could do with unwinding a little.'

'Yes, that would be great, come on then.'

'That is a good idea, I shall see you later,' the emperor smiled at them.

The two made their way between the troops tents, to the edge of the encampment; they looked towards the Twilight Kingdom.

'It is so dark over there and even here the tree leaves are turning brown as if it was autumn already. Have you noticed how the colour has gone out of the days?' Edwin asked Faith. He took her arm in his and they moved on slowly.

'I do hope that doesn't mean that the enemy is getting stronger and the darkness is spreading further,' Faith shuddered.

'Your cold,' Edwin said 'we had better return, and try to have a good night's sleep,' he turned her around and they started to stroll back. If he had looked over his shoulder he would have seen four dark shapes creep out of the woods and start making their way across the divide from the boundaries of the Twilight Kingdom and themselves.

'Look at the sun set,' Faith exclaimed, 'the sun is being obscured by some clouds.'

'That's strange, there wasn't a cloud in the sky a few moments ago,' Edwin suddenly felt uneasy and started to turn around. He was too late.

Two dark figures grabbed him and forced his arms behind his back where they were fastened tightly. Before he had time to call out a rag was pushed into his mouth and held there. He kicked out at his attackers, to no avail. The second one wrapped a rope around his legs. He wriggled and struggled but he hadn't a chance, he was firmly secured. He glanced across at Faith to see she was similarly trussed up.

Their captors flung them, unceremoniously, over their shoulders and carried the pair of them off into the darkness of the forest. There, under the trees, four horses waited. Faith and Edwin were thrown roughly over the spare horses necks before the riders mounted and urged their mounts into a canter leading the two pack horses deeper into the trees.

The horses did not slow and the low branches whipped at the head and legs of the captives. The ride was not too long; they soon arrived at the camp of the Death Riders, for that is who the attackers were. Their leader, Marwolaeth, came across greeting them.

'Well done, King Golgog will be pleased. Take her into my quarters and make her secure,' she ordered the rider who had Faith, and then she turned to the other rider and ordered, 'bring him with us.'

She led the way to a post sticking out of the ground; on this post was an iron ring. Edwin's hands were unbound then retied to the ring. His gag was removed.

'What do you want from me?' he cried.

'I need a little help,' Marwolaeth told him, 'we need you to bring Empress Gwendolyn to us.'

'Never,' Edwin replied, sounding braver than he felt.

'We will see,' she replied, and nodded at one of the waiting creatures.

It stepped forwards and unfurled a long whip, the end the whip split into three strands; each strand had a mettle barb on the end.

Edwin's face drained of all colour as he realised what was in store for him.

'You will be begging to do whatever I want in just a few moments,' Marwolaeth laughed as she raised her hand to signal the beginning of the torture.

Chapter Thirty Five

As Faith was led away she heard Edwin's first cry of pain and shuddered. Her heart beat faster as dread filled her mind, she realised they were going to torture them both until they had what they wanted.

Her captors dragged her some way down a passage until they came to a door, this they opened and pushed her roughly into a small cell. She stumbled and fell to her knees, for a few moments she remained there. The guards pulled her to her feet and cut her bonds, turning they left her and the next sound she heard was the key turning in the lock of the door. She stood there trembling as she tried to hear if Edwin was still being hurt. All was quiet, she let her breath out with a sigh of gratitude but her relief was short lived as another scream shattered the silence. They had started on the poor boy again. Faith moved over to the door and started pounding on it.

'Leave him alone, Oh please leave him alone!' She found she was crying hard. She looked around the room, for possible means of escape but there were none. The only ways in to the cell was through the strong wooden door or a very small window high up in the wall, this was heavily barred and far too high to reach.

Would the emperor or his men realise they were missing? She wondered, and even if they did how would they know where they had been taken. She sank to the floor in despair, praying that Edwin's torture would soon end.

Back along the passageway, Edwin hung limply from the post where they had so recently tied him. He was, mercifully, unconscious.

'Leave him there until the morning, he should give in then,' Marwolaeth ordered.

His torturers left and he hung there all night drifting in and out of consciousness. In the moments he was awake he became aware that his arms hurt as they were taking his full weight, but it was nothing compared to the pain from his flayed back, he tried to stand to ease the pain but it hurt so much and he drifted back into darkness.

The morning came and with it the return of his captors.

'Bring him around,' Marwolaeth growled angrily. 'He must be ready to talk by now.'

The creature with the whip dropped it and went over to a pail of water and carried over to Edwin he emptied the contents over his head.

Edwin slowly regained consciousness, as he spluttered out the water.

'Have you had enough of the whip?' Marwolaeth asked, 'or shall I fetch your charming companion, then she too could share in its agonies?'

'Leave Faith out of this!' he cried, 'What do you want?'

'I just want a little help from you. I want you to go and bring the Empress Gwendolyn here.'

'No I will not!' Edwin cried bravely, 'there is nothing you can do to me that will make me do it.'

'I was not thinking of doing anything more to you. Your friend, Faith, you say her name is. Well I wonder how long she could stand the whip caressing her back, before she begs for release. And have no doubt we will kill her in the end. So who is it to be Gwendolyn or Faith?'

Edwin hung his head in despair. He could not let Faith suffer as he had; she was only a young girl. If he agreed to fetch Gwendolyn, perhaps he could warn everyone and then they would all be rescued, clinging to these thoughts, he replied, 'I will do what you want, as long as you spare Faith.'

'Good, I am glad you have come to your senses,' Marwolaeth turned to the torturer and said, 'Treat his wounds with the special salve. I will go to fetch a goblet of wine to revive him.'

She left the room, but returned momentarily carrying a bottle and some goblets. She set these down on a side table and proceeded to pour the wine into both glasses. Her back blocked Edwin's view and he did not see her add some liquid from a small phial she had taken from her pocket. Turning she handed the doctored wine to him and took a sip from the other.

Edwin's hands had been untied and he took a deep drink. Immediately he began to feel so much stronger.

The other occupant of the room, meanwhile, was ministering to his wounds. The wine and its additive soon befuddled his mind, so much so that he did not realise that his free will was slowly being drained. The salve that was soothing his wounds was the same as had been on the spear that scratched David! Edwin was receiving very much more and he was slowly being taken under the control of the Death Riders' leader Marwolaeth.

Edwin's last conscious thought was he had to go and fetch Empress Gwendolyn, but why? He could not remember. He was led from the room and taken back to the borders between Summerdale and the Twilight Kingdom. There he was left.

Edwin looked around, not sure where he was for a moment then he shook his head and started to walk towards Emperor Godwin's camp, he had not gone very far before he was met by a patrol who had been sent out to look for the missing pair when they did not return for their evening meal.

'I must find the empress,' he muttered and collapsed into a heap at their feet.

They picked him up between him and carried him back to the emperor's tent.

'My lord, we found him wandering near the boundary of our land,' one of them reported. 'He was asking for our Lady Gwendolyn.'

'Send for her immediately,' the emperor ordered, 'and fetch Merlin to see to the poor boys wounds.'

He waited impatiently for his wife to be brought from their castle and sighed with relief when Merlin hurried in to the tent.

'Edwin is injured please tend to his wounds,' he ordered.

Merlin went over to Edwin and removed his jacket to reveal the scars on his back.

As he was doing this Gwendolyn came into the tent and rushed over to Edwin.

Merlin gasped, 'his wounds are the same as David's. I fear he too, will feel the pull of the darkness.'

Emperor Godwin looked alarmed. 'We should have taken him as far from the borders as possible, he will be watched from the other side and they will know what he is thinking.'

'The poor boy, but if you do not discuss anything of note in front of him, they will not find out anything,' Gwendolyn said. 'In fact we can learn everything the other side are saying and doing, from him. We must find out where they have taken Faith and make plans to rescue her.'

Edwin's mind was full of confusion. He smiled to himself as he lay there pretending to be unconscious. Everything would now go to plan. He felt as if his thoughts were from someone else but he was powerless to do anything about it. All he realised was Empress Gwendolyn must go over the border as soon as could be arranged.

Chapter Thirty Six

Gwendolyn had Edwin removed from the emperor's camp and returned to the comfort of his room in the palace.

'There is nothing more we can do for him for the moment. He must rest as much as possible to enable his wounds to heal. Everyone must leave him now, let him sleep whilst we decide what we can do to rescue Faith,' Gwendolyn said, 'and I shall return in the morning to see how he is.'

Gwendolyn and her servants left the room and quietly closed the door.

Edwin lay still for a few more moments but once he was sure he was alone he opened his eyes and looked around. He sat up and swinging his legs off the bed and climbed down. He went over to the window. Looking out in the direction of the Twilight Kingdom he concentrated hard on Marwolaeth. His mind became full of the Death Riders face as she directed him in what he should do. Once he had received his instructions he returned to the bed and lay down once more. He immediately fell into a deep sleep.

The following morning he had only just awakened when the door opened to admit Gwendolyn.

'I am glad to see you are awake,' she said on seeing his open eyes. 'How are you feeling? Do you need anything?'

'I am much better, but you must rescue Faith, only you can do it.'

'Of course we will save Faith; my husband is, even now, planning an attack to pull her out of the clutches of our enemy.'

'They will fail,' Edwin cried, 'if a large force is sent, they will be seen. If you went alone and dressed as an ordinary serving wench, the same as the women in King Golgog's court. None would suspect you.'

'My husband would never let me go on my own.'

'Don't tell him then,' he replied.

Gwendolyn looked sceptical.

'While I was escaping I overheard the leader of the riders telling them to take Faith to the king's castle. They are sending her with only one guard and she is to be moved this afternoon, at three o'clock. So you only have a short time to save her. You must go, please!' Edwin made a convincing show of anguish as he pretended to sob at the thought of Faith in the clutches of the evil that existed in the Twilight Kingdom.

'You are sure there will only be one guard?'

'Yes,' Edwin lied. 'They will be bringing her on the path that runs close to your boundary so you don't have to venture far in to the forest. I would come with you but they would see my mind and you would be in danger.'

Gwendolyn was convinced. 'I shall go and change right away and my maid can accompany me as far as the edge of the forest. Then I can slip over the border and save Faith. I shall send one of my pages to my husband's camp and inform him of my plan then he will be able to follow me.'

'You have no time to spare; I shall go and tell your page to take the news to your husband, while you set off. They will be there nearly as soon as you,' Edwin swung his feet off the bed and stood up. He pulled Gwendolyn's arm, 'come on we both must hurry,' he implored.

Gwendolyn believed him and so they both left his room.

As Gwendolyn went to change, Edwin did go to find a page and instruct him to go to the emperor's camp.

'Tell him that the message is from the Empress Gwendolyn. Tell him she asks that he should do nothing about rescuing Faith as she has heard that they are taking Faith deeper into the forest and will be too far away for rescuing. Tell him he must wait for the Lady Gwendolyn to join him before he does anything.'

The page left to collect a horse and rode off to the emperor's camp. He passed Gwendolyn as she came back out ready for her mission.

'I go straight to your husband with your message, my lady.'

'Good, tell him time is of an essence.'

'Yes, my lady,' the page replied, a little puzzled, but he shook his head and rode off quickly.

Gwendolyn and her maid were dressed in drab clothing, with dark cloaks over their shoulders to disguise them more. They went to the stables and mounted the horses they had ordered to be ready and set off for the border.

They made fast time and arrived at the nearest boundary within the hour. They dismounted under the shade of the forest. Gwendolyn handed her rains to her maid.

'Wait here for me. My husband will join you as soon as he can make it. I should not be much more than an hour, as it is not far, but I shall have to wait until Faith is brought past me before I can overpower her guard and bring her back here with me,' she said. She pulled a dagger from its sheath around her waist and looked at it before returning it to its resting place. Then with no more ado she set off into the forest.

By this time the page had arrived at Godwin's camp and gave him the message.

'There is one more thing, as I was leaving my lady said to tell you that "time was of an essence." my lord.'

'Thank you, you may go,' Godwin dismissed the page and turned to one of his captains. 'I wonder why she said "time was of an essence." when she had just told me to wait for her and do nothing? I'm worried. We will not wait for her as she asked, but return to the castle ourselves. Order my personal bodyguard of men to saddle our mounts, we leave immediately.'

Even as they left their camp, Gwendolyn was making her way, as silently as possible, towards the track that lead deeper into the woods and towards King Golgog's palace. She arrived at the roadside and hid behind a convenient bush, to await Faith's arrival.

Within minutes she heard the sound of horses approaching. She crouched down and peered through the leaves as two riders came trotting towards her. They went past her hiding place and she jumped up to grab the leg of the second rider. He came off the horse easily and lay on the ground not moving. Gwendolyn looked down in amazement, then realised it was not a real person but a dummy!

Shadows materialised from behind the trees. The waiting Death Riders came out of their hiding places, she was surrounded. Horrified, she realized that she had walked straight into a trap. Strong arms grabbed and bound her. She was thrown over the back of the horse that had held the dummy and led away. More horses were brought forwards and the others mounted. From her place of captivity, Gwendolyn lifted her head and saw Faith similarly tied on another horse; her eyes were large with fear.

'I'm sorry Faith, I thought I could rescue you,' Gwendolyn whispered.

'They knew you were coming, Edwin must have betrayed us!' Faith replied

'If he did it was not his fault, he has been poisoned the same way as David.'

'Will he be all right?'

'I hope so. Anyway, we have to believe that David will bring back the cure. We must take heart as I sent a message to my husband he will soon find us'

'No, the message he was told was to stay in his camp and wait for you, I heard them laughing about it.'

The rider holding the horses' reigns turned around and glared at them.

'Keep quiet or we will have to gag you both,' he growled.

Not wishing for any more discomfort they remained silent. This left Gwendolyn's thoughts in despair. She worried about their fate once they were taken to King Golgog' stronghold.

Both of them had much on their minds, as they were taken deeper into the forest and away from the safety of Summerdale.

Chapter Thirty Seven

The Death Riders horses moved easily on the soft, leaf carpeted, roadway. The branches of the trees on each side overhung, nearly touching in the middle, but the path was easily wide enough for two horses abreast.

Although it was only mid-afternoon, the light was gloomy, as if the sun had been shrouded; it truly was a kingdom of twilight.

The company arrived at a medium sized, fortified town, and having given the correct password they were allowed in through the gate. The riders had kept their mounts at a steady canter for the full journey so it had only taken just over two hours. They clattered through the cobble-stoned streets right to the back, where a castle stood. The gates to this were open and the riders went through into the courtyard within.

All the riders dismounted and the one leading Faith and Gwendolyn's horses cut the ropes around their ankles.

They were dragged from the horses' backs and pushed into the castle by a side gate and down a long, wide, flight of stairs. The air was cool and damp with no outside light. Flaming torches set in brackets on the wall lighted the way down and down to the dungeons where heavy wooden doors guarded the many cells. In the top of each door was an opening set with bars, through which the occupants could be seen. They were taken to the second cell, the door stood open. Unceremoniously they were pushed inside. The guard cut the bindings on their hands and left. The door clanged shut behind him and they heard the key turn in the lock.

Faith sank to her knees. 'What is to become of us?' she said in despair.

'You must not lose hart,' Gwendolyn said. She moved to the door and looked out. 'Is anyone else in here?' she called.

'Only me,' a voice replied.

'Who are you?' Gwendolyn enquired.

'I am Queen Josephine of the Forest People.'

'Josephine! I am so glad to find you alive. It is I, Gwendolyn, we have some very brave people coming to save you, so we all have a chance of being rescued.'

Faith looked up. 'I had forgotten about David, Freya, Thomas and my sister, as soon as they have found the cure for David, they will come to King Golgog's castle, won't they?'

'Yes my dear, but they have only been gone two days, so we will have a long wait for them to come to find us. Meanwhile we must stall our enemies if we can.'

'What is all this about?' Queen Josephine asked.

Gwendolyn told the whole story finishing with the discovery of her capture and how the four adventurers had set off to enter the Twilight Kingdom from the west, so there would be no knowledge of their movements.

'We must pray that they make it to the Tree of Healing and are still safe to come to rescue us,' Gwendolyn finished

'How have you been treated whilst you have been here? Faith asked the little queen.

'Much better than I expected, the food is not much, and the bed is hard, but otherwise they have left me very much alone. When I arrived they took my Stone away from me and they are using it to allow the Death Riders to enter into Summerdale. The more they use it the stronger they will become as the Stone becomes attuned to them. Once that is complete they will no longer need me,' the queen answered.

'They would never kill you though, would they?' Faith asked.

'Why not? I would just be in the way.'

'I wonder what they have in store for us then.'

'I expect we will be held as hostages to make my husband surrender Summerdale to King Golgog. Then our lives will be worth nothing,' Gwendolyn said.

With that gloomy thought in their minds they settled down to wait.

They did not have long as a few moments later they heard the sound of many people coming down the stairs. Faith and Gwendolyn's cell door was unlocked and King Golgog came inside, followed closely by two guards. Outside there were two more guards either side of the doorway.

'Well my dear, I hope you are enjoying my hospitality,' the king said.

'Are we so dangerous that you need four guards to protect you?' Gwendolyn retorted.

The king's face flushed bright red. 'You will watch your tongue in my presence,' he snapped at her and stepping forward he hit Gwendolyn across the face.

She staggered backwards from the force, but Faith caught her before she fell.

'How dare you strike the empress, you coward?' Faith challenged him.

'Have a care missy or you will really feel my wrath,' he spat back at her.

The guards stepped closer.

'Don't worry, I'll not hit your king,' Gwendolyn told them, 'violence serves no purpose,' she put her arm around Faith and addressed the king. 'What do you want from us?'

'You will send a letter to your husband, telling him of your capture and instructing him to meet with Marwolaeth to hand over all their arms and surrender Summerdale to me.'

'He would never do that, and I would not ask him to.'

'You will have no choice my dear.'

'I always have a choice. You can do what you like to me I will not change my mind,' Gwendolyn replied holding her head high and looking every bit like the empress she was.

'Oh I do not intend to do anything to you,' the king replied smiling, 'your friend will persuade you or you will watch her being tortured.'

Faith's face drained of all colour, she took a deep breath, 'she will not change her mind on my account,' she said bravely.

'We will see,' the king replied as he left the cell then turned he looked through the bars and told them, 'think on what I have said. I shall leave you until tomorrow night, when I will expect you to have come to your senses.'

The footsteps faded as they went back up the staircase.

'I can't let you be tortured, I will have to write to my husband,' Gwendolyn said to Faith, as she started to pace about the cell.

'I meant what I said,' Faith answered her, 'you must not give in to him and we must give the others time to come.'

'You are so brave; I don't know what to do. I think we will have to try and decide on a course of action; at least we have some time to decide. Now we had better try to rest,' Gwendolyn went over to one of the two beds set against the wall and lay down.

Faith watched her for a few moments before she too went and lay down. She closed her eyes, but she knew there would be no sleep for her, as she thought of all the terrible things that the king could do to her to make Gwendolyn write to her husband.

Chapter Thirty Eight

Gwendolyn and Faith were disturbed the next morning by one of the king's servants bringing them some bread and water. He just placed the tray on the floor inside their cells then retreated, disappearing back up the stairs before anyone could think to ask him the time or what was going to happen.

Gwendolyn sat up and stretched, she glanced across at Faith, who sat on her bed with her back to the wall.

'Did you manage to sleep at all, my dear?' she asked.

'Not much,' Faith replied, 'I think I may have dozed a few times, but there was too much going around my head to relax properly.'

'Don't worry I'll not let them harm you, I shall think of something to make them delay and give the twins time to come and rescue us.'

Faith smiled at her. She could not see what the older woman could do to help her and was very afraid, although she was determined not to show it.

After eating something, they talked to Queen Josephine for a little while before sheer exhaustion made Faith drop into an uneasy sleep. So that they did not disturb her, the queen and the empress also lay down to rest with their own thoughts.

Evening came soon enough with the guard bringing them some more water and a little broth with a hunk of bread so soak it up.

Even Faith managed to eat this, as by now they were all very hungry. The poor meal was just finished before King Golgog returned with his four guards.

'What have you decided?' the king asked Gwendolyn.

'If you give me and my companion a more comfortable bed and better food until tomorrow night then I would think I may do as you ask,' she prevaricated.

The king did not notice the subtlety in her words and agreed.

'One more day will not matter, as we will go out tonight and kill some more of your people. Just remember it is your fault that they will die.'

Gwendolyn looked horrified at his words. She had not thought of the nightly attacks. She almost changed her mind then remembered the dragons were helping. The slaughter would be more on the Death Riders side she prayed.

The king was watching her and realising her discomfort, he looked pleased with him-self. 'I will send down some bedding and arrange for you to be a bit better fed, and I shall be back tomorrow evening to give you your writing things.'

With that he turned away and disappeared up the stairs.

Gwendolyn watched them go then turned to Faith. 'That gives us another day for David's party to reach his goal and then to make his way to rescue us,' she said.

'You will not be able to put him off further. Tomorrow you will have to write the letter or else I shall go to be tortured,' Faith replied gloomily.

'Oh I have thought of that and I will ask him to leave the writing things for me to compose a note to Godwin overnight, so that will delay it even further. That will bring it to the fifth day since the party departed in search of the tree to heal David.'

'With any luck they will be on the way to us by then,' Faith said with hope beginning to glow in her eyes.'

'At least we shall have a better night and food if King Golgog keeps his word.'

Before she had finished speaking they heard the sound of people descending the stairs again. Two servants appeared each carrying a pile of bedding. A bundle was dropped outside their cell and the other one was carried over to Queen Josephine's cell. Once the bedding had been delivered the men departed leaving the captives to make up the beds with a pillow and blanket each.

'Thank you for arranging for these little luxuries,' the queen called out, 'some nights are quite chilly and I am unable to sleep. The other thing is you have taken the kings attention off me and any break from his attention is welcome.'

'Well, if everything goes as I hope we will only have a few more days of captivity to endure,' Gwendolyn replied. 'I intend to write to my husband telling him of our plight, but I must word it in such a way that he does not agree to surrender. At the moment I am at a loss how to express myself, but I am sure the right words will present themselves. For now we had better all have a good night's sleep in preparation for working our brains in the morning.'

They all enjoyed a decent night's sleep. They woke refreshed when the guard brought them a breakfast with some meat to accompany the bread and water.

Once they had finished their meal, they paced the cell to get a little exercise as they thought of different ways of writing to the emperor to alert him to the situation without alarming him too much, so that he would give them time to escape.

'We have got to make him understand that we are all right and that we hope to be rescued, but how do we word this so that we do not make the king suspicious?' Faith pondered.

The time passed by too quickly and still they had not come up with an answer to their puzzle.

They had no idea of the time of day, as there were no windows in their cells and before they knew it the evening meal was being served and that meant that the king would be coming to see them soon.

The sound they were dreading, was shortly heard as the five people came down the stairs to them.

'I have brought writing things for you. I hope you will oblige me with a letter to your husband, otherwise I shall have to take your little friend to the special cell to be punished for your refusal to help me,' the king said as one of his guards came up to Gwendolyn's cell and opened the door. He passed in a tray, set out with pen and ink and a pile of paper to write on.

Gwendolyn took it. 'I will write to my husband, but give me some time to compose a suitable text for him.'

'I don't know why you are stalling for time, but it will be of no avail as the Death Riders are getting stronger by the day and killing more of your people,' the king paused and looked at Gwendolyn for a moment whilst he made up his mind.

Faith stood with baited breath.

'You can have until noon tomorrow to compose your letter. And if it is not done by then your young friend will not be tortured, she will be killed.'

The king turned away and left with his men following.

Gwendolyn let out a sigh of relief. 'Don't worry there will be a letter. I will have found the right words by then.'

'Thomas and David where are you?' Faith whispered.

Chapter Thirty Nine

David and Thomas led the party of friends as they made their way from the lake and the Tree of Healing. They were closely followed by the four elves with Freya and Hope at the rear. They set a fast pace. David had not felt this well for a long time; he looked about him with wonder.

'I know this is a miserable place with it always being in twilight and the flowers not making much of a show, but to me everything seems brighter than I can remember. Whilst I was under the spell of the poison in my blood everything I looked at seemed misty and unreal. I was just living in a half world,' David turned to his brother, 'It seemed an effort to do anything, let alone to care about anyone. I'm so glad I'm back.'

'So am I bro. I really missed you.'

David turned and included the others as he called, 'Well I'm back now so it is time to kick the enemy and keep kicking until they give in! What do you say?'

'I agree with you,' Freya shouted, 'so let's make fast time.'

'Yes,' the others cried in unison and they upped their pace a little.

'The sooner we rescue Queen Josephine and the 'Stone of Power' the sooner we can go home,' David said as they pushed through the undergrowth. 'I'm worried about them all. We have no idea what's been happening. For all we know they may have all been captured and maybe even killed and it all would be my fault.

'How do you make that out?' Thomas caught hold of David's arm and shook it. 'Why do you always have to worry so much? They are probably fine, the dragons are there to help and protect them. Anyway the trouble with the Twilight Kingdom had started before we came here, so you can't take that on your shoulders,' he gave David a playful shove as the others caught them up.

'What's the matter?' Heddwch asked concerned at the apparent argument.

'Don't take any notice,' Thomas told them, 'David's just worrying again.'

'Sorry, I just want to look after everyone and keep them safe,' David said sheepishly.

'We know, little brother, that's why we like you so much,'

Freya put her arms around him and gave him a hug. 'Now let's go and do some rescuing,' she finished and started off again. The rest followed.

After they had been travelling for a few hours they came out onto a pathway.

'I think this leads to King Golgog's castle,' Heddwch said stopping.

'Then if we follow this road we would make better time,' Thomas said.

'What do we do if some of the king's men come along?' Hope asked.

'I think we would hear if anyone was coming, but just to be on the safe side, as we elves have extra good hearing, Llawenydd can go ahead by a few hundred metres and I shall stay a few hundred metres behind you. That way if either of us hears anything we can whistle a warning and everyone can hide in the forest beside the road,' Heddwch replied.

'The warning call could be the song of a nightingale. I am reasonably sure there will be none in this part of the world and anyone not knowing, would just hear a bird song,' Adain agreed.

Llawenydd had set off in the lead, the others followed with Heddwch holding back in the rear. They made much faster time and as they did not encounter anyone on the road only stopping for a small break whilst they had a meal and a rest in the early afternoon.

Dark was starting to descend on the forest before they saw the walls of a fortified town up ahead. Using what cover they could, from the surrounding vegetation, they drew closer to the walls and looked to see a way in. There were guards posted near the gateway and at intervals around the wall.

'We had better scout round to the other side and see if there is any easier way into the town,' David said softly setting off again.

The walls were surrounded by a moat filled with water and as they went further and further around without seeing a way in they began to despair.

'We can't give up until we have been all the way around at least once,' Faith said.

'You're quite right,' Thomas agreed, as he went on looking. 'The trouble is it is starting to get quite dark so we may miss the way in,' he went on.

'Are you looking for a way into the castle?' a small voice asked.

'Yes,' David replied, 'who is it that asked?'

'It's me,' the voice came again and a large water rat appeared from amongst the reeds on the water's edge. Following behind him were a mother and two little baby rats.

'We all live in the castle cellars, and we can show you how to get in, if you don't mind getting wet,' the rat went on. 'The river runs right under the castle and although they have bars to block the way one of them is broken so it would be easy for you to squeeze through.'

'I thought this was just the town wall, with the castle inside,' David said.

'It was the wall to the town back there, but the castle is built in the corner of the town so the walls just join its sides,' the rat told him. 'Now do you want to get in before it gets too dark to see?'

'Yes please, but is the water very deep?' Hope asked.

'I expect it will be up to your chest in some places, but the river does not flow very fast, so it will be quite easy for you to wade through. Now follow me,' the rat disappeared through the reeds and entered the moat with a small splash, his family followed him and David hurried after.

One by one they stepped down into the water and set off following the rat family towards their goal. The water only came up to their waists for the start of the journey but as they neared the metal grill guarding the way, they came into the middle of the river and the water now reached up to David's chest, they had to carry their packs over their heads. He paused and held out his hand to Hope, whom, being so much shorter had to start to swim and supported her so that she would not have to get her bundle wet.

Thomas waded past his brother. 'Wait a moment I'll go through first and then you pass everyone to me.' He easily slid through the gap in the bars, then turned and held his hand out.

David pulled Hope across until her outstretched hand could reach Thomas and he pulled her through to the other side where the water once more became shallower. Freya quickly went through, followed closely by the four elves then it was David's turn and he waded easily in and they all, once again, started to follow the rat family into the tunnel. Up ahead there was a glow of torchlight this helped them to see as they moved onwards making as little noise as possible.

Once they came to the very edge of the lighted area the rats stopped and addressed them all, the father rat said. 'Just around the corner is a block of cells that King Golgog keeps his prisoners in. You will be quite safe here as no one comes this way now. The cellars are the other way and they are only holding a few broken bits of furniture so no one visits them for anything. To get out through the castle you have to pass the cells and go up the stairs to the top. This is a side entrance, so once out you will be in the castle courtyard. The gates to this are never closed as no one thinks there is any danger. Follow the street straight to the main gates and out. No one challenges anyone leaving, only people trying to get in.'

'Thank you for all your help, but tell me, why do you stay here?' David asked them.

'We have no choice, once I was a footman at the palace and I lived happily with my wife and family in our quarters near the kitchens. Then one day, not so long ago, Morgana came and persuaded King Golgog to take over Summerdale and add it to his kingdom. Unfortunately for us, I overheard her in her room, she was talking to herself. She said she would marry King Golgog and then kill him so that she would be the ruler of the Twilight Kingdom on her own. She must have seen me because she followed me to my quarters and put a magic spell on us all, turning us to rats. We cannot go to the king and warn him because he keeps his dogs close by at all times. They would love to kill us. We cannot escape from here as we are too little to travel a long way. Anyway we are quite safe down here. The kitchen waste is left in the courtyard every night so we can sneak out and collect what we want.'

'Not to mention there are fishes in the moat if we want a change,' the mother rat added.

'But that sounds terrible, there must be a way we can help you. I shall talk to Merlin when we return and see what he can do to help,' Freya said.

'We would be grateful for your help but now we must go and find some food.'

The rat family slipped off towards the stairs, keeping well in the shadows as they went.

'Well we are here, now what are we going to do?' Hope asked.

Chapter Forty

The eight, would be rescuers, stood for a moment beside the river that had gained them entry to the king's castle.

'First things first,' said Freya, we need to change into dry clothes, 'we could go into the cellars and as we change we could put some more thought into a plan to rescue the little queen.'

'Good idea, come on,' David said and led the way into the gloom.

They easily found the door to the cellar even though there was no torch to light their way. The door was not locked and once inside they saw there was a small, barred, window in the wall letting in the moonlight.

Once they were all changed they put all their wet things out to dry by draping them over the odd pieces of furniture left in the cellar. Once this was done they started to discuss ideas of rescue.

'I think one of us should go to the cells and find out what we can from Queen Josephine,' David said.

'That's a very good idea,' Thomas agreed. 'I'll go.'

'No, I think it would be better if I went,' Heddwch argued, 'as I said before we elves have much better hearing than you humans, so we will hear any dangers long before you do.'

'All right,' David agreed reluctantly, 'but just go and find out when the guards come and if she is unhurt.'

'I'll be very quick, you will hardly know I've been gone,' Heddwch said as he eased open the door and disappeared out and around the bend to the cells.

There was no one on duty, but Heddwch could hear voices in two cells, he went to the first door and peeped through the grill. Inside he saw two women pacing up and down and talking to each other in low voices, they were saying something about writing a letter.

'Psst!' Heddwch hissed, 'who are you? And where is Queen Josephine?'

Gwendolyn and Faith turned in amazement and went over to the door.

'Queen Josephine is in the next cell, but who are you?' Faith asked as she looked out. 'Are you with Thomas and David?' she added hopefully.

'Yes,' he replied, 'my name is Heddwch; I am one of four elves who have come with David's party to rescue the queen. You haven't answered my question, who are you and what are you doing here?'

Gwendolyn pushed Faith gently aside and quickly told him who they were and why they were being held. 'They are coming at noon tomorrow for the letter for my husband so we don't have very long.'

'Don't worry everything will be in hand before then,' Heddwch replied with more confidence than he actually felt. 'Now I shall go and have a word with the queen before I report back to David.'

He went to the next cell where the little queen had flown up to the door and was looking out.

'Your majesty,' Heddwch cried, 'are you unhurt? We have come to rescue you and the 'Stone of Power', so that order can be restored to all our lands.'

'I am unhurt, but King Golgog has the stone and he is using the power against Summerdale. Every day he is becoming stronger and if we do not rescue it from him soon the stone will only obey him and he will have no further use for me.'

'Why does he need you now if he is already using the stone?'

'At the moment the stone is still technically mine and it is drawing power from me. Once King Golgog becomes all-powerful the stone will turn to him.'

'You still have some power over the stone then?' Heddwch asked as a germ of an idea started to form in his mind. 'We may be able to use that to our advantage,' he mused. 'Now, back to the matter in hand, when do you expect the next visit from anyone?'

'We have our breakfast delivered early in the morning, and then the king and four guards will return for Gwendolyn's letter at noon. Otherwise we see no one. Do you think I could meet your companions?'

'Yes of course. I will go immediately to fetch the others.'

Heddwch ran quickly back to the cellars.

'The queen is quite safe and would like to meet you all. The empress and your friend Faith are in the next door cell.'

'How on earth did they end up here?' David wondered as they all followed Heddwch back.

'Are they all right?' Hope asked worried about her sister.

'We are fine, at the moment, as you can see for yourself,' Faith said looking out through the bars on the door.

The empress explained to them all what had happened.

'You say you are expecting no one until the morning,' David mused.

'The easiest way of affecting your escape is by getting hold of the key,' Llawenydd said.

'I know we could lie in wait for the guard when he brings breakfast and capture him. Then we can use his key to release you and we can escape the same way as we came in,' David said.

'We should be well away before anyone notices we are gone,' Thomas agreed.

'The only thing is we will be on foot and they will have horses. Once they realise we have gone they will set off after us,' Hope argued.

'They will think we would go back to Summerdale, and if we did they would overtake us. No, we will have to go back to the mountains and the elves.'

'Once we are out and on our way, I could call the dragons,' Freya said quietly.

'How?' Faith asked.

'I have half of a calling charm; I gave the other to Shimmer when we parted at the edge of the Forest. If I hold it and concentrate hard on her she will pick up my thoughts and bring the dragons to help us.'

'That is good news,' Empress Gwendolyn said, 'then they could give us a lift back.'

'Right, if we are all in agreement we have to wait for the morning,' David looked around at everyone, they all nodded. 'Well there is nothing more we can do tonight so let's all try to have some sleep then.'

The eight went back to their cellar and the others made themselves comfortable as they all tried to rest in readiness of the exertions they would face the next day.

Chapter Forty One

David quietly woke everyone up just as the light was starting to come through the little window. They had packed all their belongings in readiness for leaving and stood anxiously awaiting the guard. .

At last they heard him coming down the stairs with the prisoners' breakfast, they crept around the bend in time to see the back of the guard as he opened the queen's cell door and put the food and water on the floor before backing out and closing the door again.

David and Thomas ran silently forwards and while Thomas grabbed the guard around the chest, David pulled the keys out of his hand. The guard called out but before he could make too much noise Freya, armed with an old chair leg she had found, hit him over the head, knocking his helmet off and rendering him unconscious. He collapsed into a heap on the floor.

'Is he dead?' she asked fearfully.

'No, but I don't think he will be bothering us for some time,' David replied after feeling his pulse. 'I think I shall take his jacket and helmet, you never know whether they may come in handy at some time.'

David handed the keys to Llawenydd who immediately went over to the other cell to let the prisoners out.

Queen Josephine came out of her cell and went across to greet Empress Gwendolyn and Faith as they came out of their cell. The little queen was so small Gwendolyn had to bend down so she could hug her, while Faith went into her sister's arms.

'I am so glad you're safe, but if we want to remain that way we had better make a move,' Hope said.

Thomas and Llawenydd carried the unconscious guard into the first cell; they put him on the bench and covered him with the blanket. They also put the pillows under the blankets in the other cell.

'They will think they are still asleep. Well he will be for a short while and any extra time will be a bonus,' Thomas said as he locked the door behind him.

'Which way do we have to go?' Gwendolyn turned to David.

'This way,' he said as he led them around the corner to the side of the river. 'I am afraid we are all going to get wet.'

'I shan't' the queen said as she opened her wings and flew over the water.

'You are the lucky one,' Freya said laughing. 'Come on, standing around is just wasting precious time.'

She pulled her backpack onto her shoulder and jumped down into the cold water.

'At least when we have to hurry on the other side we will be relatively cool,' Gwendolyn said as she took Freya's hand to steady herself as she stepped into the water.

The others shouldered their packs and quickly followed. Thomas and David pushed ahead ready to give a helping hand to everyone as they went through the deeper water. The little queen flew through with no problems, although she did get her feet wet as she ducked under the grill, much to Gwendolyn's amusement.

'Even you have managed to get a little damp,' she chuckled.

The queen laughed back and then flew over to the bank. 'Hurry up it is getting very light out here the sun will be fully up soon,' she said.

'Don't worry too much; it does not come out properly as everywhere stays in this twilight. It must be something to do with the evil that is practiced here,' Freya answered her as she waded across and started to climb out on to the bank. 'Can you help me David? I don't seem to be able to get a grip on the side here.'

David waded over and gave her a push up the steep side of the river. Once she was out he did the same to the others. When everyone else was out Thomas reached down and hauled David up.

'Everyone Ok?' David asked.

They all nodded, except Freya who was standing still clutching her charm that hung around her neck. She just held her hand up and closed her eyes for a few moments. Then a smile came to her lips.

'I have contacted Shimmer and she is going to arrange for the dragons to come to our aid. I have told her we are going back through the forest towards the elves mountains.'

'Brilliant, but we had better set off before we are seen by the guards on top of the walls,' David ordered.

They soon disappeared from sight in to the trees that ran beside the road.

'We will only be able to follow the road for a short time,' Heddwch said. 'We will have to go away from it if we are to make for our homeland.'

'Also they will be sending out riders as soon as they discover we have escaped,' Gwendolyn said.

'I have been thinking,' Enfys said pausing, 'If Adain and I went back to the gate and when the outcry starts we could set off the other way, letting the guards see us. That way they will think we have gone on the straight road back to Summerdale. As soon as we are out of sight we will head back towards you through the trees.'

'That is very brave of you but they could catch you as they will be on horseback and you will just be running,' Gwendolyn said doubtfully.

'You haven't seen an elf running have you?' Heddwch said, smiling.

'There are very few horses that can run as fast as we can over a short distance,' Llawenydd added.

'In that case, thank you, that would be a great help,' David replied.

The two girl elves immediately set off back the way they had come leaving the others to go as fast as they could in the other direction.

Heddwch set a fast pace, but they all managed to keep up. They were running for sixty paces then walking for sixty alternatively. This way they kept it up for a long time before a halt was called.

'We are some way away and I think it is time to have a refreshment break. None of us has eaten since last night,' Heddwch said as he pulled some food out of his bag and passed it around. Llawenydd did the same with his drink.

'What is in this?' Freya asked. 'I have only eaten and drunk a little and yet I feel full and refreshed.'

'It is our special food and drink prepared especially for journeys' the elves replied. 'It means we do not have to carry much to go a long way.'

"On that note, it's time for us to go on now.' Heddwch looked up at the hazy sun. 'It must be midday and they will be after us soon,' He added.

'When will Adain and Enfys join us again?' Hope asked.

'I would expect them within two hours. We have been travelling for about five hours now, but they will be cutting straight across towards us. Don't worry they will be fine.'

They all set off again and as predicted, just less than two hours later Adain and Enfys appeared. Everyone gathered around them as they reported their progress.

'Just after noon a great commotion started when they must have discovered you were missing,' Adain looked at Gwendolyn and Faith. 'The Death Riders came out of the gate at a fast gallop; we let them see us and ran off towards Summerdale. As soon as we were around the corner and out of sight we cut off through the forest.'

'That is when we really started running,' Enfys carried on, 'but they will only follow the road for a short time before they realise we have not gone that way. They will come back and search the sides of the road until they find where we left.'

'We did our best to disguise where we entered the forest but we did not want to spend too much time there in case there were others coming behind,' Adain added.

'It's only a matter of time before the Death Riders are on our tail, so we had better make good time to reach the clearing where we can meet the dragons,' David said.

'I hope we can reach the dragons before the Death Riders reach us,' Hope muttered, worrying as usual.

Chapter Forty Two

Shimmer had gone to her father, Greor, and told him of her contact with Freya. Greor immediately called the other dragons over and Shimmer once again told what Freya's thoughts had been.

'Freya said they are making for a clearing near the edge of the Twilight Kingdom. It is just before the start of the mountains that lead to the elves home. Two of the elves are laying a false trail for King Golgog to follow, but they will eventually catch up with them as there are now eleven in their party, these include the Empress Gwendolyn, Faith and Queen Josephine, but they have not found the 'Stone of Power' yet, so the Death Riders will still be attacking Summerdale.'

'That's a shame not to have recovered the stone. We will have to fly quickly to save them from the kings men. Then we will have to return here as quickly as possible to help you all,' Greor said.

'Why don't we separate and Shimmer, Jade and I go to help David and his party while you, Greor with Caw and Cawson stay to fight on these boundaries of Summerdale and the Twilight Kingdom,' Sherna asked flicking her long green tail.

'We would only have to make sure that they were safe from any pursuers, and once they are into the elves' mountain, the kings men would not dare to follow,' Shimmer said.

'I also suggest that you bring back the emperor's wife and perhaps Faith and Hope, this will relieve the fears that are abounding here as to whether they are alive or dead. Also it would leave a smaller party to escort the queen home to her people, and that way their journey would take less time,' Caw said as he brought his big red head down to the level of Shimmers small green face. 'Have we ever told you what a brave little dragon we all think you are?' he added.

'Well said Caw,' Greor said looking pleased, 'she takes after her mother,' he looked at his mate Sherna, making her cheeks turn a lovely shade of rose pink

The little dragon looked all confused, and then it was her turn to blush.

'Thank you, but you are the ones that do the most dangerous work; I just help where I can.' Her gaze took in all the full grown dragons as they stood around in the sunlight, their scales on their backs sparkling red or green depending which colour they were,

'Before we get carried away with compliments, I think we have a job to do,' Sherna said briskly to hide her embarrassment. 'Come on Jade and you too, Shimmer, we must go and help our friends.'

With no more ado the three female dragons spread their wings and jumped into the air. Off they flew towards the northwest, to rescue their friends.

Greor, Caw and Cawson watched them go, before they set off towards the east on their own mission, ready to do battle with the forces of darkness once more.

Shimmer set the pace as she had the smallest wings and could not fly quite as fast as her mother or their friend Jade. They flew first to the west then turned north following the edge of the Twilight Kingdom. Even now they did not want to draw too much attention to themselves, as they did not know the full extent of King Golgog's powers. They knew he still had the 'Stone of Power', but they had been beginning to suspect there were other powers in the kingdom that they could not account for.

Even with Shimmer's slower pace they arrived at the clearing well before their human friends arrived with their companions. They sat down to wait.

After a few moments Shimmer got up and paced to the edge of the clearing to peer through the trees.

'We can't just sit here,' she said agitated, 'they may have been caught.'

'Why don't you tune into Freya's thoughts again?' Jade asked.

'I have been trying on and off for a little while, but she is probably concentrating on escaping. I shall try again,' Shimmer sat down once more and this time closed her eyes, a frown appeared on her forehead as she concentrated on reaching her friend.

A few moments later she opened her eyes.

'They are in danger!' she exclaimed. 'They are still some way away from here and they can now hear the sound of the riders following them. Gwendolyn is not that young and is finding it difficult to keep up. Freya fears they will be captured again.'

'We will have to go into the Twilight Kingdom and rescue them, we have no choice,' Sherna said, immediately taking off, closely followed by Jade and Shimmer.

'Which way?' she called to her daughter.

'Over here,' Shimmer replied, 'hurry… hurry. They are in dreadful danger. They are being pursued by the Death Riders, even though it is still day. That shows how strong their power is becoming.'

They flew onwards for a few more moments and then from their vantage point, up in the sky, they saw the band of friends moving through the trees so slowly now and not very far behind the first of the black figures was urging its horse in and out of the trees at a breakneck speed, he was closely followed by a dozen more as they started to sense their goal in front of them.

All three of the dragons saw their prey at the same time and not pausing for a wing beat they all dived towards the first rider, then they spread out in a line and when they were within striking distance all three clicked their claws as they breathed out, each sending a long flame towards the oncoming riders.

The lead rider and its mount just disappeared. The surrounding vegetation caught fire causing the closely following horses to scream and rear. None of the riders were unseated, and they turned to go around the flames. The ones further back had easily avoided the fire and riding round it were even now closing on their quarry.

Shimmer flew down amongst the trees and grabbed Gwendolyn with her claws. She immediately regained height carrying the older woman out of danger.

The others no longer hampered by Gwendolyn, picked up speed. The riders were too close now for them to make the safety of the elf's territory. David shouted to them to get behind the trees and prepare to fight. They did not have long to wait. Just moment s later the first of the riders came upon them and seeing Faith peeping out behind her tree went straight for her, its sword drawn and ready to kill. The little Queen realising that Faith had no means to protect herself, quickly flew up to the top of a tree and directed some spells at the rider. Her spell was only a blocking spell but when it hit the horse and rider crumpled to the ground, as if it had hit a wall.

Sherna seeing this flew in; letting out flames which dissolved the enemy where it lay.

Sherna and Jade flew backwards and forwards sending out flames at the enemy. On the ground David and the others were shooting their arrows at the oncoming riders. They seemed to be holding their own, when one of the riders broke away and went round, coming in from a different angle; it came in behind Hope, who turned at the last moment seeing her danger. She did not have time to think just drew her sword and parried the blade from her attacker. The rider came off its horse but quickly jumped up before Hope had had time to reach it to stab the fatal blow. The black shrouded thing howled a terrible sound as it came at Hope once again. Shaking, she again parried the blow; she had to hold her sword with two hands, as the attacker was so strong. Back she was driven, away from the others, back and back until she could go no further as she had come up against the trunk of a tree.

She fought like one possessed, but she was tiring. It was only going to be moments before she was too tired to even lift her sword in defence.

There was a whoosh of an arrow and her attacker disappeared! Adain appeared, holding her bow.

'Are you all right?' she asked as she ran over to Hope, 'You haven't been cut by its sword have you?'

'No I'm perfectly all right, thanks to you,' Hope smiled then turning they both rushed back to where the battle was still going on.

They came through the trees just in time to see Shimmer had returned and she with the other two dragons came in low to blast the last of the enemy away.

The undergrowth was still alight in a few places, but it did not take much to put it out. The vegetation was dank and wet so did not sustain fire well.

The companions came out and looked up at the dragons circling overhead.

'Thank you, once again you have saved us,' David said.

'Where is Gwendolyn?' Freya asked.

'She is safe; she is waiting in the clearing for you. It's not very far. We will go back there and wait for you,' Shimmer called down.

The dragons flew off and the weary party followed at a slower pace.

Shortly afterwards they met up again Safe now as they were over the border into elf country.

Up in the top of one of the towers in King Golgog's castle, a pale, beautiful face was looking into a crystal ball.

'Those dragons have thwarted me again. I will kill them somehow and their meddling friends,' Morgana ranted. Then an evil smile came over her face as she thought of a way to stop them.

Chapter Forty Three

David and the others arrived at the clearing and Freya ran across to Gwendolyn to hug her. The others gathered around.

'You are OK, aren't you?' Freya asked.

'I'm fine and once I overcame the shock of being grabbed by a dragon and flown into the air, I quite enjoyed the experience.'

'Yes, well, I did apologise at the time. I didn't want those horrible Death Riders to catch you. I knew you would have nothing to fight them with and thought it safer to have you out of the way,' Shimmer said.

'As I said I enjoyed the experience of flying and wouldn't mind trying again under slightly different circumstances.'

'You are going to have the opportunity sooner than you thought, as we are going back to Summerdale and thought you and the two girls would like a lift. We would take you all back to your homes but as long as the Death Riders are strong enough to ride during the day we need to go back as soon as possible to help the other dragons defend the boundaries of your country,' Jade said.

'Don't worry about us, we are only going to escort Queen Josephine back to her people, then we will return to help you in Summerdale,' David reassured her.

'Once you have reached the Forest, let me know with your thoughts and I shall come with two others to fly you home, that will save you at least a day's travelling,' Shimmer told Freya.

'Thank you that will be a help, in the meantime could everyone try to think of a way to rescue the

'Stone of Power' from King Golgog and the Death Riders,' Freya said.

'If we don't regain the stone we will never stop the attacks until they have killed us all or we have surrendered,' Gwendolyn said, looking very worried.

'Talking of surrender, we had better get you back to your husband before he thinks of surrendering to the enemy to rescue you,' Shimmer remarked as she came over to Gwendolyn. 'Climb on my back and I will give you a flight to remember on your way home.'

Gwendolyn did as she was asked and Faith and Hope mounted on the backs of Shimmer and Jade.

'Are you sure you don't mind me going straight back now,' Hope asked David.

'Of course I don't,' David replied, 'I'll have one less person to worry about.'

'What do you mean? Did you think I was a nuisance?'

'Oh Hope! Stop being so paranoid! All he meant was you will be back with the Emperor Godwin and safe, so he wouldn't have to worry about you,' Faith answered her sister with exasperation in her voice.

David laughed. 'You are a ninny Hope. I'll see you when I get back.'

Hope smiled back sheepishly; they all waved to the ones left behind as the three dragons leapt into the air and returned with their passengers to Summerdale.

The little queen had been sitting quietly on a tree stump all the while the talk had been going on. She stood up and addressed her remaining companions.

'What Gwendolyn said is right, we have to think of a way to retrieve my stone otherwise all will be lost. Without it my power will slowly get weaker until I am no longer able even to fly. The worst thing is all my people will be the same and then we will slowly fade into nothing.'

Freya looked horrified and David came over to her. He took her tiny hand into his whilst looking straight into her eyes.

'Don't fear, not for one moment, we will bring back your stone. Won't we Thomas, Freya?'

Thomas came up beside his twin and taking the queens other hand said.

'David's right; we'll have your stone back as soon as we have finalised our plan.'

'I, too, promise we will bring your stone back.' Freya said with feeling.

The queen smiled at them. 'Well why are we waiting? I must return to reassure my people that all will be right in time.'

The four elves came forwards. 'Come back to our home for the night and then we will lead you back to your people tomorrow after a good night's rest.'

'That sounds wonderful,' Thomas said, 'let's go!'

Heddwch went over to the fairy queen. "I would be honoured if you would sit on my shoulders for the remainder of the journey today. This will save your tiny wings as they must be tired after travelling all that way from King Golgog's castle.'

'Thank you, I would be grateful. I am rather tired. It's not often I have to travel any distance at all and then it's usually on the back of a bird or dragonfly.'

'In the morning we will see if we can find one or the other to be of assistance to you, and if neither is readily available we can all take turns to carry your majesty. I am just sorry we did not think of this earlier,' Adain said.

The rest of their way back to the elves' caves was uneventful, though they were all relived to reach the hospitality of the elf King Brenin.

Chapter Forty Four

The friends who were left to escort Queen Josephine back to her home had a restful night and the day of their return journey dawned bright and sunny, but the searing heat was starting to fade from the days as the year moved into autumn.

David, Thomas and Freya stood at the doorway overlooking the plains where the cat creatures roamed.

'It's hard to believe that a week has not passed since we sat on this ledge wondering how we would survive as the cats waited below,' Freya said.

'At least the animals have gone,' Thomas replied.

'We should be able to make better time now I am well again,' David mused.

'I have just been told that the cats keep a lookout around the base of the cliff, they must be waiting for your return,' Adain said as she came up behind them.'

'You will not be able to out run them, if they are expecting you,' Llawenydd told them as he joined them. 'But not to worry, we have been told we can go with you, back to the edge of the grasslands anyway.'

'Yes,' Heddwch added, 'as we can run so much faster than you we are to go first and draw the cats away from you.'

'We can't ask you to risk your lives for us,' David said.

'You didn't ask and anyway we are coming to protect Queen Josephine as much as you three,' Enfys said joining them with the little queen sitting on her shoulder.

'You three have got to get back to help overpower the dark forces that are attacking Summerdale and rescue the 'Stone of Power' for the Forest, until you do we are all in danger. You don't think for one minute that King Golgog and his allies would be satisfied with only taking over Summerdale. Once that has been taken, the darkness will spread and he will turn his eyes towards the mountains and even further until we are all his slaves. Or worse, we could become like the riders who follow Marwolaeth, they are the living dead who, have had their minds so poisoned that they can only do as she tells them. Her name means death and that is what her riders deliver.'

'That makes it even more important that we recover your stone,' David said to the queen.

'And I know you will succeed; you, your brother and sister are remarkable people. Gwendolyn told me all about your adventures to help save King Arthur's life. We all have absolute faith in you,' she replied.

'No pressure then!' Thomas muttered as he turned away.

'Did you say something?' Adain said grinning.

'I said "no problem then",' He lied, blushing.

'I think we had better climb down and start our journey, if we all have everything,' Freya said, picking up her backpack.

They had each been given some food and drink to last over the journey, so they would not need to make any detours for more water. They were going to try to do the whole journey in one go. They were now ready to start and the sun had only just started to peep over the hills in the east.

Some of the other elves had come to see everyone off. They lowered a rope ladder over the cliff ready for the decent.

'We will go down first and scout ahead of you, then if we see the cats we will immediately lead them away from you,' Heddwch said starting to climb down. The other three elves followed. Queen Josephine flew down and that just left David, Thomas and Freya.

Once they were all down and the ladder had been pulled back up. David turned to the queen and asked.

'Do you want to start on my shoulder?'

'Thank you, but no. I shall fly along, to start with, that way we can all move faster.'

The elves set off at a steady run and were soon out of sight over the rise. David and the others set out at a slightly slower pace, doing as they had done before sixty paces at the run then sixty at a walk. Once they had established a rhythm they were covering the ground fairly fast.

After about an hour they had to slow to a fast walk as they were starting to suffer from the heat. As they went along they kept a wary eye open for any signs of the cats.

Lunchtime came and a halt was called to have some refreshments. Heddwch and Enfys re-joined them.

'Any sign of the cats?' David asked.

'We saw some in the distance, but they did not pay any attention to us,' Heddwch replied.

'We think they may have been following Llawenydd and Adain's trail. Which means they will be far away now,' Enfys added.

'Will they be all right?' Freya asked.

'Yes, don't worry. They were laying a trail with the aid of a dead rabbit. Once they are far enough away they will abandon the rabbit and head back in a roundabout way,' Enfys replied.

'We have come back to you to make sure you do not encounter any stray animals, which are not hunting with the pack. Though we do not expect to find any,' Heddwch said, sitting down to eat some food.

A short while later David rallied everyone ready to start again. This time the little queen admitted to being a little tired so Thomas carried her on his shoulders for a while, then after about an hour David took over carrying her. They kept swapping over and that way they managed to keep going at a brisk pace.

The afternoon passed and the sun slowly sank towards the west.

The travellers were beginning to tire and the pace had dropped to a weary walk. Freya had been slightly in the lead and she suddenly stopped.

'Look!' she called, turning excitedly to her brothers, 'isn't that the Forest on the top of that hill?'

'I do believe it is,' David said coming up beside her.

'We don't have too far to go then,' Thomas said.

'We'll run ahead and let the little people know we are returning with their queen,' Heddwch said, and he and Enfys set off at a fast run. They soon became specks in the distance.

'I wish I had that much energy,' David said smiling. He turned to the queen who was sitting on Thomas's shoulders. 'We will soon be back with your people and safe for the moment.'

'I wonder what has happened to Llawenydd and Adain, I do hope they are safe,' Freya said looking around, 'but standing here is not going to do any good, we had better finish our journey.'

They moved off again and had only gone about a kilometre when they heard their names being called. Turning they saw the two missing elves coming towards them at a fast jog.

'Keep going!' Llawenydd called, 'we have not been able to shake the cats off our trail and they are not very far behind.'

Chapter Forty Five

Llawenydd and Adain came up beside Thomas 'I'll take you, Queen Josephine, that way the others can move a bit faster.'

'I shall look after myself, thank you,' the queen replied. 'I can still do some magic and when the cat creatures come a little closer they will be in for a surprise,' she called as she flew off Thomas's shoulder and hovered around their heads.

'Now go…go! Get as far ahead of them as you can. My people will be coming to meet you so we will be safe soon.'

David and Thomas took Freya's hands and the three of them ran towards the safety of the distant trees. The little Queen flew along just behind them and she kept glancing over her shoulder to see if the danger was in sight.

They were about half way to safety before the first sign of the cats was spotted. The lead animal came over a rise; nose down as it followed the elves trail. Then it paused and moved around, it must have been the place when the elves had met up with the queen's party. Many more animals' arrived and all started taking in the smells. The leader stopped and sat up on its haunches as it looked around for signs of its quarry. Although its eyesight was good it was only the movement made by David's party that drew their attention. It let out a loud cry and all the other animals turned in the direction of David and the others. The lead cat set off at a gallop followed by the others.

Freya had glanced back when she heard the cat's cry and seeing the animals coming after them once again; she gave a little scream and put more power into her running, this time she was dragging her brothers for a few seconds before they too put an extra spurt into their running.

The cats were closing fast, and David was beginning to wonder how much longer they could keep up the pace. There was a bang and the lead cat flew into the air before tumbling backwards.

'I put a stop spell on it and it still works!' Queen Josephine shouted with joy.

She proceeded to "stop" the other leading animals. The pack stopped and sniffed at their fallen leaders whilst they looked around nervously.

'Go on as fast as you can because it will not stop them for very long, also if they all come together then I may not be able to stop them,' the queen urged them.

It was not more than a few moments before the animals came on again. The queen directed another spell at one and missed it just sending a bunch of grasses into the air. The animals were now coming in a wide line abreast, almost as if they knew how to beat the little queen.

Llawenydd and Adain took hold of David and Thomas's free hand and ran with them, helping them pull Freya in the middle. They ran five abreast, but still they were losing the race. Nearer and nearer the cats came, then disaster befell them, Freya tripped and brought her brothers down with her.

Llawenydd and Adain turned to face the oncoming animas. Suddenly the air became full of the little people flying to their aid. Every one of them had their bows and arrows at the ready. They let fly at the oncoming animals, the arrows were not big enough to kill them but they could hurt, especially when half a dozen embedded in the animals' nose. The cats stopped chasing their quarries as they rolled around trying to dislodge the little needle like annoyances, thus giving our heroes a chance to regain their feet and run on to reach the safety of the trees.

The cat creatures, realising they were beaten slinked off to lick their wounds and search for easier pray.

David, Thomas and Freya sank to the ground and lay there for a while to catch their breath. Queen Josephine flew over and landed beside them. Her people immediately surrounded her, with Prince Owen and Princess Poppy in the front.

'Oh it is so good to see you all,' the queen cried, pulling her son and daughter into her arms, 'I sometimes wondered if I would ever be free. If it hadn't been for these brave people,' she indicated the three where they lay watching, 'I expect I should have still been a captive of King Golgog.'

'Where is your stone?' Owen asked.

'I'm afraid it's still in the hands of the enemy, but we are working on a plan to rescue it,' David said as he rose to his feet. 'We must make haste back to Summerdale and Merlin. We need to consult with him.'

'How are you going to get back?' The queen asked.

'I shall ask Shimmer to bring other dragons with her to carry us back,' Freya said, 'I'll do that straight away.' She moved off a little way and took out her charm. Whilst she held it she concentrated hard on Shimmer and asked her to fetch them all.

When she returned to the group, it was to find her brothers being hard pressed to tell the tale of their travels.

'We must not forget to thank the four elves, without whom we would not have survived the journey,' David turned to indicate them as they stood on the edge of the gathering.

'We only did what anybody would, in the circumstances,' Llawenydd spoke for them all and the others nodded their agreement.

'Now we, too, must return to our people, we will ask them to prepare for a battle against King Golgog and the Death Riders,' Heddwch added.

'Shimmer is on the way, so perhaps you could delay your departure until you have heard what she has to report?' Freya asked.

'It would be a good idea, then we will know as much as you about the situation,' Adain said.

'We had better escort you to the other side of the forest ready to meet with the dragons,' Queen Josephine said walking deeper under the trees as they began to sway and moan in confusion.

The little queen began to sing; her voice was clear and haunting. The trees stilled to listen, the other fairies joined in the chorus. There appeared to be a small breeze floating gently amongst the leaves, as they rustle in time to the music. When the song ended, a feeling of peace descended on the troubled trees and they no longer tried to move around.

'They will let all friends of the Forest people come through unhindered, our enemies, they will confuse, much as they did to you before,' Queen Josephine said and set off to lead everyone through to the other side of the forest ready for the arrival of the dragons and news of the battle.

Chapter Forty Six

David and Thomas stood side by side and watched the sky for the first sight of the dragons. The others stood in a group making an occasional comment. No one quite knew what to say as they realised the time for the parting of the ways was fast approaching. They did not have long to wait before they saw Shimmer and her mother Sherna flying in towards them.

Once the dragons had landed everyone crowded around them to hear their news.

'It's not good,' Shimmer reported, 'the attacks are lasting longer. The Death Riders are getting as strong as they were when they attacked King Arthur. The 'Stone of Power' is starting to work for them. If we do not rescue it from them soon, they will win. Emperor Godwin's people are losing heart; they are being either killed or taken as slaves by the invading armies. It is only a matter of time before they surrender.'

'We had better go back to report to out king and ready ourselves for a war,' Heddwch said. 'Perhaps you could send word of your plans and then we could coordinate our attack with yours.'

'I have a better idea,' Shimmer said, 'why don't you let Enfys come with us; she is small enough to ride on my back with Freya. Once we have our plan, I could fly her back to her people to report to your king.'

'That is a good idea,' Heddwch agreed. 'We will leave straight away and tell King Brenin to wait for Enfys's return.'

Llawenydd, Adain and Heddwch took their leave of the Forest people and the royal party, before hugging the two girls and shaking David and Thomas's hand.

They turned and ran off through the trees, back the way they had come.

David's party said their farewells and climbed on to the two dragons' backs. Once airborne they set off back to the emperor's castle. The riders waved back to the little people as they faded into the distance. On and on flew the dragons faster and faster. Then in hardly any time they started to circle around the meadow, ready to land just outside the white walls of the castle.

'Thank you Shimmer and Sherna for giving us a great flight,' David said, as they all slid of the dragons' backs.

They turned to see the other dragons flying over to join them. From the gates of the castle Faith and Hope came rushing out to greet them, closely followed by Edwin and Emperor Godwin, Empress Gwendolyn with Merlin, came behind at a more sedately pace.

'It's good to see you again,' Faith cried hugging them all.

Hope followed around. 'I worried about you and the cat creatures,' she whispered to David.

'You needn't have, we had our good friends, the elves, to help us,' he turned to the emperor. 'May I introduce Enfys? She has come to join in our war council and then she will report back to King Brenin, who has said he will help in our war against the Twilight Kingdom,' he turned back to Enfys. 'This is Emperor Godwin of Summerdale.'

Godwin stepped forwards and took Enfys's hands in his own. 'Thank you so much for all you have done and for being here.'

'If Summerdale falls to the evil forces coming from the Twilight Kingdom our kingdom would no longer be safe either, so we have all to join together to stop this happening,' Enfys replied.

While Godwin and Enfys carried on talking Freya went over to Edwin.

'How are you, did they torture you when you were captured?' she asked concerned. 'Has any one checked you over?'

'There is no need, I am fine,' Edwin smiled at Freya. 'Now do excuse me I want to hear what is going to be decided for the battle,' he brushed past her as he went to listen to the talks that David and Thomas had now joined.

Freya turned to follow with a frown on her face. It was not like Edwin to be so short with his answer. He had always been full of fun. Perhaps the continual raids from the enemy had been taking their toll. She pondered as she came to stand behind her brothers. She resolved that she would have a talk to Faith, who had spent more time with him.

'We are seriously thinking of surrendering to King Golgog, my people cannot take much more of this fighting. See how the light has changed, we do not have the full strength of the sun anymore, twilight is spreading into my land,' Emperor Godwin was telling the gathering.

A deep rumble came from the dragons. 'We will never surrender to evil' Greor stated for his companions.

'Neither will we!' Empress Gwendolyn agreed. 'Not unless there was no other way to save the lives of our people,' she amended, looking over at her husband. 'Give us a few days to try to find a way to defeat them, before we talk of this again.'

'All right,' Emperor Godwin reluctantly agreed with her. 'it's Monday now, if you have not come up with something by Friday, I shall call a meeting with King Golgog and discuss terms of surrender.'

On that depressing note the gathering dispersed.

'Faith and Freya, Merlin has asked for you to come to my rooms this evening and we will try to think of some magic to help in our fight,' Gwendolyn said coming over to the girls.

'Can I be of any use?' Hope asked.

'I am afraid not, little sister, you never studied magic,' Faith said gently.

'Don't worry there will be plenty of other things you will be able to do to help,' Freya added. 'Could you look after our guest, find her a room and see to her needs. That would be a great help.'

Hope went off with Enfys. 'Perhaps you will tell me all about your journey after I left you. Were you all in any danger?'

Enfys laughed. 'Well not real danger,' she said and she put her arm around Hopes shoulders and they walked away.

David, Thomas and Freya left too and went to their rooms to freshen up.

Whilst the others went, Edwin stood and watched them before he hurried off to the stables. He ordered a mount to be brought for him and on having it delivered he rode off towards the boundary of Summerdale. No one saw him go save for Freya who happened to be looking out of her window as he rode off.

Wondering where he was going she left her room and ran down the stairs and outside intending to fetch a horse and follow him. As she ran across to the stable block she saw Shimmer was still outside in the meadow. Freya ran straight to her.

'I need your help, can you give me a lift and follow Edwin, there is something not quite right, but I can't put my finger on it. He is behaving very strangely and I need to know where he is going and what for.'

'Climb on, we will soon find out what's happening. I'm glad to do something, the other dragons have gone to check on the boundaries but my father thought I should stay here in case I was needed. He didn't realise how soon that would be,' Shimmer finished as she and Freya soared into the sky. A few moments later they saw Edwin below them so they slowed their flight, not wanting to be noticed, they stayed some way back.

Edwin rode on oblivious of his watchers.

He made good time and soon disappeared into the edge of the forest dividing the Twilight Kingdom from Summerdale.

Shimmer came down and landed and Freya jumped off her back.

'You wait here while I try to follow Edwin,' she said and ran into the trees. Luckily she did not have far to go. A few hundred metres into the trees Edwin had stopped and was talking to a tall dark lady. Freya hid behind a tree and peeped out between its branches. The lady turned and it took all of Freya's control to stop herself from gasping. It was Morgana. What evil was she up to? No wonder the Death Riders were getting stronger. Freya knew she would have to get closer to hear what was being said, but could she do it without being heard?

Chapter Forty Seven

Freya crept forward, keeping low behind the undergrowth. At last she could hear what was being said,

'You must bring me Faith or her sister Hope. One of them will be my bait to draw Freya and her meddling brothers into my clutches,' Morgana told Edwin.

'How am I going to do that my lady?'

'I have this flask; it contains a potion to confuse the girl. You will add it to her drink this will make her do whatever you tell her. You will do this and bring her to me tomorrow night. Once I have her, we can demand that Freya, David and Thomas surrender to me to save the rest of Summerdale. Morgana smiled, 'Once I have the whole family I shall no longer need King Golgog so I shall take the power away from him and the Death Riders. It is only because of me that they can use the 'Stone of Power' anyway,' she added as she handed a small bottle to Edwin. 'Be very careful when you give this drink to her and you must make sure she drinks it, do not, on any account, give her a second draft, as this will only neutralise the original spell.'

Freya realised the meeting was coming to an end. She was very careful as she slowly made her way back out of danger and returned to Shimmer.

'Edwin will be returning any minute now, so we'd better go before he sees us.' She climbed on to the little dragon's back. 'Morgana is here and we had better warn everyone of what she is planning.'

They were well away before Edwin emerged from the trees and made his way back towards the white castle.

On the flight back Freya told Shimmer what she had heard so that it could be reported back to the other dragons. The moment Shimmer set down in the meadow, Freya jumped off and went to find Merlin and told him the news.

'We had better call a meeting for everyone,' Merlin said.

He and Freya went in search of the empress and on finding her she explained what was happening.

Gwendolyn immediately called for her maid and a page, these she sent off to find her husband, David, Thomas and the two sisters to ask them to join her in her room as soon as they could.

Once everyone was assembled Freya told them what she had just witnessed.

'We have only got until tomorrow night to come up with a plan,' Emperor Godwin mused, 'we have to have a fool proof method of defeating Morgana. We also have a problem with King Golgog, She might have said that she would no longer help him but there are too many of our people held prisoner by him so we will not be out of danger.'

'I suppose it rather depends on what she wants to do to us when she has us in her clutches,' David said.

'Nothing very nice, I would expect,' Thomas mused.

'She is almost certainly going to use magic against you,' Merlin added, 'perhaps we could use that to our advantage.'

'What do you mean?' Gwendolyn asked.

'All the time you were away I have been working on a rebound spell. The idea is that whatever magic is sent at you it will rebound back to the person who cast it?'

'That must have taken a lot of work, is it ready?' Gwendolyn asked.

She went over to Merlin and looked over his shoulder, at his book on the table.

'What are we looking at?' Faith asked also coming over.

'This,' Merlin said opening at the page he had marked. 'I need you to help me put it all together,' he read out the list of ingredients.

'Most of those I have in my room, and the others we can easily go into the garden and collect,' Gwendolyn assured him. 'Freya, you can make the little pouches to hold the ingredients while Merlin and I go and collect everything.'

'Why have you not started already?' Freya asked Merlin

'It will be many times more powerful if all of us make it together, so I had to wait for you all to be here,' he replied.

'Right, I'm all for anything that will help us to make a strong returning spell,' Faith said, 'My magic is still not very strong so I would be better helping you others keeping Edwin occupied,' she added.

'No!' Merlin said abruptly, 'I don't think it would be a good idea for you to go anywhere near Edwin until we have finalised our plans. Remember he has been ordered to bring you to Morgana. We cannot allow that until we know you will be safe.'

'Merlin's right,' Freya said, 'and anyway your little bit of magic could make the difference to the strength of the spell.'

'I hadn't thought of that, I don't want to endanger our plans so I'll gladly stay and help,' Faith agreed.

'What about me? I'm no good at anything to do with magic,' Hope asked, 'but I do want to help in some way.'

'You come with me. Godwin said, You with David and Thomas can help to keep Edwin busy, we don't want him to find out that we know what he is plotting,' The four of them left the room, leaving the three females, with Merlin, looking at the page of the huge spell books making notes of what was needed.

'I wonder why Edwin has turned against us.' Hope mused as the door closed behind them.

'I think it must be to do with when he and Faith were captured; we don't know anything about what happened to him. Do you think he could have been given something to drink, like he is planning to do to Faith?' David speculated.

'He may have or he may have been tortured or bribed, we must treat him as the enemy until we can find out for certain,' Thomas added.

The emperor led the way down to the entrance hall and called to one of the pages. 'Have you seen Edwin anywhere?'

'Yes my lord, he went into the sitting area, I believe he is looking for Faith.'

'Ask him to meet us in the stables.'

'Yes my lord.'

The emperor led the others out towards the stables 'I am going to send you all to check on the dragons at our boundaries, to keep Edwin away from Faith for as long as possible.'

They had only just ordered the grooms to saddle the horses when Edwin arrived. He glanced around the stables.

'Where is Faith? I need to speak with her.'

'She is with Freya at the moment. Is there anything I can do to help?' Hope asked.

'No, thank you I just wanted to be sure that she was all right,' Edwin replied.

'Well she was fine a few moments ago, when I left her, we will join up with her in a little while. The emperor has asked us to ride out to visit the dragons and find out from them what is happening, so that we can report back.'

Edwin turned to Emperor Godwin.

'There is no need for all of us to go; I could stay in case I am needed here.'

'I want you all to go, most especially you, as you have had more experience with the situation as it stands. I think there is more safety in numbers after all,' the emperor replied.

Edwin realized that he could not win this argument and reluctantly agreed to accompany the others. After all Faith was not going anywhere so he would deal with her later.

The four of them mounted the horses when the grooms brought them out and cantered off towards Summerdale's boundaries leaving the Emperor Godwin watching them go with a worried frown upon his face.

Would Merlin be able to make a strong enough spell to save them all and were David, Thomas and Hope safe in the company of Edwin now that he had become a tool of Morgana and the side of evil. Only time would tell.

Chapter Forty Eight

Merlin, Gwendolyn, Freya and Faith worked through the day. The servants brought food and drink and left it on a side table where it remained untouched.

First they had discussed the spell that Merlin had found, and then they had modified it a little until they were satisfied it would be as strong as they could make it. They gathered the necessary materials together and mixed them in a big bowl. As each ingredient was added to the mix they took it in turns to say a strengthening spell.

Once it was ready Faith brought over the little squares of cloth and precise amount was measured into the middle of each square. These were fastened with cord leaving a large loop on the end to enable the potion to be worn around the neck. Now it was ready.

'I just hope that it is as strong as we think it is, because your life may depend on it,' Freya said to Gwendolyn and Faith.

'I'm sure it's going to be perfect for its purpose,' Gwendolyn replied.

'I agree, it will be fine,' Merlin added. 'There's so much love and caring introduced to the mixture, no amount of dark magic could break it easily.'

'Why have we made so many bundles? I thought it was only going to be Empress Gwendolyn and myself going to meet Morgana.'

'I thought if we all wear one it will be safer. Especially as I have no intention of letting you both go on your own,' Freya answered.

'Yes,' Merlin added, 'Freya and I intend to be close by; this gives four times the amount of power to the turning spell. We should be fine, especially as Morgana doesn't know we are aware of her little game.'

'Well I suggest we all put one on now, before we go downstairs to wait the return of the twins with Hope and Edwin,' Freya said.

Everyone fastened the pouches around their necks and tucked them out of sight in their clothes.

When the others had left the room Gwendolyn took a last look around to see that there were no signs of their activities for Edwin to find. Satisfied she followed the others down to the dining room where their evening meal would be served shortly.

They were standing around trying to look relaxed when Hope came in.

'Oh good, you are all here. We have just reported back to the emperor that it's fairly quiet where the dragons are patrolling. Everyone is coming for dinner now,' she warned, and as she finished speaking the door opened and Edwin came in followed closely by Thomas and David. Edwin went straight across to Faith.

'I've been waiting to talk to you, are you all right?' he asked.

David shot a look of alarm at her. She just smiled back and replied.

'I'm fine; I've been with Freya and Empress Gwendolyn. We've been looking at new recipes for the use of herbs,' she said truthfully. Merlin was standing in the corner of the room, just out of Edwin's line of vision, so did not see as the magician raised his eyebrows at Faith and smile.

'I don't understand you girls and all this thirst for knowledge of new cooking recipes,' he replied, 'but I would like to spend a little time with you. We have not seen much of each other since we came back from our adventures and I miss your company.'

He sounded so sincere. It was difficult to believe that there was anything wrong with him and for a moment Faith was almost taken in. She did miss his company; he had made her laugh before. Then she remembered he was playing a part, as he was Morgana's pawn.

'Perhaps you two could go for a little walk together after dinner, but don't forget you promised to lend me your wrap for the evening,' Freya said thinking fast how she could get a few moments alone with Faith to make sure she knew how to be safe with Edwin.

Faith looked a bit bemused for a second but recovered her wits in time, understanding the reason for Freya's remark.

'I'd forgotten that I promised to loan it to you. As soon as I've finished my meal I'll go and get it and take it to your room, then I can go and meet you, Edwin, by the front door.'

Emperor Godwin swept into the room and took his place at the head of the table. Everyone else then took their places and the servants started bringing in the meal. Talk turned to general things. The meal passed pleasantly enough and at the end Faith excused herself, closely followed by Freya.

'I shan't be very long, Edwin, I'll meet you by the front door in about ten minutes. Will that give you long enough to finish your wine?' Faith asked as she passed Edwin's chair.

'Yes, that will be perfect,' he smiled back at her. His innermost thoughts were in turmoil as he felt the pull of Morgana's spell to take Faith to the lady herself. A very small part of him realized what he was doing was wrong but this only lasted a split second before the black mist descended on his mind again. The potion

Morgana had given him was very strong, and once Faith had drunk it she too would be completely in Morgana's power. Then it would only be a matter of a short while before everyone would be in her power.

Faith hurried up the stairs and Freya ran after her to join her in her room. She glanced up and down the corridor before closing the door behind her.

Freya went to Faith and took hold of her arms staring into her eyes.

'You must be very careful when you are with Edwin. He is to give you a draft of something that Morgana has made. You will be completely in her power. Somehow you will have to swap the drinks around and make him drink yours. If what I hear is true, Edwin will be released from the spell and you will be safe.'

'I understand, but how is he going to make me drink something. He has suggested we go out for a walk?'

'I expect he'll ask you to accompany him back indoors. It probably would be better if you could suggest going into the little sitting room, that way you would be in control.'

'How am I going to make a switch of the drinks?'

'I have an idea. What if I should be outside, behind the lavender bush; there is a good view into the room from there. Once I see Edwin go over and pour the drinks I will see which one he puts the potion into. I can then knock on the window to distract his attention. Whichever side of the window I tap will show which glass he has put the draft in. If it's in the one near the window I shall tap on the left hand side and if the other I shall tap on the right hand side. So when he is looking at me you can quickly pick up the other one then you will be safe.'

'Right, I'm a little nervous, what if I get it wrong?'

'Don't worry; I'll not let him take you away whatever happens. Now you must go before he becomes suspicious,' Freya gave her a hug and pushed her towards the door. 'Oh I nearly forgot your shawl you were going to lend me.'

'That would never do, he would have smelled a rat it you had returned without it. Here this one matches your dress,' Faith handed Freya a blue silk shawl and then they both hurried out of the room.

'Just give me ten minutes,' Freya whispered as the two girls parted company,

Chapter Forty Nine

Edwin was outside waiting for Faith when she came out through the door, he smiled at her. Faith went up to him and put her arm through his.

'I think we should go for a little walk, but not too far as it's a little chilly tonight,' she said smiling up at him.

They walked through the gardens towards the gates. The moon shone down and illuminated their way. The grass took on a silver sheen and the trees rustled in the slight evening breeze. It was a perfect evening for a romantic stroll.

A face looked out at them from the upstairs window, Merlin was watching anxiously. He was ready to hurry down and raise the alarm if Edwin tried to take Faith out of the grounds   Even as he watched Faith turned to Edwin and laughed up into his face, she said something and they turned, starting to walk back the way they had come. Merlin heaved a sigh of relief; she had obviously suggested returning for a drink. So far everything was going to plan. Earlier he had seen Freya slipping out of the side door and making her way around to the lavender bushes outside the little sitting room window.

Faith and Edwin strolled back in and made their way to the little sitting room.

'I'll be much warmer inside,' she said opening the door and moving over to stand in front of the fire that had been lit.

'Would you like to drink a toast to the brave dragons, for all they have been doing to keep the land of Summerdale as safe?' Edwin asked.

This was the moment Faith had been dreading, what if Freya could not see which glass Edwin put the drink in? Not letting any of her doubts show in her face she replied.

'I would love to; I wouldn't mind a small glass of whatever you are drinking.'

She realized she had to have the same drink so that Edwin would not notice when she swapped glasses.

'I thought you only drank milk or fruit juice,' Edwin replied, 'I was going to have a glass of mead.'

'One glass of mead won't hurt me,' Faith replied with more conviction than she felt.

Edwin inclined his head in acceptance and moved over to the sideboard where glasses and bottles were set out. He picked up the bottle of mead and poured a little into two goblets then he pulled a small phial from his jacket pocket, slipped the stopper out and added a few drops to the right hand drink. He reached forward to pick them both up. There was a rapid knocking on the right side of the window, Edwin jumped and nearly knocked over the drinks. He spun around to see Freya's laughing face through the window. She knocked again and beckoned to him. Annoyed he went over to her and as he did so Faith quickly swapped the goblets around. Edwin opened the window.

'What so you want?' he enquired gruffly.

'Sorry, I had been going to go for a walk, to join you both, when I saw you through the window,' Freya lied. 'Would you mind if I joined you for a drink? This shawl is lovely and warm but walking by oneself is not much fun.'

'We don't mind, do we, Edwin? We were just going to have a toast to the dragons and I was going to be naughty and have a drink of mead. Do come around and have one too,' Faith said not giving Edwin a chance to answer for himself.

Freya hurried off and Edwin closed the window before returning to the sideboard. He picked up both glasses and offered the right hand one to Faith.

'Drink up. We can always have another when Freya arrives.'

He watched as she raised the goblet to her lips and took a sip.

'This is rather nice,' she said, as she tasted the sweet liquid.

Edwin smiled and raising his own glass he said.

'Here's to all the dragons may they have long lives,' he put the goblet to his lips and drained it in one go.

'I second that,' Faith said as she followed suit and drained her glass.

Edwin turned to Faith with a satisfied look on his face.

Freya came into the room and noted the empty goblets.

'I see you didn't wait for me,' she smiled at Edwin as a strange look came over his features.

'What's happening?' he gasped as he staggered to a chair and sat down. A glazed look came over his face. 'I feel funny. Where am I?'

Faith and Freya went over to him and held his hands.

'It's all right, you're with friends,' Freya reassured him.

''I'm meant to take Faith to Morgana,' Edwin said. 'Everything is so strange, I can't think straight.'

'Rest a moment, the others will be here soon and we will give you the cure.'

Freya went to the door and opened it as Merlin arrived followed by David.

'How is he?' Merlin asked.

'He is muddled still, but I think the drink has reversed the hold Morgana had over him.

Unfortunately he still is under the spell of the Death Riders. Faith replied.

'I have the cure for that,' David said and took out some of the berries he had collected from the tree of healing. He gave two to Edwin,

'Eat these; they will make you feel better.'

Edwin did as he was told and after a few moments a look of wonder came over his face.

'I feel better, what was I doing, I had a dream that Morgana had made me come to capture Faith to use her as bait to capture the rest of you.'

'It wasn't a dream, you really tried to make me drink something to make me become a pawn to Morgana,' Faith told him.

'Yes but you didn't,' Merlin said. 'Now comes the difficult bit, you are both going to have to go to Morgana, so that she does not suspect anything, then we must recapture her before we can take the 'Stone of Power' from King Golgog.'

'I hadn't realized that I'd have to go in on my own,' Faith said worriedly.

You won't be on your own. I'll be there to protect you. I'll not let anything happen to you don't fear,' Edwin said gallantly.

'All we have to do now is to plan it,' David said.

'And make it work,' Merlin added.

Chapter Fifty

Edwin told them what he could remember of his ordeal. He was having difficulties understanding that the parts he thought he had dreamed were actually true. He had been part of a plan to enslave Faith so she could bring Freya, David and Thomas under Morgana's spell.

'The last proper memory I have was of me being tortured. The pain was so bad! Then they said they would start torturing Faith unless I agreed to help them. I couldn't let her go through all that, so I agreed to help them. They took me and bathed my wounds with something that made everything go hazy, then I was given a drink and everything seemed to be unreal. I just knew I had to help Morgana,' Edwin shuddered. 'I came so close to it too. How did you find out and save us both?'

'You can thank Freya for that, she followed you and heard your orders,' Merlin told him. 'Why she decided to follow you is beyond me.'

'I just knew there was something wrong with Edwin, he was so abrupt, not like his usual cheerful self,' Freya told them.

'Thank goodness one of us had their wits about them,' David said as he walked over to his sister to give her a hug.

Merlin brought them back to the point in hand. 'We must get down to work. How are we going to handle the next part and capture Morgana?'

'There's only one way we can go,' Faith said looking at Edwin. He nodded.

'We are going to have to go back to Morgana as if her plan has worked and wait for her to send the ultimatum to you three.'

'Once David, Thomas and I go to her we can then overpower her and bring her back to you Merlin,' Freya said.

'She will try to use some pretty nasty magic against you,' Merlin reminded them.

'We will have our talismans around our necks to rebound any spells she sends at us onto her, that should confuse her enough to capture her.'

'No that will not work, she would suspect something if her spells were to rebound, I'll only agree if you let me come with you,' Merlin said. 'My magic is stronger than any of yours so if something unexpected happened I would be there to help. I could not let you all go and risk your lives without me doing something,' he added.

'I have to admit we would all feel safer if you were near at hand,' David agreed.

'What do I have to do, exactly, to convince Morgana that I am under her spell?' Faith asked.

'That's easy,' Freya said, 'don't answer her back and keep your face showing as few emotions as possible.'

'Also do whatever she says straight away and I mean whatever she says,' Merlin added. 'You just have to act as if you have got nothing in your thoughts. You must not show any interest in anything going on around you.'

'Was that what I seemed like?' Edwin asked.

'Yes, it was as if you had no feelings at all, you became a cold calculating person,' David said with a laugh.

'You had better get going or Morgana will be getting worried about you.'

'Gosh, can I do this?' Faith asked.

'Of course you can, and I shall be with you,' Edwin said and gave her a kiss on her cheek.

'Now we can't have that kind of behaviour from a cold calculating person,' Thomas added and they all laughed.

The tension eased and they went together to the stables to see the two brave adventurers off.

As the horses were led out Hope came haring down the path.

'You can't go without saying goodbye to me,' she said as she catapulted into Faith's arms. 'You have to stay safe otherwise our father would never forgive me.'

'Don't worry we have it all worked out. They'll be back in no time at all,' Merlin told her and gently pulled her away from her sister.

Edwin and Faith looked at each other, and then taking a deep breath they both mounted their animals and headed off towards the Twilight Kingdom and Morgana.

Chapter Fifty One

Edwin and Faith rode quickly to the border of the Twilight Kingdom, and then plunged into the murky forest beyond. They soon picked up the trail that led them towards King Golgog's castle. Even riding hard it still took them some hours to reach it. The gates were opened immediately and they were escorted to the stabling area where they left their mounts and proceeded to Morgana's chambers high in the castle.

The guard knocked on the door.

'Enter,' an imperious voice called.

They went in.

'At last, you are late!' she said to Edwin and turned to the guard. 'You may go, have my servant come to attend me.'

Edwin and Faith stood waiting keeping their faces blank. Inside, they both quaked with fear. Morgana turned back to them.

'What did you instruct Faith to do?'

'Only to accompany me to see you and that she had to do whatever you wished.'

'Excellent, now Faith I wish you to sit down and write a letter to Freya and her brothers,' Morgana indicated a table set with writing things.

'Yes, my lady,' Faith said moving to the table and sitting down. 'What shall I write?'

'You will tell them that you are in danger for your life and that they must come immediately to rescue you. They must tell no one and come entirely on their own. Tell them if they do not do as I ask I will put you and Edwin out in the swamps and leave you tied up as a meal for the Trolls.'

Faith could not repress a shudder.

Morgana looked at her sharply a frown upon her face.

She turned and stared at Edwin. He stood with his face completely blank.

Faith finished writing and handed the message over for Morgana to read.

'Perfect,' she mumbled after reading it and went over to the door and opened it. Outside her servant was waiting. 'Take this to the Emperor Godwin's house and make sure it is put in Freya's hands only,' she said then lowered her voice, 'ask the guards to return here and wait outside the door until I call them.'

'Yes, my lady, at once.'

Morgana retuned into her room smiling. 'I think you both deserve a drink to celebrate,' she said as she moved over to her sideboard and poured out three small drinks.

Faith and Edwin watched fearfully, wondering if they were going to have to drink some of her magic potion and become under her influence. This fear was reinforced as they heard the sound of the guards returning outside the door.

Morgana returned with the three glasses on a tray. She looked at their faces and smiled.

'No my dears, there is nothing in the drink; it is some of the best quality wine. I just wish to drink to my success at capturing you and through you the meddling family that has caused me all my grief.'

'You haven't caught them yet,' Faith exclaimed before she could stop herself.

'I was right you are here under false pretences,' the lady gloated.

Faith looked across at Edwin. 'Sorry, she tricked me.'

Edwin just stood gazing ahead, as if he had not heard.

Morgana laughed. 'It appears that you are on your own, my dear. Tell her Edwin, who you work for.'

Edwin turned and looked at Morgana then at Faith he smiled, 'I work for my lady Morgana,' he said.

Faith gasped, they had been fooled; Edwin hadn't been cured at all.

'Now we will drink to success, hand the drinks out Edwin.'

Edwin did as he was told and took the tray of drinks, he offered it first to Morgana and then moved over to Faith, he had his back to the dark lady and as he offered the tray he looked straight at Faith and winked.

Faith took the drink wondering how she could keep a straight face; to cover her confusion she took a deep drink.

'I shall drink to success, ours not yours,' she said defiantly as the relief rushed through her now she knew she was not on her own.

'You can dream. Now Edwin, you will take her to my workroom and guard her well. I shall no longer need the other guards, with you still loyal. I am going to speak to King Golgog and await the arrival of our invited guests.'

Edwin finished his drink and replaced his and Faiths glass on the tray. Taking a firm grip on Faiths arm he led her from the room. Once they were out of earshot he said. 'No more outbursts please, I nearly died when you rounded on her. I just thought it was worth a try to convince her that I was still her servant. It was the look on your face that really convinced her, if looks could have killed I would have been dead.'

'I thought you hadn't been cured and were still under her magic spell,' Faith confessed, 'but do you have to hold me so tightly, you're hurting.'

'Sorry, I had to make it look convincing.'

'Well there is no one watching now.'

Edwin let go of her arm and they went up the stairs and into a large room. There was a big table in the middle of the room where a pile of books had been placed, some open but most in a neat pile. On each side of the fireplace were shelves upon which were many jars containing different liquids and herbs. A fire burned brightly in the hearth giving the room some warmth, but the overall feeling of the room was uneasy.

Faith went over to one of the windows and looked out.

'Look you can see some of the road leading back the way we came.'

Edwin joined her, 'We can keep watch for the others.'

'If we can see them, won't Merlin be seen following behind?' she asked.

'Don't worry; I'm sure he'll find a way of arriving unannounced.'

'I can't help it I come from a family of worriers, you only have to ask Hope,' Faith said as she tried to make light of it. She could not relax and spent her time walking around the room picking up things and putting them down. As she glanced at one of the books open on the table, she stopped and read it, then turned the page, her face going paler and paler.

'Edwin this is a very powerful spell to turn people into statues. There is no cure, only time will weaken it, only another powerful magician can release the petrified person.'

Edwin came over and read it. 'I don't know much about magic, but it does seem that one spell can't block it, we are going to have to escape to warn them of the danger they will face.'

Faith took his arm. 'Come on then let's go.'

Edwin led her to the door and opened it, he looked out. There was a sound of someone ascending the stairs.

'Too late, someone is coming. Don't let on you know anything,' he said as he closed the door again.

Faith moved over to the fireplace and Edwin remained where he was.

The door opened and Morgana appeared.

'Our new guests will not be here before the morning so I have arranged for your accommodation,' she said to Faith. 'The guard will take you to the cell so recently vacated by yourself. But don't worry he will remain outside all night so you will not be disturbed by anyone,' she laughed at the despair on Faiths face.

Edwin made up his mind that as soon as Morgana retired he would make an attempt to go to warn their rescuers. His hopes were dashed as Morgana turned to him. 'You will rest in my spare, chamber off this room, I shall be here all night preparing.'

Not knowing what else to do Edwin went into the anti-room and any thought of escaping went when he heard the key turn in the look.

Faith was led away to her cold cell with worry her only companion. How were they going to avoid the strong spell? Freya, David and Thomas were riding to their doom.

She could not see how Merlin was going to be able to save them now.

Chapter Fifty Two

David and Thomas were waiting with Merlin when the emperor's servant brought the message for them. David opened it and looked at Thomas.

'Faith has written saying Freya, you and I must go immediately to King Golgog's. She says that she and Edwin are in danger of their lives. If the three of us don't go alone Edwin and Freya will be left in the swamp for the Trolls to eat!' he read.

'That means you won't be able to come, Merlin,' Thomas added.

'I don't think you'll have to worry about me coming with you, I've already come up with a plan,' Merlin replied.

'What do you mean?'

'You brought back one of the guard's tunics and hat, well I thought I could accompany you wearing those items of clothing and no one will look twice at me.'

'Very cleaver, I knew they would come in handy,' David laughed. 'I can't think Morgana is very interested in Summerdale as she hasn't asked for anything from the emperor.'

'I agree, I think this is purely revenge against you. After all you stopped her in her attempt to kill King Arthur and take over his crown,' Merlin mused.

'That means we have to get King Golgog involved so that we can retrieve the 'Stone of Power' for Queen Josephine and her people,' David said.

'How are we going to do that?' Thomas asked.

'I can't think of anything at the moment, we will have to make the situation up as we go along,' Merlin answered.

'Well we'd better go and find Freya and capture Morgana,' David said leaving the room.

'There are a lot of untied loose ends. I just hope we can think of the answers on our way to the castle,' Merlin said as he followed the brothers to find Freya.

Freya was found in the meadow talking to her little dragon friend, Shimmer. When she saw her brothers approaching she called to them.

'Have you heard from Faith?'

'Yes, we must leave immediately.'

'Is there anything you want me to do for you?' Shimmer asked.

A glimmer of an idea popped into Merlin's mind. 'Yes, Shimmer, could you first go and find the emperor and ask him to hold his army in readiness, in case there is a sudden attack. Oh yes, warn your father and the other dragons too. Then I was wondering if you could fly and land on the roof of King Golgog's castle. Make sure everyone can see you, that way I think King Golgog will run to Morgana for protection. He will think the dragons are about to attack his castle and he'll want Morgana's help. That way, with any luck, both of them will be together when we do the rebounding spell. That should catch them both.'

'There is an awful lot being left to chance,' Thomas said, looking doubtful.

'What other choice do we have?' David said. 'Actually, even if the king doesn't go to Morgana's the dragons will be able to help us catch him afterwards.'

'You're right we have to have a go at it. We always knew it wouldn't be easy and King Arthur wants his sister back,' Freya added.

'Well what are we waiting for?' Merlin said and they all moved off towards the stables.

Once there, Merlin collected the guard's outfit and put the tunic on, then he tied back his long hair and pushed it up under the helmet. He became a perfect match for any of the guards around Morgana's hiding place.

As the four rode through the woods towards the castle, David slowed his mount slightly to bring him alongside Merlin.

'I'm a little worried about your disguise, Merlin, after all Morgana knows you very well and she will immediately recognise you.'

'I think you're wrong, no one actually looks at guards they are treated as part of the furniture. I'm willing to stake my reputation on her not noticing me.'

'It's not only your reputation but your life as well,' David reminded him.

'Don't worry, my friend, I think there will be too much going on for any attention to be spared for the likes of me. You have to remember the talisman that we are all wearing around our necks; any magic that is sent at us will be returned to the sender. What I am actually hoping for is Morgana sending a spell to include us all at once, that way the combined protection of all of us will work together.'

'Have you used this rebounding spell often?' David then asked aware that Thomas and Freya were now listening to the conversation.

'Well, no actually, this will be the first time,' Merlin replied, 'but I have every reason to believe it will work.'

David let out a loud laugh. 'You are so reassuring,' he said and kicked his horse forward, calling over his shoulder. 'Come on everyone, let's go and meet our doom!'

'Well I, for one, believe in you Merlin,' Freya cried as she too kicked her horse onwards.

Thomas and Merlin followed suit and as they drew nearer to the castle they saw Shimmer fly overhead on her way to do her part.

'I do hope I don't let you all down,' Merlin muttered to himself as he followed the others around the corner into sight of the castle.

Chapter Fifty Three

The castle guards were causing a commotion and someone was sent to warn the king of an imminent dragon attack.

Shimmer had landed on the roof, well away from the danger of any arrows reaching her. She shot out a token blast of flames at one of the trees nearest to the castle walls. It burst into flames, causing even more excitement.

King Golgog looked out of his window, but could see nothing except the burning tree. He immediately left his room with his two favourite hunting dogs at his heels and went to find Morgana.

David's party arrived at the same time and they too were sent to Morgana's room.

Merlin knocked on her door. They heard heavy footsteps crossing the floor then the door burst open to reveal an agitated King Golgog, behind him, sat in a chair was Morgana with Edwin at her side.

'What do you want?' the king asked.

'I have brought the prisoners to my lady,' Merlin replied bowing his head.

'Bring them in,' Morgana called, 'and then you can go to the cells and bring back the other one. Faith I think her name is.'

Merlin stood back as David, Freya and Thomas passed him into the room, then he went off to find Faith. He was surprised to find out she had been discovered but once she was fetched things would once more fall in with his plan.

Merlin did not know exactly where the cells were but guessed that they would be in the lower reaches of the castle. As he made his way downstairs he saw some other guards walking towards a doorway.

'One of you come with me,' he called, 'I need the keys to let out the prisoner to take to the lady Morgana.'

'The keys are still down there in the guard room. We are needed to ward off the dragon attack,' one of the men replied.

The other man looked fearfully out of a window at the burning tree.

'He will need assistance to bring the girl out,' he said to his colleague, 'so I will help him then get back to you as soon as possible.' He went over to Merlin, not giving the other man a chance to disagree.

'All right but be quick about it,' the first guard replied and went off.

'It's this way,' the guard said looking at Merlin strangely 'I haven't seen you before have I? You must be new not to know the cells are over here.'

'I've only just arrived,' Merlin replied truthfully. 'Now lead on, Lady Morgana is waiting.'

At the mention of Morgana's name the guard hurried forward and led Merlin through an archway that he had not noticed. They ran down the steps and came to the cells at the bottom. The guard took the keys and unlocked Faiths cell door pushing it open to let her out.

'Come on we're in a hurry,' he put his arm out and dragged Faith forward. Merlin stood behind him with his finger to his lips, warning Faith to say nothing. Her eyes widened but she quickly looked away and went past the guard.

'Why don't you stay and make sure everything is in order,' Merlin suggested to him and the guard looked relieved. He didn't want to go back to fight the dragons.

Merlin caught hold of Faiths arm and pulled her towards the stairs.

'Come on Morgana is waiting,' he said.

Once they were out of hearing Faith told Merlin about the petrifying spell that Morgana was planning.

'I gave the game away the first time Morgana set a trap but Edwin is still pretending to be her servant and so far she does not know any different,' she finished.

'Don't worry; I'm almost sure that the combined power of our talisman's protection will work. You and Edwin are wearing yours aren't you?'

'Yes we are wearing them. What do you mean, almost sure?' Faith asked as they hurried on up the stairs.

'As I explained to David, I have never had cause to use it before, but it should work in theory.'

'Great we are all going to risk being turned into statues on your theory,' Faith muttered.

'What was that my dear?' Merlin asked.

'Nothing, I was just talking to myself, come on let's get it over with.'

They had arrived at Morgana's room. Merlin knocked then opened the door and stood back for Faith to enter first. He followed and closed the door standing with his back to the door and his head slightly bowed in deference to the king's presence and to stop Morgana having a good look at his face.

Freya, David and Thomas were stood over by the fireplace with Edwin slightly behind them, appearing to be keeping watch over them. Morgana was standing beside the table and King Golgog was sitting nearby with his hounds at his feet.

'Good, you are all here now. I was waiting for you my dear,' Morgana turned to Faith,' I need you to see what I shall do to your meddling friends and take the news back to Emperor Godwin, you will tell him that I will do the same to him and his wife if he does not surrender to my good friend King Golgog.'

'What are you going to do to us?' David asked.

'I am going to turn you into statues,' she replied.

'The dragons and Merlin will rescue us,' Freya said glaring at Morgana.

'No they won't. First Merlin is not here to stop the spell and once in place it takes years to weaken and secondly, if the dragons don't leave here and agree never to trouble me again, we will take you all out to sea on a boat and throw you overboard, that way no one will ever find you'

'You're wrong on the first count because I am here,' Merlin said as he stepped forward and removed his helmet allowing his hair to fall around his face.

The shock showed on Morgana's face.

'You're too late, you will not have time to find a way to deflect the spell,' she cried and picked up her wand. Chanting some words while pointing her wand at all of them, not even bothered if Edwin, whom she thought on her side, was in the way.

The air filled with electricity as a flash shot from the end of her wand it surrounded the friends and sparked the light around them turned from yellow to red, then purple. Then six silver lights glowed from each of the recipients of the spell before it exploded back at Morgana.

There was a screech as the purple lights spun around her and slowly from the feet up she turned to white alabaster.

King Golgog jumped up from his chair and made for the door. His face contorted with fear. He had to go right past Merlin who merely pointed at him said an incantation. With a puff of smoke the king disappeared and on the floor was a fat rat sat in the middle of the kings garments. The king's hounds jumped up and made for the rat. It let out a squeak of alarm and rushed towards the bottom of the door, where there was a small hole. The rat dived through the hole, and let out a squeal of fear as it stuck; it scrabbled and scrabbled until it made it through just as the dogs arrived. One of them snapped at the tail and took off the end. There was another scream from the other side of the door, then silence. The dogs scratched to be let out then, Freya went and opened the door and the dogs shot off down the stairs following the rat to the dungeons.

Freya turned to Merlin. 'I told you I believed in you,' she said with a smile.

Edwin hugged Faith while David and Thomas went over to Merlin and shook his hand.

David looked where the dogs had gone.

'That was a good choice of spells for the king. Now what do we do with Morgana?' he asked.

'We'll have to take her back to King Arthur as she is his sister, at least she'll not be bothering anyone for a long time,' Merlin replied.

'What about the 'Stone of Power?' we need to find it and return it to its rightful owner,' Thomas said.

Freya had gone over and picked up the king's discarded clothes.

'I don't think we will have to look any further,' she said as she pulled a small dark grey coloured stone, the size of a pebble, out of a pouch that had obviously been around the king's neck. 'It doesn't seem much does it?' she added.

Merlin came over and took the stone from her. 'Remember Queen Josephine is only small; anything bigger would be too heavy for her.'

They all crowded around and looked at it.

'Look its changing colour,' Faith said in wonder.

It was slowly turning a lighter grey.

'The evil is fading. It's returning to what it should be like, for the furthering of all things good in the world,' Merlin said. 'We will return it to Queen Josephine and then it will turn to pure white.'

Chapter Fifty Four

Merlin went out of the room and called all the guards together.

'Your king has gone away and Morgana is going to return to her brother King Arthur in Camelot. The Emperor Godwin of Summerdale will send a steward to look after the castle until your king returns. In the meantime there is no longer a threat from the dragons, so there shall be no more wars.'

There was a loud cheer from the men. With the threat from the dragons lifted they all felt safe again.

Freya took out her calling charm and sent her thoughts to Shimmer asking her to meet them outside the front of the castle; she was needed to carry a statue for them.

While she was doing that David turned to Merlin and asked. 'Could you do one more thing?'

'What would you like me to do?'

'Well, when we came to the castle first we were helped by a family. They had been turned into rats by Morgana. I just wondered if you could change them back.'

'Of course I could. I'll send something with the new steward to give to them to change them back into what they were.'

'Thank you, well with that settled we had better get the statue of Morgana outside to Shimmer.'

David and Thomas, between them, managed to carry it down the stairs and out through the gates, where others came and helped them load it on to Shimmers back.

'I will take the statue back to Camelot and explain to King Arthur what has happened. Shall I tell him you will be following shortly?' she asked.

'Yes' Merlin replied. 'Please ask Fredlie to come back with you to collect me. Then we'll all come back home ourselves.'

The little dragon left on her long journey and our friends set out on their shorter one back to Summerdale.

Once they left the forest of the Twilight Kingdom they entered a totally new Summerdale, the sun was now shining with its full strength, the trees leaves were beginning to go back to green and the birds were singing again.

As they rode up to the emperor's house Hope and Enfys ran out to meet them.

'Where have you been? We looked all over for you,' Hope cried taking her sister hand and helping her down off her horse.

'We have been to defeat Morgana,' Faith replied.

'You must have retrieved the stone, as everything is returning to its normal state. Also the dragons said the Death Riders did not come today,' Enfys added.

'Yes we have the stone, we have just to return it to Queen Josephine and all will go back to normal,' Merlin said dismounting. He walked over to the emperor and empress who had followed at a much more leisurely pace. 'You should not have any more attacks from over the border. The Death Riders power has been withdrawn. Morgana is at this moment on her way back to Camelot and her brothers keeping.'

'Could she escape again and come after you?' Emperor Godwin wanted to know.

David laughed. 'She has turned herself to stone and on her own admission the spell will take years to weaken and allow her to be released.'

'And what has happened to King Golgog?' Gwendolyn wanted to know.

'He is a little occupied at the moment, I suggest you send a steward to look after his kingdom and educate him on his return,' Merlin replied.

'Who could we send?' Godwin asked his wife.

Edwin looked at Faith and she nodded.

'May I be of assistance? Faith and I would like to remain here and serve you both in any way that you desire,' he said and smiled at Faith.

'That would be wonderful,' the emperor said beaming, 'and what about you others?' he asked turning to everyone else.

'I shall return to Camelot and serve my king,' Merlin said.

'We'll also be returning,' Freya said, 'as David is now cured.'

'What about you, Hope?'

'I shall follow David,' she replied.

Merlin turned to Enfys. 'What about you, will you return to your people to let them know the good news?'

'Yes,' she replied, 'but first I shall return the 'Stone of Power' to its owner.'

'Look here come the dragons, just in time for the fun.'

The sky became red and green with the colour of the dragons as they flew down to the human friends.

'Come on every one, let us go and celebrate with them tonight. Tomorrow you will all go your separate ways. We are going to give the best party you have ever seen.' Empress Gwendolyn declared smiling fondly at everyone.

Shimmer was just leaving King Arthur to return with Fredlie to collect Freya and Merlin. As she took off she glanced down at the statue of Morgana and thought she saw a spark coming from the end of the stone wand held in Morgana's right hand. She shook her head. No it must have been a trick of the light. After all how could Morgana escape and seek her revenge and what of King Golgog, would he outwit his dogs?

Well that's another story.

Lightning Source UK Ltd.
Milton Keynes UK
UKOW05f0423310713

214618UK00001B/43/P